Stones

by

Marilyn Baron

Stones

Cover Art by *Kim Mendoza*

The Wild Rose Press, Inc.
PO Box 708
Adams Basin, NY 14410-0708
Visit us at www.thewildrosepress.com

Publishing History
First Mainstream General Edition, 2014
Print ISBN 978-1-62830-441-1
Digital ISBN 978-1-62830-442-8

Published in the United States of America

To go or not to go to Palm Coast is no longer the question. The question is what will I do once I get there? Will I really have the nerve to reconnect, or as my daughter Natalie likes to say, "hook up," again with Manny Gellar? How will I feel tomorrow when I see him alone for the first time after twenty-five years? Will I finally reveal what I feel compelled—no, what I'm busting a gut—to tell him? That he has a beautiful son, that our son Josh is getting married in just three months? I'm probably rationalizing, but I think he finally has a right to know.

If I could, I'd fix what is wrong with my marriage and put it back the way it was before, as easily as Ricardo fixed my washing machine. *Before* Matt yanked me out of Miami by my roots as if I were a noxious weed he was tossing out of a flower garden and carelessly transplanted us to Atlanta. *Before* we moved a state away from my family and my best friend and a business I'd worked a lifetime to create.

Before Matt sold his freight-expediting business to a German conglomerate for mega-millions and agreed to run the company for them from Atlanta for the next two years, barely consulting me. *Before* the *German occupation*, or rather before he became *preoccupied* with his sexy-sounding German second-in-command, Gretchen. *Before* he stopped sleeping with me in the biblical sense. *Before* I turned fifty.

All I really want is closure. I'm convinced that meeting Manny Gellar again is the only way I will ever come full circle and reconnect with my life.

Praise for Marilyn Baron

"Baron offers a bit of everything…. There's humor, infidelity, murder, mayhem, and a neatly drawn conclusion."

~*RT Book Reviews (4.5 Stars)*

"I just finished reading *UNDER THE MOON GATE* and really enjoyed it. I was fascinated by the intertwining of the characters in the stories from the 1700s to present day and I especially enjoyed the segment that took place during WWII. Great writing. Marilyn did a great job of bringing Bermuda during the WWII era to life in this book."

~*PJ Ausdenmore, The Romance Dish*

"[*UNDER THE MOON GATE*] is a surefire blockbuster…a treasure trove of mystery and intrigue. It sparkles with romance…. I couldn't recommend it more."

~*Andrew Kirby*

"An enjoyable read from start to finish…family, friends, enemies, intrigue and suspense…sadness, laughter, romance and ultimately love."

~*Romance Junkies (4 Blue Ribbons)*

"*SIXTH SENSE* has a great mix of romance, spine-tingling suspense, and real hope for two jaded individuals for a happily-ever-after ending. I'm looking forward to reading Book Two in the Psychic Crystal Mystery Series."

~*Tami Brothers*

"An intriguing, albeit reluctant, psychic detective in this paranormal romantic suspense story…a strong and captivating heroine ."

~*Pauline Michael, Night Owl Romance (3 Stars)*

Dedication

To my wonderful daughter, Marissa,
whose stories make me laugh
and who inspires me
to be true to myself in my writing.

Awards

Finalist, Georgia Romance Writers Unpublished
Maggie Award for Excellence, 2005, Single Title
(*STONES*, originally titled *The Colonoscopy Club*)

~*~

Winner, Georgia Romance Writers Unpublished
Maggie Award for Excellence, 2012,
Paranormal/Fantasy Romance (*SIXTH SENSE*)

~*~

First Place, Suspense Romance Category
2010 Ignite the Flame contest
(Central Ohio Fiction Writers chapter
of Romance Writers of America)

PART ONE: THE ROAD TO PALM COAST

PRESENT DAY

Chapter One:
Desperately Seeking Closure

Atlanta

Thank God for lint.

It's the one area in my life where I've been able to achieve closure. I can wash a load of towels, toss them into the dryer, fold them, and, after opening the lint filter, peel back a glorious, thick, colorful strip of lint, admire it, and throw it into the wastebasket. Then I can cross that task off my to-do list. Now, *that* is closure! And, by the way, I have a new dryer that gives really good lint.

I'm sure you're thinking that anyone who's turned lint-making into a fine art must be either crazy or desperate. But before you jump to the conclusion that I'm totally insane, I should tell you I am *not* crazy. Now that I've reached the unenviable milestone of fifty years, I am, however, officially old. I have to face facts. If I didn't know it before, I'm reminded daily by all the e-mails I get about the signs of depression, regaining my mobility with a power scooter, and burial insurance.

The good news is my best friend Mackie and I are

growing old together. If you walked out of a bathroom trailing toilet paper, wouldn't you want someone to give you a heads-up? For me, that someone is Mackie Shack. And, like toilet paper, Mackie is the kind of friend who sticks till the bitter end.

To celebrate our coming of age, we even scheduled our colonoscopies on the same day, but in different cities. That's one rite of passage I could have done without. I'm here to tell you that even though the colonoscopy itself was anticlimactic, the prep for that operation (my husband Matt minimized the whole thing by calling it a *procedure)* was nothing short of traumatic. Besides, Matt has no right to comment, seeing that both he and Mackie's husband, Little Jon, have been "too busy" to schedule theirs, and they are rapidly running out of lame excuses.

Mackie and I have decided to form The Colonoscopy Club, since that seems to be the favorite topic of conversation among the fifty-something crowd these days. It's always a contest between us as to who had the worst colonoscopy prep experience. I, of course, consider myself the hands-down winner. Some of our friends say their prep was a walk in the park. They waltzed out of their doctors' offices and into a restaurant to have breakfast or went right back to work. Needless to say, they weren't invited to join our club.

Right now, Mackie and I are the only two members of this exclusive organization. And we like it that way. There's no formal program or structured format to our club meetings. They are not even meetings in the strict sense of the word. They can be held online or over the telephone. We can't meet face-to-face because my "dearly beloved" dragged me out of Miami last year and dumped me into what Mackie calls the Deep South, although, on the map, Miami is technically far south of Atlanta, which makes absolutely no sense. All I know is, Mackie and I are now worlds apart.

We can talk about whatever happens to touch us or tick us off. We've got sort of a foam-at-the-mouth, stream-of-consciousness dialogue thing going on, like real friends do. We don't take club minutes. Neither of us really needs an official record, because time has branded memories on my brain like a hot iron. And Mackie is my Rosetta Stone. She is best at helping me decipher my life because she lived through it with me.

Now that half my life is over, I've somehow become disconnected, and I'm breaking apart at the seams. It's as if some giant Hoover is hovering over me like a rain cloud or an alien spaceship, sucking all the happiness and energy out in steady, soul-severing whooshes, leaving me stuck on the spin cycle, permanently pressed.

How do I know I'm unraveling? I used to be a news junkie, and now I never read the newspaper—except for my horoscope in the Living section—and I can no longer tolerate the babble and the blare of TV. I guess if I lose my grip on reality I can always find it on any number of network reality shows I *don't* watch. I may be the only person on the planet who doesn't watch *Dancing With the Stars* or *American Idol*. How did I ever survive? I figure if I miss something really important someone will let me know.

Last week, Matt came home from a business trip and found me fast asleep on one end of the couch with a book over my face and my Bichon Frise, Abercrombie, asleep at my feet, both of us comfortably settled under the same wool afghan. He took a digital picture, printed it, stuck it on the refrigerator (thank God he didn't upload it to Facebook) and created a screensaver for my computer, in case I needed a reminder that I was sleeping my life away. Or that my ass was leaving an imprint the size of Savannah on the sofa.

The dog is not growing old gracefully, and neither am I. At least Abercrombie has an excuse. The vet says she has doggie dementia.

"You're kidding," Matt said when I brought her home from her most recent checkup.

"No," I countered. "He says she's lost her purpose in life."

"And how would anyone know what that was?" he replied. "Are we supposed to ask her? Just what *is* her purpose in life?"

"To love me unconditionally." *Like you used to do.*

Matt says he's worried about me because I never consider weighty matters anymore. He might be surprised to know that, in fact, I'm considering a very serious matter right now. One that never would have entered my mind a year ago. But a lot of things have changed since Matt moved us from Miami so abruptly, announcing that Atlanta is a better place to do business. Matt believes that Miami is a good place to live—if you're a drug dealer. I think even Matt would agree that contemplating whether to meet my first love, Manny Gellar, at my oceanfront condo in Palm Coast, Florida, qualifies as a pretty weighty matter.

To go or not to go to Palm Coast is no longer the question. The question is what will I do once I get there? Will I really have the nerve to reconnect, or as my daughter Natalie likes to say, "hook up," again with

Manny Gellar? How will I feel tomorrow when I see him alone for the first time after twenty-five years? Will I finally reveal what I feel compelled—no, what I'm busting a gut—to tell him? That he has a beautiful son, that our son Josh is getting married in just three months? I'm probably rationalizing, but I think he finally has a right to know.

My bedroom is scattered with slip-on summer dresses and slip-off sandals. My suitcase is bulging with sexy bathing suits, frivolous beach accessories, and freshly purchased, frothy unmentionables. Not that my husband is interested in my frothy unmentionables anymore. Maybe Manny Gellar will be.

Mackie says I have a severe case of tropical depression. Which is a coincidence, because at this very moment a hurricane (formerly a tropical depression) is heading toward Florida—and so am I. I told Matt I was going to our condo to batten down the hatches, just in case. I knew he wouldn't go, of course. He's always too busy with work.

Mackie thinks I'm in a funk because, for the first time in my life, I'm trying to negotiate an empty nest. She might be onto something. I'm in the middle of planning Josh's wedding, and my daughter Natalie has just gone off to college out of state. She's already dating a boy named Barnyard. Now, before you ask, his real name is Bernard, and no, I don't know why his fraternity brothers call him Barnyard—I don't want to know.

Mackie asked me about it this morning as we sipped hot chocolates at our respective Starbucks. Since Matt and I moved to Atlanta last year, Mackie, one of my last links to sanity, and I have a standing weekly date at Starbucks, via our iPhones, with matching purple OtterBoxes®. Natalie wanted me to buy her an iPhone, too, but I thought I could save some money by mating my iPhone with Mackie's and giving the by-product to Natalie. That didn't work out. Apparently the gadgets don't reproduce. Sometimes we call; sometimes we e-mail; sometimes we Instant Message. My screen name is *Jewels*. Mackie's is *DoubleMac*. Both nicknames are courtesy of our mutual friend and my ex-boyfriend, Old *Un*faithful, Manny Gellar, now "Realtor to the Stars."

Mackie calls in religiously from Miami; I report from Atlanta. Things haven't been exactly the same between Mackie and me since I moved away. There's a subtle strain, a distance I pick up on whenever we talk now. I hope it's all in my mind.

From my corner seat at the coffee shop, I inhale the steam and touch my lips to the liquid warmth, letting the drink conjure all the feelings of home. I can almost feel my mother's hand pressing a mug of sweet cocoa into mine as we try to stay warm, cocooned in the cramped kitchen in the house where I grew up, around a portable heater, on a rare chilly 40-degree Miami morning.

"Is Barnyard an animal?" Mackie wants to know.

"No. I've never met the boy, but according to Natalie, he seems perfectly respectable. And the best part is he has a small family. You know how big Josh's fiancée's family is. The Suarez side of the guest list is growing like kudzu."

"Kudzu?" Mackie asks.

"It's a hyperactive vine with an attitude that's trying to finish the job General Sherman started," I explain. "Anyway, I promised Natalie that if she married Barnyard his mother could invite as many people as she wanted to the wedding."

"That's very generous of you, Julie," Mackie observes, before her tone turns serious. "What do you think that means for Natalie and Greg?"

Greg is Mackie's son, and we've been planning their wedding since the kids were in diapers. And Greg would have made a fabulous son-in-law, and he will, only for some other mother-in-law. The happily-ever-after ending is never going to happen for Natalie and Greg, because, although Natalie loves Greg, she's not *in love* with Greg. And I don't know how to begin to tell Mackie or if I should even be the one to tell her. So I resort to a little white lie to keep from hurting my friend.

"You know how girls can be when they get their first taste of freedom," I say. "Remember how we were? She just wants to experiment. Barnyard is nothing more than a starter college boyfriend. She'll come back to Greg. They were meant to be together."

We don't always get what we want. I thought Manny Gellar and I were "meant to be together" too, but that didn't exactly work out either.

Mackie's sigh of relief is audible.

Natalie thinks I'm crazy to bring up marriage, since she's only been out with Barnyard four times. Now that I'm no longer working full-time at my jewelry boutique, *Stones,* in Coral Gables, Florida, my daughter says my new job seems to be supervising every move she makes. She accuses me of hovering and meddling in every aspect of her business and encourages me to "Get a Life!"

She made an exception one evening last week when I picked up the phone, heard her wavering voice at the other end of the line, and imagined her beautiful, pale face crumpling.

"Mama," she cried.

"Honey, what's wrong?" I pictured a horrific car crash, a nuclear accident, or a terrorist attack on campus.

"It's Bernard."

"What about Barnyard?" I said, my parental radar picking up flashing Natalie danger signals.

"I found out he has a girlfriend back in Boca."

Small family or not, I wasn't going to let Barnyard get away with saddling my daughter with ex-girlfriend issues.

"Those long-distance relationships never last," I assured her.

"When I confronted him, he told me they'd broken up. And now they're back together."

We had made such progress in the last three years, I wasn't about to let Natalie founder in rough relationship waters. She had to be protected at all costs. No matter how far away she roamed, I would never stop trying to smooth the way for her.

"There are other fish in the sea, or in this case, animals in the barn," I counseled. "There are a ton of boys at the university. I'll bet if you look, you'll find one who is perfect for you."

"I know. But I like Bernard. He kissed me."

"That's all he did, I hope," I managed, trying not to strangle on the words. I wanted to wring Barnyard's neck for hurting my baby. And I didn't want what had happened to me in college to happen to my daughter. I didn't want history repeating itself by having her hung up on the wrong man for half a lifetime.

"I have to see him all the time. He lives in my dorm. He's in most of my classes. He still wants me to go out with him, even though—"

"Well, if you're asking my opinion, don't go out with that farm animal until he gets his act together. Ask one of your sorority sisters to fix you up. Maybe if he sees you with someone else, he'll get jealous."

"Mom, that's sneaky."

"Yes, well, sometimes your old mom can be a sneaky Pete." *If she only knew.*

Natalie laughed at my attempt to lift her spirits. My daughter is brilliant, so much so that it sometimes boggles my mind. But she is also oversensitive and serious, so I have a tendency to overcompensate by being overprotective.

In the past there have been a whole range of subjects that were off limits to talk about between us. Boys, clothes, and food (especially food) are just a few of the parent traps. If she baits me by asking about one of those "hot button" topics, I refuse to comment because I have learned that there *are* no right answers. Mackie's husband, Little Jon, my psychiatrist, says Natalie was just acting out because of separation anxiety as she mentally prepared to go off to college. But that rocky period is behind us, now that her eating disorder no longer defines her. And she's very resilient. She's already survived a shaky period in her young life, so I have to believe she'll be okay. It doesn't stop me from worrying, though.

I don't know how many times in the past month I've fallen asleep on the couch in the den only to wake up in the middle of the night, disoriented, looking for my precious Natalie, who up until a month ago had been my little shadow. Is she up in her room? Sleeping at a friend's house? Out with Greg? Why isn't she here in the house with me? Then I remember she is away at college, Matt is out of town, and I'm alone, except for the ever loyal and affectionate Abercrombie, who dutifully follows me around like Mary's little lamb. And it takes a few minutes for the ache of missing my little girl to disappear.

The line at the cash register at the Starbuck's is snaking out the door. I take another sip of my hot chocolate, which is no longer hot. I've been sitting at my table for so long the other patrons are giving me dirty looks. I do the only thing I can do. I look away.

"Being a concerned mother, I even went a step further," I admit to Mackie after I've filled her in on my latest conversation with Natalie.

"At the risk of being too stalkeriffic, I tried surfing the Web to find Natalie's profile on that Internet dating service she subscribes to. I didn't have much luck. There was this one hot-looking guy listed, but he doesn't make enough money."

"Enough for you or for Natalie?" Mackie asks.

"His profile says he is looking for a woman between the ages of 19 and 51," I report.

"Hey, we just make the cutoff," Mackie replies, her voice perking up an octave.

"He reminds me of Ricardo, the man who fixed my washing machine yesterday," I muse, biting my bottom lip.

"Ricardo? You two are on a first-name basis?" Mackie sounds suspicious.

"Well, yes, he's very interesting. He told me how he escaped from Chile on a cargo ship. He's going to school to learn English. He can speak it but can't write it."

"You learned all that on a service call? So what are you telling me, that you're interested in the Maytag repairman?"

"Just to look, mind you. You know how lonely these washing machine repairmen can get. He has the most adorable little butt crack when he bends over behind the washer."

"You're hitting on the washing machine repairman?" Mackie sounds horrified. "This is serious. We need to find you a hobby, or you need to start wearing a warning sign that says, 'Dangerous when bored.' Natalie's right. You obviously don't have enough going on in your life. And she'll flip out if she finds out you're looking up her profile. Besides, what does she need with a dating service when she has Greg?"

"True, but as long as she's looking, I need to know what's out there, to see what she's up against." I continue to vet the candidates on my laptop as Mackie listens politely, secure in the delusion that my daughter and her son are ultimately headed for matrimonial bliss.

"The best match I found was a guy named Danny Fier. He's pre-med at the University of Florida."

"What does it say about his perfect first date?" Mackie wants to know. "You have nothing to *fear* but *Fier* itself?"

"Okay, then what about a guy who says he likes to work outdoors with his hands?"

"Beware of men wielding power tools," Mackie

cautions. "Everyone knows power tools are just penis extensions."

"Mackie, you're outrageous!" That is one of the things I love about my best friend. Nobody has ever accused me of being outrageous. But that is all about to change.

"I did find another attractive guy, but there's a red flag," I point out. "It says his hobby is decoupage."

"Doing decoupage is not a red flag," Mackie objects. "It's a frigging deal breaker."

"Well, then, what about a handsome man in uniform? He's in ROTC. You know he has to be brave to be willing to defend his country."

"Hmm," Mackie says thoughtfully. "ROTC...isn't that for boys who need structure and *like to kill*?"

I hesitate. "Maybe I should let Natalie find her own dates. I think I've passed on enough advice to my daughter for one week."

"Has it ever occurred to you that you're great at giving advice but you just can't take it?" Mackie asks, with what sounds to me like latent hostility. Met with a stony silence (she knows I don't like to be criticized), she tries to lighten the mood. "By the way, have you passed on the secret ingredient in your grandfather's brisket recipe?"

"Not yet. Natalie isn't interested in cooking."

"She takes after her mother."

"I can cook—when I want to," I object.

"Frozen pizza," Mackie says.

"Matt won't even eat that anymore. He has an aversion to anything that might be convenient for me. You have to admit, I do make a great brisket!"

"Yes, you do," Mackie concedes, trying to wriggle

her way back into my good graces. "And hey, I know I'm not family, but after all these years, I think I deserve to know what the secret ingredient is."

Mackie is closer than family, and I tell her everything, well almost everything. I still haven't been able to bring myself to tell her how bad things have gotten between Matt and me in the bedroom, or about Natalie's battle with anorexia, and keeping those secrets is killing me. I don't know who I am trying to maintain the illusion for, Mackie or myself. But in any event, she is like the sister I never had, so she deserves to know. *About the brisket, not the bedroom.*

"Chewing tobacco," I whisper conspiratorially into the cell phone.

"Are you serious?"

"I am. My grandfather always had a cheek full of chewing tobacco, and my grandmother swore he spit some into the brisket to add flavor."

"Remind me never to eat brisket at your house again."

"Well, that's what I've always heard. But you're safe. I substitute Worcestershire sauce."

Now I am considering a substitute for the man in my life.

Matt says I have no goals. But he's wrong. My goal is to achieve closure. In this world, that is very difficult, maybe even impossible, to accomplish. Bottom line—nothing can ever be accomplished in the first go-round. Everything has to be redone. As a result, there is never any closure.

Take, for example, the call on my answering machine urging me to call the Breast Health Center right away because there was an area on my mammogram that required further evaluation. The radiologist recommended I return for special views of my left breast. If I want special views, I can get a room with a balcony on a Mediterranean cruise.

The message said I needed to come in for a follow-up mammogram and possible ultrasound. Which meant another visit for additional imaging. Lucky for me the results of the further evaluation turned out to be normal.

And of course there was that horrible month that I was considering a hysterectomy. Or rather, my doctor was considering giving me one.

"You're in a lot of pain," I remember him saying as he bobbed his head with all the sympathy of a politician's nod.

"I'm not in any pain," I disagreed, interrupting his unimpressive flow of empathy.

"But you *are* experiencing heavy bleeding," he reasoned.

"I'm not experiencing any bleeding," I protested, in case he was looking for my opinion, which he wasn't. *Hello, are you even listening to me?*

"You have a growth the size of a small grapefruit in your uterus...it measures seven centimeters!"

I couldn't relate to that concept. I had been told to avoid grapefruit or grapefruit juice because it reacts negatively with the medicine I take to reduce my cholesterol.

"I read that tumors can dissolve," I offered hopefully.

"Reading can be dangerous to your health. I'm your doctor, and I recommend an operation right away."

Then, as a casual aside, he remarked, "You don't

really need your uterus anyway. You already have two children. At your age, you don't want any more."

Well, what if I *do* want more? And anyway, you're a man—translation: moron—so how could you possibly know whether or not I still need my uterus? It's a part of me and I still want it, whether I need it or not.

"What I *want*," I calmly told my doctor, clenching my teeth, "is to be able to have that choice."

So I went for a second opinion, which of course meant a second appointment, this time with a female gynecologist. Believe me, it was a lot more complicated than having my washing machine fixed. In the final analysis, the radiologist who read the ultrasound confirmed that, in fact, I didn't have a growth. Apparently, it had disappeared. It was a miracle. I still believe in them, even at my age.

"Could it have dissolved?" I asked Dr. Second Opinion.

"Of course," she replied.

So I changed doctors and kept my working parts intact, just in case. Closure, at last.

Now that I'm planning my son's wedding, I can't help flashing back to the time I married Matt and put an end to the life I thought I was meant to have with Manny Gellar. No matter how much, in my imagination, I try to reengineer the twists and turns of my life, or how much I'm eaten up with regret, I can't alter that outcome. Or achieve closure.

At my age, closure is an extremely important concept. Because—let's face it—I'm running out of time here.

Closure. That's what this trip to Palm Coast tomorrow is all about. Knowing that I'm about to reconnect with my old boyfriend while I'm still married—no matter how much I rationalize that Matt has driven me to it—poses a question I've been grappling with for days and still haven't resolved.

If I could, I'd fix what is wrong with my marriage and put it back the way it was before, as easily as Ricardo fixed my washing machine. *Before* Matt yanked me out of Miami by my roots, as if I were a noxious weed he was tossing out of a flower garden, and carelessly transplanted us to Atlanta. *Before* we moved a state away from my family and my best friend and a business I'd worked a lifetime to create.

Before Matt sold his freight-expediting business to a German conglomerate for mega-millions and agreed to run the company for them from Atlanta for the next two years, barely consulting me. *Before* the *German occupation*, or rather before he became *preoccupied* with his sexy-sounding German second-in-command, Gretchen. *Before* he stopped sleeping with me in the biblical sense. *Before* I turned fifty.

From my experience in the jewelry business, I know that precious gems and metals may sparkle and appear perfect on the outside. But at fifty, I'm finding that, more often than not, there are flaws and inclusions if you look beneath the surface. And soul-searching involves a heavy dose of looking beneath the surface.

I've been so busy fretting over the pros and cons of this trip to Palm Coast and thinking about the kids, the wedding, the viper Gretchen, and how out of hand things have gotten with Matt in the bedroom, that I have somehow lost the core of myself. Or maybe I'm just trying to justify the actions I know I'm about to take.

I'm not just some pathetic, premenopausal woman reacting to the fact that she will never again have sex in her life. Or that sneaking around behind my husband's back isn't taking its toll on me.

All I really want is closure. I'm convinced that meeting Manny Gellar again is the only way I will ever come full circle and reconnect with my life, maybe find my way back to Matt.

Tomorrow, I'll be one step closer to closure.

Chapter Two:
Hormones Trump Hurricanes

Jewels@aol.com: Matt's been talking to some chick in Germany named Gretchen. She calls at all hours of the night. They seem to be joined at the hip and who knows what other body parts. Apparently they've formed their own European Union. He says it's just business, but it sounds more like monkey business to me.

DoubleMac@aol.com: Maybe she calls late at night because of the time difference.

Jewels@aol.com: Too convenient.

DoubleMac@aol.com: She's probably some mousy-looking fräulein with glasses.

Jewels@aol.com: I wear glasses. And she doesn't sound mousy-looking. She sounds...irresistible. Like some sleek, cream-swallowing cat. She purrs.

DoubleMac@aol.com: In German?

Jewels@aol.com: Yes!

DoubleMac@aol.com: Did you listen in?

Jewels@aol.com: They were speaking German!

DoubleMac@aol.com: I didn't know Matt spoke German.

Jewels@aol.com: Neither did I. There's a lot I don't know about Matt. My mother said he ordered an exquisite piece of diamond jewelry from *Stones,* and he was so anxious to get it, he had her ship it to Germany.

DoubleMac@aol.com: Matt never buys you jewelry.

Jewels@aol.com: Bingo. That's why I think Gretchen is getting my diamonds!

DoubleMac@aol.com: If that's true, she's getting something much more valuable.

Jewels@aol.com: I thought Matt was different. But he's just like all the rest of those snakes who come into my shop hiding their dirty little secrets; looking for the perfect diamond for the perfect mistress or the not-so-perfect parting gifts for the wives they've grown tired of who don't have a clue they're about to be sacked. The stinker is cheating on me. He's buying diamonds for Gretchen, from *my* mother!

DoubleMac@aol.com: Matt would never cheat on you. He's not wired that way.

Jewels@aol.com: He's a man, isn't he?

****

My hand is trembling. In it is an unopened RSVP, from the *fräulein*, received in the mail today after I got back from Starbucks. I know it's from Gretchen because it has a Berlin postmark. Okay, so now is the moment of truth. Is she or is she not coming to my son's wedding? I'll never know if I don't open the envelope. If Matt has the audacity to flaunt his colleague/lover in my face by asking me to invite her to his son's wedding, then I should have the courage to open this stupid reply.

When my husband told me to include his business associate Gretchen Kleinmann on the guest list, I had to ask, "What's she like?"

"Very smart," he'd answered.

"Pretty?"

"Yes."

"On a scale of one to 10?"

"Do you want me to lie?"

"Yes," I pouted. "No. Maybe."

"She's an unattractive spinster with no social life, so this wedding will be the highlight of her otherwise pitiful existence. How's that?"

"Is it true?" When the question I really wanted to ask was, "Are you boinking Gretchen's brains out?" But I didn't want to hear him say: "Do you want me to lie?"

"No."

So now I'm waiting for a drum roll, or at least an appearance by a representative from the firm of PricewaterhouseCoopers, responding to a call for "the envelope, please." When no one and no sound comes forth, I tear it open.

Gretchen has underlined the appropriate spaces and written in the margins in broken English: *Gretchen Kleinmann* will be *pleasured* to attend.

That's *pleased*, you bitch. I wander over to the living room and pick up the seating chart I left on the coffee table. Where can I place her? As far away from Matt as possible. Maybe at the kids' table? Ha! Perfect.

Then I notice my answering machine flashing with three new messages.

"Mama. Just wanted to let you know that not only am I burning the candle at both ends but I'm also pushing the envelope. Ha. Ha. Bernard is going home again this weekend (dramatic pause) *to break up with his girlfriend! Guess the jealousy thing worked. He says he can't wait to get back to me. Thanks. Oh, and I want to bring him as my date to Josh and Zandy's wedding.*

Bye. Love you." Beep. Natalie.

"I know you don't read the papers or listen to TV anymore and you don't know what's going on in the world, so I thought I'd tell you that there's a killer hurricane heading to Palm Coast. I hope you're not going anywhere near that place. Don't go down there thinking you can call me for help if you get stranded. I have nothing to do with this hurricane. It's run by God. Beep. My mother.

In case you don't know, Sylvia Goldsmith and God are on a first-name basis, as in, "I was going to buy that Little Black Dress at Macy's yesterday, but they don't make the Little Black Dress in big sizes anymore. But God must have been looking out for me, because I waited until today and I found my size *and* it's on sale!"

I'm sure God has better things to do than make sure the merchandise my mother wants is marked down at Macy's.

"Hello, número uno. (My father always calls me his number one daughter, even though I am his only daughter.) *"I have one word for you. Hegira."* Beep. My father.

My dad issued the obscure word like a verbal challenge, stumping me again. I chuckled and took a second to look it up on the Internet. *Hegira. Any flight or journey to a more desirable place.* Maybe my father was trying to tell me something.

Mackie says I'm decathexing.

"Defecating?"

"No, that's what we did the night before our colonoscopies. You're experiencing decathexis."

"Is that word even in the dictionary?"

"I assure you it really exists. I should know. My husband's a psychiatrist. It's when you've already left a place in your mind and moved on to your new destination, invested yourself in your new life."

Is that what I'm doing by going to Palm Coast? Disengaging from my marriage? Hiding my head in the sand? People frequently accuse me of hiding my head in the sand to avoid life's unpleasantries.

My mother, who believes she's an authority on absolutely everything, thinks I have sand in my *shoes*.

"You were born in Florida and you're trying to get back there—to the sun and the sea and the sand," she says.

Well, actually, I am trying to get back there. But not just for the beach. I do crave the soothing feel of sun on my skin and the scratchy sensation of sand under my feet. And I don't even mind the heat, if it comes with a sea breeze and a water view. But there's something else—someone else—in Florida I crave. Or want to find out if I still crave after all these years. The someone who's been on the back burner of my mind—the proverbial old flame who has chosen the perfect time in my life to turn up the heat.

It's probably too late to call anyone back tonight, I rationalize. If I call my mother, she will immediately sense something is wrong, because besides being a conduit to God, that woman has X-ray vision, I'm convinced, and can see through telephone lines. If I tell her I am going to meet Manny Gellar, she will rat me out to Matt, because she and my husband are, and always have been, in cahoots.

My mother can stop anyone cold with The Look. The Look could turn a Gorgon to stone or stop a train.

My mother can get anyone to do anything she wants just by giving someone The Look. I'm mostly immune to The Look. She's used it on me so many times over the years that I've developed a resistance to it, sort of like penicillin. But I can feel The Look, even over the phone. I can't call Mackie before I leave, either, because she thinks this walk down memory lane is a big mistake, and she will try to talk me out of going to Palm Coast, again. And I need to take this trip.

Just yesterday, I read in the Perspectives column of *The Miami Herald* that "history chases us and catches us by surprise." That is what is happening to me. My past and present are on a collision course.

Chapter Three:
Doing It at The Home Depot

DoubleMac@aol.com: You can't fix your marriage by meeting another man at The Home Depot. If it's a matter of intimacy…

Jewels@aol.com: ☹Matt's idea of intimacy is leaving town.

DoubleMac@aol.com: What if you get there and you want to go through with it? Where will you do it? In the restroom of The Home Depot? And how are you going to sneak Manny into the women's restroom? Come to think of it, you hate The Home Depot.

Jewels@aol.com: I know. That's why I chose it. It's Matt's favorite place. He says you can get anything you want at The Home Depot.

****

Maybe Matt is right. But The Home Depot scares me to death. They sell too many tiny things like nails and screws and nuts and bolts, and it freaks me out to even walk into that store. So maybe I'll see the place, take one look at Manny Gellar, and turn around and walk right out of there.

The thing about all those tiny things is that in the store they're all alone and isolated but when you take them home they all fit with something. And that's the thing about me. Right now I don't feel like I fit anywhere anymore.

And speaking of intimacy, when did my marriage deteriorate beyond repair? When did Matt stop noticing me? To say my marriage is going through a rough patch is an understatement. I'm talking about more here than just a random bump in the road, something closer to a street-swallowing sinkhole. The road construction crew is already descending into the cavernous depths of a crater that Natalie would call *huge*.

The glaring, gaping hole in our marriage wasn't so noticeable when the kids were still in the house, but now that it's just the two of us, it's become painfully obvious that more than just the kids are missing. In terms that Matt, the Frequent Flyer, can understand, we share the same airspace and we're both circling, but neither of us cares enough to make our connection.

So it looks like my marriage is not going to end with a bang (no pun intended). The spigot will simply shut off gradually until the flow narrows to a trickle and all that is left of it will come out in fits and starts, drips and drops. *Plop, plop, plop.*

Now, whenever Matt tries to joke with me outside the bedroom, or cajole or disarm me, or share a confidence, I think, *No fair, you bastard.* If you aren't going to give me intimacy on all levels, then I won't accept any at all.

Behavior that has only mildly annoyed me before suddenly sticks in my craw like a sharp chicken bone.

I am almost desperate enough to seek advice from my mother, until I remember that she once told me my father doesn't say, "Good night, Sylvia," before he goes to bed. Instead, he makes pronouncements, like "Eggs," or "Oatmeal," so my mother knows what he wants her to fix him for breakfast the next morning. Hardly a relationship model to emulate.

Okay, what am I missing? Something is very wrong in my own marriage. Matt is either boinking Gretchen's brains out, which is why he doesn't feel the need to boink my brains out, or maybe his libido is seriously out of whack. Either way, I'm screwed. Or not. All I know is that, intentionally or unintentionally, he is systematically destroying our marriage with his neglect.

When I tried making just my side of the bed to drive home a point, Matt wasn't interested in my point. And that is the point, isn't it? Matt is a great father, and the years we were married were some of the most wonderful times of my life. I wish we could get that feeling back. But the magic is missing. Maybe our marriage could benefit from a reassessment period. I'll bring that up after Josh's wedding. I just can't think about it now. Hey, since I'm in Atlanta, there's no reason I can't channel Scarlett O'Hara.

All I know is, Matt no longer gives me what I need. I get more support from my eighteen-hour, cross-my-heart, hold-my-boobs-in bra. I'm out of practice and frankly out of patience with being a wife without privileges. Any sex we have at this point seems obligatory, and I am through settling for that. We've both just stopped trying, and now the well of resentment I am drowning in has become an ocean.

Matt pretty much falls asleep the minute his head hits the pillow. Sex is no longer important to him. But it's still important to me. He keeps to his side of the king-sized bed, which leaves me alone on mine. Which is a problem, because I'm a snuggler.

Most nights we go to bed without saying a word,

facing away from each other, lying still as statues, barely breathing (well, Matt claims I snore), each of us engrossed in our own private thoughts, me in my own private hell. Sometimes I actually ache at night for wanting Matt inside me. The emptiness and the loneliness are not vague, frivolous states of mind. They are real, and they are making me desperate. One minute I want to burrow into Matt, be banded by his arms, but then he makes some innocuous remark and I blow it all out of proportion, until the moment and the opportunity pass and it becomes easier to hang onto the old familiar anger.

It's a civil enough situation—less like an armed camp and more like an uneasy truce that we almost break the night before I leave for our condo. I am determined to give my husband one more chance to make love to me and change my mind about going to Palm Coast, but he fails the test he doesn't even know he is taking.

After what seems like hours of tossing and turning and stewing, I throw the sheet and the blanket off my bed. It feels like somebody is stoking a furnace inside my body.

"Turn the air on, Matt. It's roasting in here," I complain. "I can't breathe."

"There's nothing wrong with the thermostat," Matt says, in a voice still groggy from sleep. "You're the one who needs a tune-up. You're going through the change. Now go back to bed so we can both get some sleep."

"Are you a gynecologist now?"

A strangled sound escapes from Matt's throat.

"That better not be a laugh."

"It's a cough. I was coughing." He couldn't resist.

"But I know what I see."

My new gynecologist, Dr. Second Opinion, has probably seen it, too, during her exam on my last visit. I am at the end of my reproductive line. I am never going to have a period again. She just failed to let me in on her little secret.

Too worked up to sleep, and too nervous about tomorrow, I jump out of bed, grab my purse, and riffle through it in the dark until I feel the damning pink mini-pillow of plastic. I haven't had a period for forty days and forty nights. Is there a biblical significance to that number? I don't think it could be a coincidence. Being an optimist, I always carry around a maxi-pad, just in case. I crush my fist around it, switch on the bedside lamp, drag the entire bag of maxi pads out of the hall closet, and stuff the package into the wastebasket.

"Does this mean you're going to be in a permanent bad mood?" Matt wants to know, before I grab my pillow and give him a resounding, satisfying thwack on the head.

This sudden onset of meanness and mood swings surprises me. One minute I'm content and the next belligerent, feeling put upon and entitled to my rage. The weight of the world is pressing in on me, choking off my breath.

"You're crushing our marriage with your neglect."

"You're the one who's crushing our marriage with your unrealistic expectations. I thought women going through the change were supposed to have a lower sex drive."

"What's wrong with my expectations?"

He had no answer for that. It was a stalemate.

I'm sure the advice experts would toll the warning bells—that Matt is looking outside the marriage. Matt has needs, and he isn't coming to me to fulfill them. So who is he going to? There has to be someone else. And I think I know who that someone else is.

I've pretty much heard every excuse from Matt. At night he claims he's too tired. In the morning he lifts weights and runs on the treadmill, and then he's too sweaty. During the week he's never in town. The stars are never perfectly aligned. According to Papa Bear, the porridge is either too hot or too cold. The time for having sex is never Just Right.

"I'm exhausted," Matt says. "I've been working hard." Left unsaid is, *"And you haven't."*

"You need to find a job or a hobby or something to do," Matt chides. "You need some stress in your life, and you need to engage your mind. Otherwise you're just a protoplasm."

Me, a protoplasm? I don't know what that means, but when I look it up, the word is defined as "the colloidal and liquid substance of which cells are formed, excluding *horny*, chitinous, and other structural material." Horny is a concept I can definitely relate to. Maybe I've already turned into a protoplasm, like Abercrombie.

"You know, we're not twenty anymore," Matt says defensively whenever I bring up the subject of sex, or the lack of it. "We used to do it all the time, remember?"

Frankly, I don't, and that's part of the problem.

"I'm not asking for all the time," I counter. "Just once, again. I'm fifty, not eighty."

"You've been reading too many romance novels."

"You're gone all the time," I say.

"I've always traveled. I was never romantic. I'm the same person you married."

"You're not," I insist.

"Nothing's changed."

You're wrong, Matt. Inside my head, everything about you has changed.

"Maybe you need to see someone," Matt suggests.

"Oh, so now *I'm* the one with the problem? Maybe I *do* need to see someone, and I don't mean a shrink."

"What's that supposed to mean?"

The room resounds with silence.

"Is it someone else?" I whisper, not really wanting to know the answer to that question. "All those times you had to go to New York to meet with the investment bankers? And to Germany to meet with the buyer, when I asked you to take me with you and you refused?"

"No, of course not. It was all business, Julie, I promise you. We wouldn't have had a spare minute to spend with each other. I was in meetings all day and night." *Meetings with Gretchen.*

A year ago, I would have believed him. Sexy as the fräulein sounded, I didn't think then Matt would ever cheat on me. He hated change. He's had the same secretary for the last twenty-five years, the same job, the same house (until he moved us out of it unexpectedly), and the same wife. But he might be tempted. The Germans almost conquered the world— twice. How hard would it be for one German woman to conquer one man? My man! Things between us haven't been the same since Matt started traveling to Germany a year ago. I know there must be more to the story.

"I'm not having an affair, and I can't believe you

would even think that," he insists.

I wonder whether disinterest qualifies as an explanation.

Apparently he isn't turned off by all women, just me. "Well, then, is it *me*? Do you still love me?"

He pauses, considers his answer. "Of course I still love you."

"Talk to me, Matt," I urge, as the tears slide down the side of my face. I reach for his hand. Even in the darkness, I see a look cross his face that I have never seen before. Beneath his hooded eyes, it appears almost venomous. Like he wants to punish me. And then it is gone. Maybe I've imagined it.

He only hesitates a minute before he says, flippantly, "I think I have indigestion."

"That's lame, Matt. That's like saying you have a headache." Matt doesn't get headaches, he gives them. Matt is a consummate power player. He likes to mess with my mind, not my body, and is looking to lay blame. I am just looking to get laid. In fact, I am so frustrated that if the next UPS man who comes to the door shows even the slightest interest, I will be tempted to see just what Brown can do for me.

"When's the last time we did it?" I ask Matt lightly, trying not to sound too judgmental. When he doesn't answer, I try a humorous approach.

"I know for sure we've done it at least twice," I joke, while seriously trying for the umpteenth time to seduce my own husband.

Then it is my turn to be contrite. Because I know what he is thinking, although he'll never say it to my face. He'll be contradicting me in his mind, "At least once." But saying that would be a betrayal of Josh. And

Matt thinks of Josh as his own, even though he isn't my son's biological father. I never doubted Matt's love for my son. In all the years we've been married, he's never once thrown Josh's paternity back in my face. The bond my husband has forged with my son is one of the things I love most about him.

When the kids aren't around, we call Josh "Fabio Jr." because Matt still believes my son was fathered by an Italian playboy who got me pregnant when I was going to school in Florence, Italy, during my senior year abroad. He doesn't know who Josh's real father is. And he married me anyway. He made a commitment to my son and me, and he kept his word and honored it. I tried to tell him the truth about Josh on several occasions, but he didn't want to have that conversation. He dismissed the whole thing by announcing, "The past is in the past."

But I can't seem to put the past behind me.

When Manny Gellar began his e-mail seduction campaign in earnest, it was only a short slide from shock to vulnerability, allowing the sly wolf that had been my friend and former lover to seductively blow his way into the house of straw that has become my life.

The first dozen yellow roses arrived the day after Manny's first e-mail. There was a card: "Meant to Be Together." I didn't need a signature to know who had sent the arrangement. The flowers seemed harmless enough. Who could get hurt by this distraction? Not Manny's wife, my longtime rival, Nita, who I blame for stealing Manny away from me. As far as I am concerned, she doesn't have feelings.

The flowers were followed by late-night phone calls.

"Are you alone?" Manny asked in his husky, sneaky, still-so-sexy voice. Always, I thought, and then, not anymore. "Jewels. I can only talk for a minute—"

"I know," I whispered, praying he wouldn't mention *her* name. "I got your flowers. They're my—"

"Favorite, yes, I remember," Manny says. "I had to call to hear your voice again."

More huffing and puffing on the wolf's end.

"If I can't have you, it's the next best thing to being there. I want to be there with you now, holding you, kissing you." More heavy breathing by the Big Bad Wolf.

"Jewels, I need to see you again," he implored.

"Why should we get together?"

"To complete the circle."

"What good would that do?"

"I think we both want a taste of what we once had. Besides, this thing between us isn't over." Same old confident Manny.

"I…" was all I could manage, still flustered and tongue-tied whenever I was around him or even heard his voice. I can listen to Manny's voice forever. I usually have trouble sleeping when Matt is away, but I drift off easily after one of Manny's calls, until the guilt sets in.

"I've got to—" I manage, "hang up now."

When I tell Mackie about our encounter, she says, "Did he ask if you wanted to join in any reindeer games?"

"He didn't quite put it that way," I answer. "It was more like—"

"Do me, Rudolph?" Mackie speculates.

"Not quite that crude, but close."

It's true what they say, "It takes two to tango." Or not to tango. The tango is what Matt and I have NOT been doing for the past year. While Matt's mind is focused on acquisitions, I have the urge to merge. And maybe that's just what I'll do when I get to Palm Coast.

Chapter Four:
The List

Jewels@aol.com: My horoscope says I will exude
sex appeal today. But who will I lure? Manny? Or my
husband of twenty-five years?

DoubleMac@aol.com: You make your marriage
sound like a life sentence. What horrible crime did Matt
commit? Did he leave the cap off the toothpaste?

Jewels@aol.com: How would I know? He's never
around. I don't even see him brush his teeth. He's just
not romantic, you know, passionate, any more.

DoubleMac@aol.com: LOL. Little Jon says
"unbridled passion" has a half-shelf life of eighteen
months.

Jewels@aol.com: Well, then I guess that puts me
on the shelf permanently.

DoubleMac@aol.com: It would be hard to stay
passionate for twenty-five years. When you're young
you just can't get *enough* sex, and when you get older,
you just *can't* get enough sex.

Jewels@aol.com: What about the next twenty-five
years? The average life expectancy is 77.6 years. It
must be nice to be married to your own private
therapist.

DoubleMac@aol.com: He's so drained—
emotionally and physically—after a long day of seeing
lunatics, and then he has to come home to the lunatic he

married, so there's not much left over for me. He shuts up tighter than a drum. You know that recapturing the past is just a fantasy.

Jewels@aol.com: No, it's a real thing. There are a couple of books out about first loves and second chances. Apparently it's common for old flames to reconnect. They say first love is powerful, and the attraction is practically chemical. That's what's pulling at me. I'm having trouble fighting it, getting him out of my mind, not thinking about the way things were. This psychologist who wrote a book about it said it had something to do with imprinting.

DoubleMac@aol.com: You mean like ducklings and goslings following their mothers?

Jewels@aol.com: I guess, something like that. Bonding with someone who shares your history.

DoubleMac@aol.com: Is that what you're trying to do? Rekindle an old romance? Manny is just playing games, and you're playing with fire. That's the thing about old flames—you can get burned.

****

Why am I even contemplating meeting my old flame? When I was growing up, my father never even let me play with matches. Now I am about to start a firestorm. Am I just looking for validation that I am still an attractive, desirable woman, not a dried-up old prune praying for menopause so I can finally have sex with my own husband without birth control? Or is it the fact that Matt has become more like a roommate than a husband?

I don't want to talk about sex to my best friend, or anyone. I've read the surveys of couples who argue about having sex only two or three times a week, which is considered average. Apparently my sister-in-law is above average, because she confides that my brother Joel wants to do it every day.

There's even a category for couples that have sex fewer than ten times a year. *I don't need a survey to tell me I am stuck in a "sexless" marriage.* The horrifying thing is there isn't anything my husband does for me that I can't do for myself. The expiration date on my marriage has long since passed. The truth is right there in front of me, gasping desperately for air, flailing like a fat, slippery tarpon slapping on a hot pier before it stills and loses consciousness. I want to throw the tarpon back, but, like with a train wreck, I can't seem to look away.

I am not the type to write to an advice columnist or see a therapist, at least not for that problem. So I suffer in silence. Is it abnormal for a fifty-year-old woman to think about sex? Not according to a landmark sex study conducted by the AARP about sexuality in midlife and boomers and a second sexual revolution.

Fifty or not, I want a spicier sex life, and I am not ready to be put out to pasture. I'll even settle for a bland sex life. What I really want is the exciting kind of love I read about in my romance novels and see in the movies or hear about in songs. I guess I'm going through the classic midlife crisis. I just never imagined anything so colossally mind-altering would happen to me.

Am I just looking to fulfill my sexual fantasies with Manny? I already know he is capable of doing that. For example, Matt is not into breasts. At least not *my* breasts. In fact, he never comes near them. And I can't even remember whether he ever did. You know, like some men treasure the special spot behind a woman's knees, or crave some other part of her body. Well, Matt doesn't crave or cherish any part of my body, that I'm aware of. On the other hand, my breasts were always the focus of Manny's attention.

So when Matt and I are in bed together, I have to imagine that someone is pulling my hands roughly over my head and overpowering me, someone is teasing my nipples with his tongue, and plunging himself deep into me, because Matt doesn't do that. And the person I almost always imagine doing that is Manny.

I know what I want, but I don't ask for it. So Matt probably has his fantasies about what he'd like me to do to him, and I have my fantasies about what I'd like him to do to me. In the end, even when we're together, we're not really together at all.

No, there is more to it than sex. Much more.

When I called Matt from the road and told him I was heading to Palm Coast early to open up the condo before he got there, he sounded suspicious. But there was no way he could have known what I was contemplating. He was just upset that I'd left for Palm Coast without telling him. He said he was worried about me, but I didn't believe that.

"Did you take the garbage can down?" Matt began. "Tomorrow's garbage pickup day."

"I did that this morning," I replied.

"Good. Did you pick up my shirts from the cleaners?"

"Yes."

"What about my prescription?"

"Taken care of."

"Did you go grocery shopping?"

"There's plenty of food in the fridge. I even made

you a brisket for tonight. *You're lucky I don't chew tobacco.* And anyway, you'll be in New York the rest of the week."

"Hmm. Did you deposit my paycheck at the bank?"

"Yes. I did everything on your list."

I waited.

"What about Carlos?" he asked. "Did you leave the check for Carlos?" *Carlos the Jackal* is our nickname for the man who cleans our house. His real name is Carlos Santana. Seriously. We couldn't call him that. There was only room for one Carlos Santana in the world. Carlos works for a company called Delta Cleaners. I'm convinced Carlos is the original hit man, employed by Delta Force to get on my nerves.

His weapon of choice? The vacuum cleaner. He follows me from room to room vacuuming behind me. I try to stay out of his way. When I'm comfortably settled with a book in the living room he starts vacuuming around me. When I move to the office, he moves with me. Next, I seek refuge in the den and he's right there behind me, wielding his weapon of mass *dust*ruction. I wouldn't mind, except Carlos does not have an adorable butt crack when he bends over, like Ricardo, the washing machine repairman. But back to *The List.*

"It was on the list, wasn't it?" I countered.

"We have some bills due, Julie. Did you pay the bills?"

"Yes," I said evenly, even though I hate it when he treats me like his secretary or his errand girl. I'm sure he doesn't treat Gretchen that way.

"Did you stop the mail and the paper?" Matt asked.

"Yes."

Silence.

"I don't report to you," I hissed. "You're not the boss of me."

"Now you sound like Natalie," he replied, trying his best not to sound amused.

My first-class pout was wasted on Matt because, unlike my mother, my husband can't see through telephone lines.

"You *know*, Julie," he sighed, in that low, slow, deliberate, newly annoying voice he uses that sounds like the Horatio Caine character that used to be played by David Caruso on the show *CSI: Miami*, "I thought we were going to drive down *together* this weekend."

"Well, yes (Horatio), I know we talked about that. It's just that you will be out of town most of the week, as usual," (I couldn't resist adding that—it had become my mantra, after all) "and Josh and Natalie are in college now. So there's really nothing to keep me there. Except the dog, and I already took her to the kennel."

Matt hates taking the dog to the kennel because the dog hates going to the kennel. She starts shaking every time we get near the place. I'm always the bad guy because I'm taking her to jail, and Matt gets to be the hero and rescue her when it's time to go home.

"I thought you wanted us to get more use out of the condo," I said.

"What about the wedding? Aren't you expecting the RSVPs?"

"They can wait a week. And besides, the bride's family is handling most of that."

"Have they heard from anyone yet?"

Matt is so predictable. I knew he could care less about wedding details. It was just his way of keeping me on the phone.

"Yes, Zandy's mother said the Red Aunt (that's what we call my mother's sister Betty Jean because she has red hair) couldn't attend because she has a CD coming due at the bank. And the Black Aunt (my mother's sister Ruth has black hair) won't come either."

"Why not?" Matt wanted to know.

"Well, as she pointed out when she called me to decline, we have a lunch from noon to 5 p.m. and the dinner reception starts at 7. She says there's nothing to do from 5 to 7."

"Your relatives are insane."

Actually, he's right about that. The Black Aunt has diarrhea of the mouth and telephones her sisters twice a day on three-way calls. And that's just when times are good. Her standard opening line before launching into her litany of troubles is, "Wait. Let me preheat the oven. It's gas, and it's big enough for the three of us to stick our heads in."

When I asked my mother why she puts up with that, she responded, "I'd better be nice to her. We'll probably end up in a nursing home together."

"What about the kids?" Matt asked, pulling my attention back to the conversation. "What if they need you?"

"The kids are just a phone call away. We've managed to raise two perfectly capable children."

"Yes, they're perfectly capable of calling their mother for help whenever they have a problem."

Matt was right about that, too. I was really good at solving problems (except my own, apparently). These days, it seems, my children are mostly too busy living their own lives to call me. Now I know how

Abercrombie must feel, hanging around waiting for table scraps.

The truth is, no one really needs me anymore. Except the dog and the frogs. I am really good at saving frogs. Every morning, I go to the skimmer to rescue some tiny chlorine-logged frog before the pool pump turns on. Or I coax a frog doing laps in the pool into the mesh leaf skimmer, tossing him a lifeline to safety. But we are about to close the pool for the season.

"Okay, then, what about the hurricane?" Matt posed. "It's predicted to make landfall in Florida tomorrow. Everyone is evacuating. You shouldn't even be going there. Remember Katrina? Remember Andrew?"

"Of course I do. But I'll be okay. Palm Coast hasn't had a direct hit from a hurricane in a hundred years."

"So the realtor says. I think the hurricanes were just churning out there in the Atlantic, waiting until we closed on our condo before unleashing their full fury. And it's all part of a hyperactive storm cycle that will last for the next two or three decades."

"Great. Now you sound like my mother. Stop reading the papers. I did. I'm much happier. And the storm is not expected to hit Palm Coast."

"You're an ostrich with her head in the sand."

"You know how much I like the sand," I countered, letting him mull that over for a minute. "Daddy," I whispered, trying to stop Matt from continuing on his rant. "Aren't you going to ask me if I did all my homework?"

Matt already thought I was a child. My snotty attitude just confirmed it. I knew he couldn't find fault with me for anything else, but I could tell by his deafening silence that I still needed to bolster my case.

"And we have so many things to bring down to the condo. I think we needed to take two cars anyway. I brought that Turkish carpet we bought in Istanbul, the light fixture for the foyer, that pewter mirror I got from The Pottery Barn, and some pillows and sheets for the twin beds. And it's good that I'm going down early so I can prepare the condo in case the hurricane *does* hit."

"You've never driven down there alone before," Matt pointed out. That was true. If Matt doesn't drive, I usually fly into Jacksonville or Daytona and we rent a car for the short drive to the condo.

"Well, I'm fifty years old. Isn't it about time I did?" I countered. "Look, Matt. There's a lot of traffic on the road. I need to pay attention."

"Yeah, you're probably the only car driving *into* Florida. The traffic is all going the other way."

"I'll call you when I get there, and I'll see you this weekend," I said, cutting off any future arguments.

I drive in peace for a few hours until Mackie calls.

"Mackie, I tried to stay away from him," I tell my best friend as I pass Valdosta, heading for the Florida border. "I looked for signs the whole way down. Heavy rain, a lightning bolt, a tree in the road, a flock of birds, anything. There was nothing."

"What about a Category Five hurricane? I know you don't watch TV. Did you know you are heading right into the path of a killer storm?"

"Now you sound just like Matt. And my mother. She called last night to warn me about the hurricane. Y'all have weather issues."

"Since when do you say y'all?"

"Since I moved to Atlanta. I'm practicing my Southern. Look, Mackie, I'm having hot flashes every fifteen minutes just thinking about Manny."

"It sounds like you're about to give birth. And anyway, my flashes are hotter than yours."

"They're sympathy flashes."

"Very funny."

"I'm sorry," I say. "I even ignored my horoscope. It said, 'You may yearn for a new romantic partner. But you're headed for stormy weather if you hook up with an old love.' "

I believe in signs of all kinds, including horoscopes and even fortune cookie predictions. Last night I picked up Chinese takeout and my fortune read, "Happy Life is Just in Front of You." Well, I am determined to reach out and grab that happy life.

"Julie, why would you let Manny back into your life again after everything he's put you through?"

"I guess it's the feelings we share."

"Did you ask him what this is really about, why he got in touch with you after twenty-five years?"

Mackie has heard rumors that Manny's wife, Nita, threatened to kick Manny out of the family real estate business if he didn't shape up.

"She thinks he's been fooling around with one of his clients, you know, that Latina singing sensation in Miami who just came out with a new crossover album, 'Magdalena: Singing in the Key of Country,'" Mackie says. "Her new hit, '*If You're Not Devoted, Then This Gun is Loaded,*' is off the charts. Apparently, Magdalena was more than grateful when Manny found her an Italianate mansion on South Beach. It wouldn't surprise me a bit if Manny was sleeping with that woman, and, if the rumors were true, his entire stable of clients."

"Does Nita know that Manny's been back in touch with me?" I ask.

"You would have heard about it if she did," Mackie says.

"What does Little Jon say?" I inquire.

"Don't use Little Jon as an example of fidelity," Mackie says bitterly. "He doesn't exactly hold up under close scrutiny. He should have gone into real estate like Manny. He has trouble staying off other people's property."

"What are you talking about?"

"Nothing." Mackie sighs.

I had already asked Manny why he was suddenly so interested in getting together.

"I miss you, Julie," he'd told me. "I've been thinking about you, and I wanted to see you. Does there have to be a reason?"

"After twenty-five years, yes," I said.

"It's seasonal. I start feeling this way every spring," he admitted, hesitating. "That was the time we were the happiest together, before you—got married, had the baby. Before I knew it was not going to happen for us. I'm having trouble concentrating. I'm having memory problems. I can't stop remembering the way we were together."

Jeesh! He sounded sincere, but maybe it was scripted. Or a plea for help.

"I know he initiated the contact and he won't leave you alone," Mackie says. "He just keeps sniffing around, playing you. Wanting what he can't have. He hasn't changed at all."

"Mackie, in all fairness, it's not all his fault. I want this as much as he does. But I really think all his big talk on the Internet is just that, talk, Internet innuendos. I'm finally calling his bluff by agreeing to meet him for lunch. I can't go on like this. I think I could be content with Matt if Manny wouldn't intrude on my life, fracture it, you know, churn up all these old feelings. Letting go of him and the hold he has on me is the first step, and I'm almost all the way there."

"I think addiction is a twelve-step program," Mackie observes wryly. "Admit it, you're still obsessed with him."

"Well, whatever happens, I plan to get him completely out of my system, exorcise the devil so I can get on with my life," I insist. Maybe find my way back to Matt.

I pause as another, much more terrifying, thought occurs to me.

"You don't think he knows about Josh, do you?" I say, clutching the wheel, suddenly worried. "And that's why he wants to get me alone?"

"I don't think so," Mackie stated. "Not after all these years."

But there had been some close calls. Like the weekend of Josh's Bar Mitzvah. Since our families were still close, I was expected to invite Manny and Nita to my son's Bar Mitzvah. There was Josh standing up at the bimah in the synagogue, chanting his Torah portion, and all I could think was, My God, Manny is going to see it. He's sitting there right in the second row, and he is finally going to see the resemblance. And Matt is going to see it. And everyone in the family is going to see what I see. The thing I'd been trying to avoid for thirteen years. The thing I had worried about every day since Josh was born. How could I not think about Manny when his face was forever staring back at me?

I could see it as plain as day. It made my heart stop every time I looked at my son. He was the spitting image of his father. With his dark and brooding good looks, even at thirteen. And those dreamy eyes. There was no mistaking whose eyes he had. Or whose son he was. And here they were, in the same room. People were finally going to put two and two together. And I would be so screwed. I'd be branded like that woman in *The Scarlet Letter*.

Last year, when we moved Josh out of his apartment after he completed his undergraduate degree, I almost choked at the mess. And I almost blew it.

"This place is a rattrap, Josh." I laughed. "I can't believe Zandy is going to marry you. You're a total slob, just like your father." My hand flew to my mouth as soon as the words were out. Luckily, Matt had just left the apartment to haul the TV out to the car. Josh just stared at me like I was losing it. Everyone knew Matt was immaculate. Nothing in his life was out of place. It was Manny who was the pig.

I was saved from the certain doom of discovery only by the fact that Matt, like Josh, had dark hair but his was curly and springy. And he had a light complexion, almost white. There was nothing of Matt in Josh in the looks department. But I guess people see what they expect to see, and after a while, like pets that grow to resemble their owners, kids tend to look like their parents.

Last month, I caught Matt gazing wistfully at

Josh's college graduation picture as if he were trying to conjure a resemblance. So I crept around the house trying to hide the evidence, and pushed all of Josh's photos into the shadows behind Natalie's, or into drawers.

"Mom, should I be developing a complex, or something?" Josh inquired, surprising me as I placed his photo face down on the desk in Matt's home office.

"I'm j-just d-dusting," I stuttered.

"But Mom, you don't dust."

"True," I said, improvising, "but you know Natalie is going through a stage. She doesn't think she's beautiful enough and you're the star of everything. I thought we'd put her front and center for a change."

"I think Natalie is really pretty," Josh said. "Maybe it would help if I told her."

"Maybe it would," I agreed, falling in love with my son all over again as I righted the frame and put it back where it belonged, beside Natalie's.

I looked at my daughter's picture. Natalie was so obviously Matt's she could have been stamped from his mold. She had his black, crinkly hair, sheep hair, chronic bad hair, which would cause her fits for the rest of her life. But it suited her. To compensate, she had the most remarkable green eyes, Matt's eyes — how could I have forgotten one of the features that had drawn me to Matt in the first place? — a peaches-and-cream complexion, a beautiful, almost arresting face, and a sassy spirit to match. But no amount of ironing would straighten that hair to her satisfaction. We always want what we don't have.

Even if Manny had suspected anything about Josh's paternity, we never could have discussed it.

Because his witchy wife would never allow me to get within an inch of him or she'd pounce, a mother tiger protecting her cub. Nita Weinstein Gellar had been territorial ever since she'd set her sights on my boyfriend in college and finally snagged him.

"Julie, are you still there?" Mackie asks, as I refocus my attention on the road. "Are you still determined to meet Manny Gellar in Palm Coast?"

"Yes," I answer, in a voice that leaves no room for argument. "Don't worry, we're not going to do it at The Home Depot. We're just going to meet there, and if things go well and we feel like it, we'll have lunch at one of the seafood shacks on Flagler Beach. Then we'll see what develops. At first, we'll just talk."

"You're not going to take him to your condo, are you?"

"I haven't decided yet. I could take him to that new La Quinta Inn & Suites."

"I always wondered, what does La Quinta mean in English, anyway?" Mackie asks.

"My Spanish is pretty rusty, but roughly translated I think it means, 'Next to Denny's.' "

"You *have* decided," Mackie accuses. "I know you. You've already hatched a plan, and you're going to do it in the bedroom you share with Matt. He bought you that beach condo because that was *your* dream. Living on the water means nothing to him. He burns to a crisp the minute he steps out in the sun."

"Don't you think I know that?" I counter. "You're beginning to sound like my mother. You're starting to guilt me out. That's not something I'm planning. If we decide to…do it…well, then, there's always the guest room. It has a new queen bed."

"Cheating in the guest bedroom instead of the master bedroom is still cheating," Mackie points out. "You have your head in the sand if you don't think so. Can't you see Manny is hitting on you when you're the most vulnerable? I'm just trying to save you from yourself."

"I can't help myself with Manny. You know our history."

"And you know you're making a big mistake, don't you?" Mackie warns.

"What I *know* and what I *feel* are two different things. I don't want to deal with any negativity."

"Well, that's going to be difficult, because there's nothing positive about what you're planning to do," Mackie scolds. "I can already tell you just what is going to happen. He's going to leave you broken and bleeding by the side of the road, *again*. I'm just trying to save you the trauma of the crash."

I don't answer.

"You're going to get screwed," Mackie says simply.

"If I'm lucky."

"Your mother is right. You do have a smart mouth."

"No," I correct her, "that's what she says about you. This is me, Julie, remember. I don't talk back and I don't talk up."

"I'm just saying, you can still turn back."

"It's too late. I'm almost at the toll gate," I say, blowing out a breath as I pull my toll card from my purse. "I can't talk now. I need to concentrate. I'll call you later and tell you how it went. You're the only one who knows I'm doing this, so if there is a hurricane and

I die in Palm Coast and they discover my body with Manny's...you need to come up with a plausible explanation for Matt and my mother."

"You might have thought of that before you went down this road."

"I've been giving this a lot of thought, and I think Manny is my road not taken, you know, like in the Frost poem. How many people get a second chance like that?"

"I think you're missing the point of the poem," Mackie explains. "When you married Matt you took the road less traveled by. Everybody's been down Manny's road. I'm just trying to protect you."

"I'm losing the signal," I say, trying to create some fancy pseudo-static before hanging up.

How will I feel when I pull into the parking lot of The Home Depot and spot Manny's car? I know he is driving a blue BMW with the vanity plate The Big Man because he told me the day he bought the car, online, which is where we've been conducting our off-again-on-again "secret cyber romance" for the past year. He has been shamelessly flirting with me, relentlessly pursuing me, until I finally caved.

Manny can run hot and cold. I honestly think he might be bipolar, or at least schizophrenic. One day he's all over me and the next I'll say "hi" and he'll say, "Forty people are trying to shoot the breeze with me, and I don't have time for all of you." Maybe he has multiple personality disorder.

Then I will either block him or remove him from my contact list so I won't be tempted to talk to him the moment his name appears. A few days later, he'll do the dance again and sweet-talk me when he knows I am the most susceptible. And I'll be sucked right back into his sexy aura with another cyberspace come-on.

The truth is I am thrilled every time I receive one of his messages.

"Does DoubleMac know about us?" he types.

"I don't have any secrets from Mackie," I write back.

"But you do have secrets from Matt."

"Yes, well...that can't be helped. I assume you haven't told Nita about us?"

Big mistake to use the *Us* word. There isn't even an *Us*. *Us* implies that we have some kind of committed relationship, *which* we don't.

I hate being the jealous girlfriend. And I'm not even a girlfriend. I don't know how to categorize our relationship. I only know I can't resist Manny when he practically begs me to meet him halfway between Miami and Atlanta in Palm Coast. He says he needs to talk to me. *Needs!* How can I refuse someone in need?

When Manny reentered my life, his timing was perfect. Restless, at loose ends, and looking for a change, I am ready for him in every way. Our renewed Internet relationship is risky. We're playing with fire, and we both know better.

I wish I hadn't driven to Palm Coast. In all honesty, I know that isn't entirely true. Manny and I are inevitable. If we hadn't agreed to meet again, I would have wondered about it for the rest of my life. I also know I have to break this latent addiction I have to him or it is going to be the end of me. But my emotions just keep building until they turn my psyche into a feeding frenzy of feelings.

I wonder what it will be like when I first see

Manny Gellar again. How will I react? Will all the old feelings come bounding back? Will our love be so overwhelming and new again that we will be forced to find fulfillment in the most convenient place around, the women's restroom at The Home Depot or the guest bedroom at my beach condo?

My Aspen Green S-type Jaguar hugs the road and prowls through the bog of traffic clogging Interstate 95 as I slip off Exit 289, onto Palm Coast Parkway, pull into The Home Depot parking lot, and prepare to meet my first love. Suddenly, I can feel my nerve endings. My stomach is doing flip-flops. My heart is stuttering. It's just lunch with an old friend, I rationalize, again. What harm can come of that?

As I pull up in the Jag and see Manny leaning on the side of his car, hands folded confidently across his chest, that insolent smile and those dimples I remember so well lurking at the corners of his wide mouth, I know before I stop breathing that everything will be all right and that I am home again.

But I'm not ready to face him, not just yet. If I touch him or he touches me, I know my gut reaction will betray my feelings. So I back away and start to pull out of the parking lot. I don't see the aging hippy with the greasy ponytail on the motorbike behind me until it's almost too late and if he hadn't swerved, he would have been roadkill.

"Where did you get your license, lady, the Stevie Wonder School of Driving?" the biker yells. He is right. I can't even back down my own driveway. I was born without the backing gene. *But apparently I am great at backing away from my marriage.* I do my best to look apologetic. But the truth is I am in shock. In fact, Shock and Awe has nothing on the way I am feeling right now.

"Julie, where are you going?" Manny shouts, as I roll down my driver's side window.

"I—I have to unload the car, open up the condo, rest. I've been on the road for seven hours."

"Okay, I'll go with you, help you, whatever."

"No, you can't. Go into The Home Depot and look around."

"Are you kidding? The place is packed. Everyone is buying emergency supplies for the hurricane. I don't need anything at The Home Depot. I don't need anything..." he says softly, "but you."

Shit. "Well, there's a Bob Evans restaurant down the street. Go eat some sausages. I'll be right back." *Maybe.*

"I didn't come here to eat," he says as his dark brown eyes measure mine.

"Well, then what *did* you come here for?" I roll my eyes. "Stupid question. You don't have to answer that."

Did I mention I am the world's biggest coward? I know I'm just postponing the inevitable. But I have to get my breath and my equilibrium back. Get my emotions in check before we talk. I am still having trouble compartmentalizing and reconciling my feelings for Matt with my feelings for Manny. They are somehow all tied up together in the past and the present. I am literally freaking out.

"Your car must be dirty after the long drive," I comment. "There's a Psychic Reader & Car Wash around the corner." I know how much Manny fusses over his car. Maybe he could use a spiritual reading. I know I could. But my palms are so sweaty they would produce a false reading or a true one. Either scenario would bite.

"I don't need my palms read," Manny sighs patiently. "I already know what's in the cards for us."

"I'll be back," I call, doing my best Arnold Schwarzenegger impression.

"Julie!" he calls after me. And that's when my cell phone starts buzzing. Manny was calling me, and I was determined not to pick up.

Somehow I manage to back out of the parking lot without hitting anyone, ease away from the line of cars leaving the island via the emergency route, cross the toll gate, and accelerate over the bridge, the bridge leading me away from Manny, temporarily, and toward my condo. What should I do? Normally, I'd say, "I'll cross that bridge when I come to it." Trouble is, I'm already on that bridge. I know Manny will wait for me. He's waited for twenty-five years.

But haven't I waited long enough? I still believe that dreams can come true if you wait long enough. And even if everything goes like a dream, it will mess up my life. And if nothing happens and the whole romantic rendezvous is a bust, it will mess me up, too. Maybe I'll be better off just *wondering* what it would have been like to be with Manny again instead of kidding myself that he is my destiny that has to be fulfilled.

Chapter Five:
Crossing the Bridge

Palm Coast, Florida

The condo is calling me like Mecca as my car accelerates along Palm Coast Parkway, a canopied road lined with sable palms, pines, hackberry trees, and majestic, moss-draped oaks swaying wildly at cross purposes in the ocean breeze. *Translation—the outer bands of the hurricane are just beginning to gust.* I long for the first sight of the Intracoastal Waterway on either side of the bridge and a glimpse of the elegant entrance to the Hammock Palms community.

Peace washes over me the minute I see the pale yellow Mediterranean-style stucco building outlined against the glorious cloudless blue sky and the restless ocean. Not exactly Category Five hurricane conditions. But it is always that way on the beach side of the condo. Thunder and lightning could illuminate the sky on the golf course side of the building and the pool and the ocean side would be sunny and mirror calm.

I pull into my space in the underground parking lot and walk across the garage to the cart storage space. All the pool furniture has been stacked up in the parking garage in preparation for the storm. After loading the cart with all my baggage, I push it slowly toward the lobby, where I check the mail, then take the elevator to the fifth floor.

I can drive to Publix and shop later. Manny has driven five hours to get here, and my cell phone won't stop vibrating, but he'll have to wait a while longer. I need to put everything away and in its place. I have the list in my hand, Matt's list of instructions for opening and closing the condo.

Can't go anywhere without *The List*. And when I get settled I'll have to call Matt so he can ask me himself if I have turned on the water heater in the outdoor utility closet ("On" is in the up position) and plugged in the phone that he leaves disassembled in the bathroom drawer in the master bathroom so the workers don't make long distance calls. Trust But Verify has always been Matt's motto. Thankfully, the condo opening list is short. The condo closing list is daunting.

1. Shut off all fans and lights.

2. Unplug phone (both cords) and place in bathroom drawer in master bathroom.

3. Shut off water heater in outdoor utility closet. ("Off" is in down position)

4. Empty ice bucket in laundry room sink. Rinse off, shut off icemaker. (Switch is in freezer on right side inside wall of freezer.)

5. Throw out all the trash.

6. Make sure no toilet is running.

7. Shut off washing machine water supply. The shut-off valve is directly behind the washing machine. Push lever towards the wall. (Away from you towards wall!)

8. Take in all chairs on patio deck. Place in storage locker.

But Matt will be there to handle the condo closing

list, thank God, whenever he can get away from work. It's just too much responsibility in my fragile frame of mind.

I look in the living room at my new palm tree lamp with its turquoise base, slim alternating white-and-brown stem, blue-green metal leaves sticking out (Matt says someone could cut themselves on those leaves), and the impossibly funky lampshade imprinted with palm trees. I don't need a decorator to tell me it doesn't match the décor. Matt hates my lamp with a passion. But it is mine and I love it. It is the most random purchase I've ever made. It is perfect for my new life. *Good Night, Moon; Hello, Palm Tree Lamp.* Appropriate, since my mind is now a bowl full of mush.

I look out the windows at the magnificent view of the beach. It never disappoints. Living here is like being on a ship, without the swaying. Everywhere you look, from every window, all you see and hear is ocean.

I put everything away, call Matt, so I can safely lock him out of my mind for the next few days, dash into my monstrous walk-in closet, and change into the bathing suit I keep hanging there. I think I have time for a quick trip to the beach, just to get reacquainted. To get my bearings and get my feet wet. I guess it must be something like being baptized.

I grab my set of keys. Key to lock the condo, key to get out of the condo building. Key to get into the pool and cabana area. Three fountains splash playfully into the pool, sending out ripples in opposite directions. Steam swirls out of the hot tub. Beyond the pool are thick, tightly woven stands of palmetto scrub. I cross the wooden walkover bridge that arches the dunes at the ocean's edge.

The ocean has restorative powers that are so good for my spirit. I am lulled by the feel of the fresh air and the salty tang on my teeth. I can sink deep into the sand and lose myself. Or find myself. Because when I look at the ocean, I feel the old me. On the surface I am calm and happy and satisfied to go on the way I've been, smooth as glass, always trying to put the best face on things. But underneath, I'm boiling and frustrated and restless, and my thoughts are angry and traitorous. Matt thinks he knows me, but he doesn't know the real me. Not the part I keep to myself. If he really saw me, he wouldn't like what he sees. And he wouldn't love me the way he does, *if* he still does. And sometimes I don't even like what I see when I look deep into myself. One day, soon, my worlds are going to collide and the *me* inside is going to overpower the what-I-want-the-world-to-see me, and then the earth will shift and chaos will reign.

I've seen the ocean in almost every season, every time of day—in summer storms, on winter walks, spinning its magic in the spring. At night, lying back on my lounge chair, looking up at the planetarium show from a front-row seat on my balcony, I can't see the ocean but I can hear it, feel it. On my last visit to Palm Coast, I was treated to a shower of shooting stars that streaked across the sky, lighting up the darkness, as two white gulls, like holy doves, flew gracefully by.

Today, the sunlight shimmers over an emerald green sea, sparkling like the glittering diamonds at *Stones*. Sometimes the sea is blue, sometimes it's green, depending on the time of day or the weather. Other times, it is a combination of the two. It is beautiful even when it is khaki-colored under an overcast sky, heavily-laden with gray clouds against patchy blue ones, bubbling and simmering like a hearty pot of my mother's homemade split pea soup. And it is particularly beautiful during a lightning storm, frightening and spectacular as a display of fireworks lighting up the evening sky.

A flock of low-flying white gulls flaps in the foreground, dipping and diving, squawking and splashing, circling and swooping. Their wings skim the waves and dash back over land, their shadows chase each other over the dunes. The production is perfectly orchestrated, like something out of central casting. *Enter gulls, stage left.* Two dolphins race along the water—always a good sign. A dragonfly, drunk on the sun, hovers. A tiny sandpiper tests the waters, tottering on wobbly legs, trying to keep up with its mother. I feel like a fat, lazy lizard sunning myself on a hot rock. The beach is encrusted with uncollected shells.

I find a giant conch shell, partially hidden in the sand. It is misshapen, not smooth or polished—far from perfect. But it speaks to me, whispering its ancient sea secrets while I hold it against my ear.

I know now that I am going to take Manny to the condo. I'm not sure yet whether I will reveal my own ancient secrets. But I want him to see this place. I want us to watch the sunrise together. Sunrises are spectacular at Palm Coast. Sometimes the sun emerges, filtered and bound behind wispy ribbons of clouds. Sometimes it explodes out of a cotton-candy blue ocean against a Pepto-Bismol® sky, sending shimmering flecks of turquoise over the water, putting on a Technicolor dream show. On those mornings, when God moonlights as an Old Master, his deliberate use of light and color achieves dramatic effects. The light kisses the incoming waves as they almost knock each other over, in their rush to shore, giggling like a bunch of naughty, eager schoolgirls. I know Manny will love it here. We will love it here together.

Suddenly, the surf starts to churn as the sea spits foam in advance of the storm, like someone has emptied a giant box of Tide into a vast washing machine. Pieces of white foam collect at the shoreline, whipped by the wind so they skip and scatter and cartwheel across the wet sand, chasing each other like tumbleweeds.

I play in the shallow water a while and frolic in the waves. Yes, *frolic,* on my private beach (the beach is actually deserted because of the evacuation order) while all the angst, anger, and frustration I have bottled up inside me flows out. This luxury is even worth the risk of ruining my hair. I want to be fresh and clean when I go to Manny. I don't want to be carrying all my baggage. Actually, Manny comprises most of my baggage. I know I have to let it go and not overthink it. Because if I do, I will wonder, "Is this any way for Natalie and Josh's mother to behave?" Or, "Is this any way for Matt's wife to act?" Then I'll have to turn right around and go back to Atlanta before I experience the one thing I need to make me whole again.

Facing the back of my condo, I squish my brightly painted neon-green toes deep into the wet sand and then wriggle them about. I am free-floating, swinging off the handle of the Big Dipper, dangling fearlessly off Orion's belt into the edge of space. Usurping Cassiopeia's throne. I am light and limber, shooting around the solar system. I am practically naked,

Botticelli's goddess in the *Birth of Venus.*

Out here, I can pretend I'm really not fifty.

The irregular conformation of black rocks creates tiny wading pools on the sand. Lulled by the rhythmic sound of the waves, I focus firmly on my feet planted in my personal place on the planet. Am I really moving? Yes, nature's force is tugging at me, unwrapping the bonds and boundaries of my universe. As the tide recedes, I slide further, further, further back in the continuum of my life to the first time I ever laid eyes on Manny Gellar and the first time he walked back into my life.

PART TWO: THE ROAD NOT TAKEN

TWENTY-FIVE YEARS EARLIER

Chapter Six:
Can't You Read the Signs?

Miami

Manny Gellar walked back into my life the same way he entered it. Through the front door of Goldsmith's, my family's jewelry store in the now-shabby Westchester area of Miami. Only this time he came alone and this time I knew he was coming. I hadn't received any advance warning. But I could read the signs. I was a big believer in signs. Like my Grandmother Rose, I was born without a sense of smell. Nature compensated by gifting me with a sixth sense— a special ability to tap into the future. At the moment, the future was not only tapping, it was doing a pretty good impression of Ringo Starr rocking out on my psyche.

His name flooded my mind, a broken turn signal that wouldn't stop flashing. The kind of light that annoyed you as your car followed it down the road. *Manny Gellar. Manny Gellar. Manny Gellar. Julie Goldsmith Gellar.*

The nagging feeling was now so strong I knew

with absolute certainty that I was going to cross paths with Manny Gellar, and very soon. I'd been avoiding him for more than four months, since I'd left him to study in Florence, Italy (some would say to stick my head in the sand), my senior year of college.

So I wasn't surprised, as I was getting ready to leave Goldsmith's to go on my lunch break later that afternoon, when I was forced to come to grips with my past.

"Of all the jewelry joints, in all the towns, in all the world, I walk into yours," laughed a man in a familiar, gravelly voice.

Looking up, I found myself face-to-face with Manny Gellar. His dreamy brown eyes lit up the room, and his dazzling smile revealed the biggest, whitest teeth and most engaging dimples on his cheeks and chin. Bounding around the counter, he swept me up into his welcoming arms for a huge hug that literally left me breathless and blushing. It went beyond the camaraderie of an old friend and bordered on the sensual, as his strong lover's arms wrapped around me, refusing to let go.

I broke out of the embrace to give him a closer look, and my first instinct was to step behind the counter in a defensive move to hide myself from a more thorough perusal. He had hardly changed, and that caught me off balance.

When the man of my dreams walked into Goldsmith's and back into my life that afternoon, I took the opportunity to study him. As I was trained to do, I appraised what was set before me. In this case, it was Manny, and I gave him the same careful examination I would a jewel of unknown origin that had just come into the shop. Perhaps the man I surveyed seemed a bit more serious and mature than the one I had known before. But the first difference I noticed was his clothes. Black pinstriped suit. White dress shirt with a button-down collar, well starched. Subtly striped Brooks Brothers tie. Black wingtips.

Dressed in his "Mr. Sincere" suit, he was still model-handsome in the conventional sense and by almost any standard. And he seemed slightly taller than I remembered, with a dark complexion, short dark hair, a broad brow, and an angular face, tempered with the dark and dangerous looks and wild Cuban blood from his mother's side of the family. It was a combination I still found irresistible.

He'd retained the same boyish charm that had caused me to fall deeply and hopelessly in love with him so many years before. Okay, let's be honest here. I was still in love with him.

Sincerity had never been Manny Gellar's strong suit. He never took things or people seriously. An enigma, it was difficult to figure out what made him tick. I didn't always know where I stood with him. That was a big part of the mystery that drew me to him and also a big part of the problem.

With Manny, you never knew how deep the feelings went. You always had to look below the surface to catch an honest glimpse of the man. There were layers, so being with him was slippery, like sinking into quicksand or wading into a murky, man-made lake. One minute you were on solid ground. The next you were in over your head. In a crunch, he could be counted on to toss you a lifeline, but only when you were going down for the third time. And he'd put me down for the count more times than I cared to remember.

I do remember missing his voice—a carnival barker's voice that still promised delights under the Big Top. He was a natural announcer. His deep, measured, modulated cadence, magnetic and mesmerizing, still had the ability to pull me back, pull me in. I tried to remain cool, but the longer he stood in front of me, the more I succumbed to the dangerous undertow that I knew could drag me into the darkest depths again.

He hadn't moved an inch after the hug, but his hypnotic influence on me was so powerful the physical connection between us wrapped me in a stranglehold.

The truth is, I was coming undone. Manny's presence in my store was unnerving. He was standing much too close. I gaped at him and couldn't even manage a hello. It took me a minute to recover my composure and catch my breath. I hoped the shock hadn't registered on my face. But his self-satisfied smile signaled that it had.

"W-what are you d-doing here?" I stammered.

"I live here, remember," he said, flashing that infuriating, devastating trademark smile. His eyes hadn't left mine since he walked into the store.

"How's DoorMatt?" Manny asked pointedly, using his nickname for my old boyfriend because he knew it irritated me.

"*Matt* and I are not seeing each other any more, not that you ever really cared, even though he *was* your fraternity brother," I replied.

"I'm not into brotherly love these days," said Manny sarcastically. "I heard he asked you to marry him."

"Then I guess you also heard I turned him down."

"Good news travels fast. What I want to know is, did it have anything to do with me?"

"You *would* think that." I wanted to slug him. I almost wished I had accepted Matt's proposal just to wipe that arrogant look off his face.

"Why would it have anything to do with you?" I managed. "You and I haven't seen each other in more than four months." Talking about my breakup with Matt was the last thing I wanted to do.

"Your mother told my mother you'd been thinking about relocating the shop."

"My mother talks too much. Is there anything you don't know about my business?"

"Not much." He laughed.

I didn't find his latest intrusion into my life the least bit humorous.

"Maybe I can help you sell the shop and find a new location," he offered. "Have you forgotten I'm in the real estate business, big time?"

"I heard," I said, continuing to size him up and reconcile the image of the boy I knew with his new reputation as "Realtor to the Stars." From where I stood, he was still the same self-centered Manny I remembered. Always playing an angle—always looking out for *his* best interests while trying to convince me he was only looking out for mine.

"I'm not exactly your typical client—I'm not a famous rock star," I pointed out.

"I'll make an exception in your case."

"So why are you really here?" I asked suspiciously, trying to get control of the situation and my emotions.

"I'm here to see you," he said simply, and he

looked like he meant it. Suddenly, he started firing off questions and accusations rat-a-tat-tat, in staccato bursts, with the fury and speed of a submachine gun.

"You knew I'd come looking for you. Did you think you could hide out from me forever? Didn't you get my letters? Why didn't you ever answer them? And why did you go to Italy in the first place?"

He looked hurt, and, always sensitive to other people's pain, my first instinct was to apologize. But as usual around him, I could hardly get a word in edgewise.

"Jewels, you look great," he said, changing the subject and the tone of the conversation, as he continued to rest his gaze on me, assessing me unreservedly. He still used his pet name for me. I had to admit I took satisfaction from that, and it triggered another memory, actually my first memory of Manny Gellar, from when we were in grade school.

I had dropped by Goldsmith's Jewelers on my way home from elementary school, eager to be around the sparkling stones in my parents' store. Goldsmith's was my home away from home. I loved the play of lights against the polished glass surfaces that revealed the treasures displayed within. I could walk blindfolded the well-worn path in the carpet that led to the engagement ring cases. My mother's smile was etched into my consciousness as she beckoned customers to browse and cajoled them to buy. Graceful, cool, elegant, and refined, Sylvia Goldsmith's movie-star looks were as classic as the merchandise offered in her shop.

The jewelry business had been in my blood for as long as I could remember. It was in my grandmother's jewelry shop on Worth Avenue in Palm Beach that my father first met my mother. I never tired of hearing my parents tell the story.

Sylvia thought that tall, slim Tech Sergeant Sidney Goldsmith, stationed at Morrison Field in West Palm Beach during World War II, was the most handsome man in uniform she had ever seen, on or off the movie screen. My father's brown cracked leather flying jacket, adorned with medals, was still encased in plastic in the back of his closet, looking as smart and stiff as it had when he had taken it to be cleaned right after the war.

"Here I was, a poor kid, in the middle of all this Palm Beach splendor," said my father. "As fate would have it, I walked into your grandmother's jewelry shop to have a ten-dollar watch fixed, and that's when I first met and fell in love with her daughter, your mother."

"Of course, there was no charge for the watch repair," my mother explained. "The people of Palm Beach thought the men in uniforms were our saviors, protecting us from patrolling German submarines we were convinced were lurking off the coast."

Sid returned to pick up his watch and sneak another peek at the girl who had waited on him. Sylvia took Sid's breath away. He thought she looked like an angel or a movie star—Veronica Lake—with dark, smooth, shiny, waist-length hair that fell seductively over one eye as she smiled shyly and inclined her head in my father's direction. She was only fifteen and Sid was almost twenty-one, but he found her irresistible and fell in love with her on the spot. And, he found out later, when he returned from the war, she was in love with him, too.

It was the most romantic story I'd ever heard, and that was exactly the way true love happened to me.

Manny Gellar walked into Goldsmith's with his mother, Elena, and his twin sister, Estrellita. The Gellars had just moved into my neighborhood from Key West, and I had very definitely noticed "the new boy" in Mrs. Commodore's second-grade class.

Elena clutched a sturdy navy canvas beach bag tightly to her chest, guarding it as closely as if it contained the crown jewels. Manny's hand was latched protectively around his mother's elbow.

My mother introduced herself, then added, "I'd like you to meet my daughter, Julie."

Elena's hands never left her bag. Estrellita stood shyly off to the side without saying a word.

"Julie," Manny said, seriously mulling over my name. Then his dimples appeared, that first time I saw him flash his smile. "Julie. It sounds like jewelry." That's when he first started calling me Jewels.

"Make attention, children," Elena began in broken English, as she announced she had brought some jewelry in to be appraised. "You are going to be surprised really very much."

"That's *pay* attention, Mom." Manny leaned over to whisper in his mother's ear. He looked uncomfortable doing it. At the time I thought it rude of him to correct his mother in front of total strangers. Later, he told me his mother had specifically asked him to correct her whenever he thought her English could be improved. And, since we didn't know his mother, he didn't want us to think less of her. When his father was not around, it was Manny's job to protect his mother and his sister, a responsibility he took very seriously.

What came out of the common cloth bag that Elena carried was so unusual and so unexpected it left both me, normally a chatterbox, and the unflappable, unshockable Sylvia Goldsmith speechless.

There were dazzling, richly decorated necklaces of enameled gold and jewels, encrusted with alternating diamonds and rubies. I was captivated by the long strands of rare, natural black, pink, and white pearls—unblemished, iridescent, large and perfectly shaped. There were cross pendants and other faith-based symbols, as well as emblems such as the fleur-de-lis, along with hearts and other representations of love. Our visitor had enough merchandise in that one bag to open her own jewelry shop or stock an auction at Christie's.

My mouth fell open and my mother's eyebrows lifted when Elena set a spectacular collection of precious stones on the counter—oversized rubies, emeralds, sapphires, and diamonds—set in round or rosette-shaped pendants that could be worn on heavy braided gold and silver chains around the neck. It was the emerald medallion, which had belonged to Elena's sister, that drew my attention. I was already partial to emeralds, even at an early age, since they were my birthstone.

Elena explained that jewels such as the emerald, worn during the time of Queen Isabella, were crafted mostly for royalty and the court society of Spain. Each precious piece had a story and the collection was almost too much to process in the space of one afternoon.

"You take it, the bag," Elena prompted as she gingerly handed it to my mother for safekeeping. But I could tell she didn't really want to give it up. It was her history, her heritage. I watched my mother expertly catalogue the pieces and proffer a receipt, agreeing to store them in the Goldsmith's vault for Elena and promising to arrange for the valuables to be properly insured and cared for.

We later learned that Elena Zareta Gellar came from a wealthy, aristocratic Cuban family of Spanish descent. Her ancestor, a court jeweler for Queen Isabella in fifteenth-century Spain, had ultimately settled in Cuba. The Zaretas lived like kings in the island country. The jewels, which had been in Elena's family for centuries, were solid evidence of that.

The Gellars could have sold these heirloom pieces at auction and become wealthy beyond their wildest dreams, but Elena would never consider that. She refused to part with these only reminders of the family that had been tragically murdered in Cuba over a political misunderstanding. Sensing trouble brewing, Elena's mother had sent one of her daughters to safety with her cousins in Key West, weighted down with money and the jewels sewn into the bodice and hem of her dress. Elena's twin, Estrella, had stayed behind to be with her fiancé.

When her relatives told her of the murders of her family—including her beloved twin sister Estrella—Elena wished she had stayed and met the same fate rather than be cast off here in this alien country with their strange ways, alone with no one but distant cousins.

Estrella Zareta was never heard from again, but Elena never wavered in her belief that her sister had somehow escaped and was alive and safe and perhaps hiding out in Cuba, waiting for the right time to reveal herself to her twin.

Meanwhile, that day Elena brought the family heirlooms to our shop was the beginning of two friendships, mine with Manny and my mother's with Elena.

****

"What's wrong with you?" Manny snapped, when he noticed that all my attention wasn't focused on him. That jolted me out of my reverie.

"Oh, nothing," I feigned. Just that everything was a mess right now. I desperately wanted him to leave. The last thing I needed was for Manny Gellar to walk back into my life and remind me of the last weekend we had spent together. I hardly needed him to remind me. Although I didn't think it showed yet, I was carrying living proof of everything I had lost to him. My innocence, my trust, my love.

"Let me just get another good look at you, Jewels," he insisted, pulling my hand into his. "It's been so long."

Suddenly he broke his grip and smoothed his warm hand over my stomach. I flinched. Our eyes locked and I was the first to blink. I never did have much of a poker face. Absolutely all my feelings were revealed in a single look.

"Holy shit, Julie," Manny growled as he stood in front of the counter next to me. "You're pregnant. How the hell did that happen?"

I had to choke back the bitter laughter before I became hysterical. He knew exactly how the hell that had happened. He had been there.

Chapter Seven:
Berenstain Bears—Too Much Pasta

Jewels@aol.com: Why should we get together again?

TheBigMan@gellargroup.com: To complete the circle.

Jewels@aol.com: What good would that do?

TheBigMan@gellargroup.com: I think we both want a taste of what we once had.

****

"Did you hear me, Julie?" Manny uttered the angry words as he paced the length of the watch counter like a restless panther before returning to stand directly in front of me. His eyes seared mine, searching for some truth.

What I saw reflected in his eyes was shock. He sagged against the counter, like someone had just knocked the breath out of him. His naturally tanned face was ashen. After he recovered from the initial impact of his discovery and gained a little color back, he just looked lost.

"I'm not pregnant," I said lightly, calling on my keen sense of self-preservation and my ingrained need to please. But my first instinct had been to protect Manny from the truth. "I just ate a lot of pasta in Italy. You know, 'Berenstain Bears: Too Much Pasta.' "

"Are you kidding me?" he sneered. "Is this some

kind of a joke to you?"

"No," I reasoned. "That's your department. Do I look like I'm kidding?"

He looked around the showroom to make sure there were no customers, and then he twisted my arm and whispered, "I know every inch of your body, or have you forgotten? What I want to know is whose baby is this?"

Frowning, I bit my lower lip until I tasted blood.

"I told my father it was an immaculate conception."

"I'm not buying that," he said. "Did he?"

"He wanted to," I began, "considering how close Florence was to the Holy City. But, being Jewish, he's having a difficult time wrapping his arms around that concept."

What my father really wanted to do was wrap his hands around the neck of the "son-of-a-bitch" who violated his daughter and then shoot him full of holes with the nearest available weapon in his considerable arsenal. But, fortunately for the baby's father, my mother stopped him, and a speeding bullet, cold with The Look.

"Now I want a straight answer to my question," Manny insisted. "How could this have happened?"

"Do I have to spell it out for you?" I asked.

"When we were together, I was...your first," he said, lowering his voice. "Could the baby be mine?"

"Not likely," I responded too quickly, staring up woodenly at the crystal chandelier, wishing, at that moment, that I was anywhere but here with Manny. He was hurting me, and my strongest impulse was to hurt him back. Make him feel the same pain I had been feeling for such a long time.

"Explain," he said simply, tightening his grip on my arm.

"When we...after you...*awakened my passions*," I said sarcastically, "I began to crave it."

"Crave what?" he challenged, his eyes blazing.

"You know..."

"See, you can't even say it. You're such a prude. You don't mean that. Look at me, Julie."

If I were such a prude, how had I ended up pregnant?

I refused to look at him and continued to stare at the ceiling. I'd have to remind my brother to take care of the dust that was gathering on the prisms. The cobwebs on the chandelier were really getting out of hand. And Joel was the only one in the family tall enough to reach it, even with a ladder.

"And did you satisfy those cravings?" Manny demanded, boring his eyes cruelly into mine.

"At every opportunity."

"It was Matt, wasn't it?"

"I don't have to answer that," I said. "Maybe it was one of my *many* Italian lovers."

"And where are all those Italian lovers now that you're knocked up? Do you think they'll be interested in you when you're waddling around like a beached whale?"

I flinched but tried to joke my way out of it. "Manny, if I went into labor in Italy, those Italian lovers would be doing most of the panting and heavy breathing. We're talking about Italian men, after all."

I couldn't believe I was having this silly conversation with him, and I didn't want to be having it. And I couldn't believe he actually thought I was so loose that I'd sleep with someone else so soon after we had made love.

Manny grabbed my shoulders and shook me.

"Stop that," I hissed. "You're hurting me. What right do you have to come into my shop and interrogate me? You think no one else could ever want me?"

He loosened his grip and spoke softly. "I know how easy it is to want you, Julie. I had you, remember?"

The glimpse of honesty was gone in a flash. Suddenly, his mood shifted again, like the wind-blown sands of the Sahara.

"Hey, let's get out of here, have lunch, catch up on old times," he cajoled, grabbing me again, this time gently, rubbing my arm to soothe away the soreness, seeking forgiveness.

I knew I shouldn't go. But I never could resist him. I had a sinking feeling I was getting entangled in something that would lead to no good, but when it came to Manny Gellar I could never help myself and, following my natural pattern to take the path of least resistance, I capitulated. Apparently time had no lessons to teach me and history was doomed to repeat itself.

We reminisced about the past and spent a leisurely lunch catching up and covering every topic but the one that was uppermost in both of our minds, the elephant in the room (well, I wasn't quite that big, yet)—my pregnancy.

Manny talked a lot about his life since we had last seen each other. I just listened—dumbstruck as I always was around him. I confided in him about my dream of buying into Goldsmith's with my grandmother's inheritance, totally revamping the shop, relocating and modernizing it, renaming it and fashioning it into something uniquely mine. Manny was encouraging and, as we talked, my plans began to take shape. In fact, they were more than plans at this stage. But before today, because of the pregnancy, I had seriously contemplated abandoning them.

Outside the restaurant, he walked me to the car and brushed against me so I was backed up to the door. And then he kissed me. It could charitably have been considered a long-lost friendship kiss, except that his lips lingered a little too long on mine. I was pretty sure it was intentional. His lips felt warm, and the heat stirred something inside me.

"You do remember, don't you?" he whispered against my ear.

"Remember what?" I said, in a valiant but futile attempt to sound annoyed and remain unmoved.

"The way it was with us," he continued, not making any effort to let go of me and wrapping his arms so tightly around me I could barely breathe. His lips teased mine again. "How great it was."

"You have a funny way of remembering the past," I protested nervously. "This is silly. I've got to get back to the shop before they wonder what happened to me."

"You know, I never got over you," he said. He was still playing mind games. Maybe he couldn't help himself.

"You're crazy," I said trying to disentangle myself from him, although I still found him difficult to resist even after all this time.

"Crazy about you." He smiled.

"And you're practically engaged," I added. "Did you think Mackie wouldn't tell me?"

That remark sent him into retreat, scurrying like a cornered rat.

"Or have you conveniently forgotten about Nita Weinstein?" Bonita "Nita" Weinstein, my arch nemesis, was not someone I could easily overlook. She was a rattlesnake. A woman who thought money could buy everything, including love.

"I've forgotten nothing," Manny said pointedly, "and for your information I'm definitely *not* engaged to Nita Weinstein."

"Are you sleeping with her?" I posed. I hated myself for asking that question, but I had to know.

"No!" he protested and even managed to sound appropriately offended.

I wondered how true his statement was. I found it hard to believe.

"Why not?" I demanded.

"Because I don't want to."

"But you *are* in bed with her father. Deny that," I countered and slipped into the car as Manny ambled around to the driver's seat.

"I'd rather be in bed with you," he replied softly as he pulled out of the parking lot.

While I was in Italy, Mackie had kept me informed of Manny's meteoric career rise that had been propelled by his girlfriend's family connections. Nita's father, Beauregard "Big Beau" Weinstein, who headed a real estate empire that generated large quantities of cash, some of unknown origins, was a force to be reckoned with. Although he was ensconced in Savannah, his influence not only reached far down the East Coast, all the way to Miami, but everyone in the Southeast and as far away as the West Coast, it seemed, owed Big Beau Weinstein a favor. And the way he wanted to be repaid was by the addition of clients to the regional branch of the prestigious real estate firm where Manny was employed.

Manny was on the fast track, and Nita's father implied that if his future "son-in-law" played his cards right, he would guarantee a steady stream of wealthy clients.

Big Beau delivered in a big way. To his exclusive clientele, Manny sold multi-million-dollar luxury condos in Boca Raton and Naples, palatial estate homes on Star Island and in Palm Beach, and prestigious waterfront residences on the Intracoastal Waterway along elegant Las Olas Boulevard in downtown Fort Lauderdale. In a matter of months, courtesy of Big Beau Weinstein, Manny had already become a broker associate. Eventually, under Big Beau's influence, Manny was destined for a partnership.

Manny's success, of course, was predicated on the fact that he would marry Big Beau's daughter. According to Mackie, he hadn't yet taken the first step of proposing. Nita had more than hinted several times that she was ready for a lifetime commitment, but Manny, it seemed, was always more than ready with an excuse.

Despite his waffling, Nita proceeded to engineer his life and map out his path, and he was going along without protest. Manny had made the most of the opportunity he was given. Word of his talent spread and soon he had divas of all nationalities eating out of his hand and tripping over each other to sign up for a taste of Manny's personal brand of service. Between Big Beau and Bonita, I didn't stand a chance.

"Jewels, I need to see you again," Manny said.

"Why?" I protested.

"Because this thing between us isn't over." Same old confident Manny.

"I—" was all I could manage, still flustered and tongue-tied whenever I was around him.

"Listen, you said at lunch you wanted to make a total change. There are some great spaces in Coral Gables I can show you. Very classy. I know you'd like them. That area is really growing. The Gables has character to spare. A real international flavor. They've got a lot of fine art galleries, great restaurants, and I have the perfect location in mind for you. They've just rezoned a section on Alhambra for commercial, and I've got the listing for an old Mediterranean-style house that would be ideal if you converted it to a business. You and your family can relocate the shop and make improvements at that time. I can help you, and that will give us a legitimate chance to see each other."

"I don't think Nita would like me working with you," I said with certainty.

"You let me worry about Nita," Manny said, as he pulled up to one of the spaces reserved for Goldsmith's customers. "I can handle her. She doesn't own me."

I was sure he just wanted to see if I was still vulnerable to him, if he still had the same power over me, if he could draw me into his web again. He was still playing his irritating cat-and-mouse games.

Fuming, I couldn't believe I was falling for his Romeo brand of bullshit again. But at the same time I found myself thinking about the kiss and the warmth of

Manny's body next to mine. The fact that he still wanted me was flattering. But I had to face facts. I had never gotten over him and I probably never would. There was too much between us.

"When can I pick you up for our next *business lunch*?" he spun, in his smooth-as-silk tone.

"I didn't say you could," I protested, knowing even then that I would go with him. "And if I said yes, it would really *be* a business lunch."

"Like our *study dates* in college?" he taunted. "Okay, how about noon tomorrow?" Manny suggested. "I know this great Italian place out on Key Biscayne. Remote. We can talk there."

Yeah, right. Talk.

"Well, tomorrow is my birthday—" I began, and I could tell by the way he hesitated that he had forgotten. Well, what did I expect?

"Even better. See you then, Jewels."

"Manny, you never give up, do you?" I sighed. "It must be exhausting, being you," but he had disappeared before I even had a chance to turn him down.

When I went into my office and closed the door to contemplate the afternoon, I was mad at Manny all over again, and surprised at how angry and isolated he still made me feel. I had never really examined or articulated those feelings.

It was obvious I wasn't going to get any more work done, so I stretched out in my comfortable office wing chair, propped my feet up on the desk, shut my eyes, and let my mind drift into the cracks and crevices of my life that hadn't been dusted in years.

Chapter Eight:
Early Memories

I could hardly remember a time I wasn't infatuated with Manny Gellar. When we met, I was super skinny, with a smooth, creamy complexion, a pug nose, and pouty lips that seemed too big for my face at the time. My thick brown hair framed my oval face and fell to my shoulders in a perfectly manageable pageboy, except for one large, unruly curl that I was forever trying to tame and that I had to constantly blow off my face when it fell into my eyes.

Everyone said my eyes were my best feature. Big and blue, they were evenly set in my face and looked like the ocean on a calm day but flashed brightly when I was angry. I looked out at the world from behind what my best friend Mackie called the longest pair of lashes in creation.

Mine was the type of beauty you grew into, my mother explained. The beauty that adults instantly recognized as classic but that young boys didn't yet find attractive.

To make matters worse, in the fourth grade, I got glasses and braces in the same year, so my stunning baby blues were hidden behind a set of thick lenses for most of my adolescence. Not to mention my chest was as flat as an ironing board. So in my early teens, I stuffed my padded bras with Kleenex. I was a late bloomer. But all that changed when I underwent a dramatic transformation on my sixteenth birthday.

I was named after my father's younger sister, Julia Lee, who had died from rheumatic fever when she was only fifteen. My father blamed the death on malnutrition because of the extreme poverty in which his family had grown up.

"She was an angel," my father used to say. "A beautiful girl. Too beautiful for this world."

I spent my first fifteen years trying to live up to the ideal of the dead aunt I had never met. I kept a picture of my namesake under my pillow. Though the print was faded and crumpled, Aunt Julia Lee had an aura about her, with long ringlets of strawberry-blonde curls cascading down her angelic face. For most of my young life, I feared I was destined to suffer the same fate as Julia Lee had when she turned fifteen. As a result, I held my breath until the day I reached my sixteenth birthday. Then I believed the spell was broken, and I was free to grow and ready to live again and to finally put Julia Lee to rest.

But Aunt Julia Lee had other ideas. While Julia Lee's photo was safely tucked away in my bottom dresser drawer and I had dismissed all thoughts of her from my mind, my aunt's spirit somehow managed to cross over and "possess" me. If Aunt Julia Lee had been dormant, she was about to make up for lost time.

Beginning the morning I turned sixteen, my dark, straight hair grew in light and curly, and I developed curves in all the right places. Boys started to give me second looks because they now found me alluring, not aloof, and somehow they liked the total effect.

Manny Gellar had been trying to get into my pants

ever since I could remember. His pursuit of me began innocently enough the Friday night of my Bat Mitzvah. Only thirteen at the time, I hadn't been ready for a relationship. If he really knew me so well, he would have sensed that.

For the ceremony, I wore a stiff turquoise shift dress with an empire waist, two accordion pleats down the front, a matching three-quarter-length silk turquoise jacket, and a watch with a turquoise alligator strap. My strand of pearls had been passed down from my Grandmother Rose. I was still as skinny as a beanpole, but I added width by teasing my hair at the top and turning it up in a flip. Then I topped my outfit with a turquoise yarmulke, folded in half and fastened with a bobby pin.

My mother and I lit the Sabbath candles to begin the service. Manny was in the very front row, listening to me chant the familiar prayers I had practiced so diligently. Something mystical must have happened that night, because Manny sat transfixed as I sang.

After services, he tried to approach me at the Oneg Shabbat, but I was surrounded by well-wishers. My mother's friends in the Temple Sisterhood set out a beautiful spread with a braided challah, rainbow sherbet punch in a polished silver punch bowl, a tropical fruit platter, cookies as delicate as lace, a yellow cake with white icing, and all the traditional refreshments. Manny came back to my house that night to see me open presents, but again, there were so many people around, he got lost in the crowd.

He returned the next morning and called me to come outside and talk. But that day something was different. It was the way he looked at me—mournfully, soulfully, with an intensity that made me uncomfortable.

"You were great last night," he began. "The way you sang, your voice is really beautiful."

"Thanks."

"No, I mean it," he continued, staring into my eyes with longing. "You sang like an angel."

"Are you okay?" I asked, concerned that he was coming down with something. I felt his forehead, and he shuddered when I touched him. "No fever," I reported.

"Jewels," he whispered, leaning over and pressing his lips softly to mine.

I pulled away abruptly, and swayed, flustered, but he reached out for my hand.

We were the best of friends, but I wasn't ready for this unfamiliar thing that was happening between us.

"Manny, what are you doing?" I asked, and pushed him away again.

"It's okay," he assured me. "Really, Jewels. Would you go with me?" He whispered it so faintly, so tentatively, I wasn't sure I had heard him correctly.

"Go with you, where?" I asked, puzzled.

"Go steady with me."

"I've got to go…study," I stammered. I couldn't get away fast enough, closing the front door behind me as I sought the shelter of my house.

"But it's Saturday," he said, and his voice trailed off.

He sat under my window the rest of that day and the day after, gazing up at me, like a sad and lonely old hound dog, hoping I'd come out and throw him a bone. He didn't even go home after it got dark. I was afraid he might start howling at the moon.

I didn't know what to do. I was frozen, a prisoner trapped in my own house. I didn't know what to say to him. Fortunately, it was the weekend, so I didn't have to leave the house to go to school. After a few hours, I sent my older brother Joel out to test the waters and watched as they engaged in a spitting contest.

"When is Julie coming out?" I heard Manny ask.

"She's afraid to talk to you," Joel replied. "What do you want with my dumb old sister, anyway?"

"I love her," Manny said.

"Man, you are crazy," Joel said and left.

"Julie," my mother said. "You've been in this house for two days. You can't just ignore the boy forever. He'll starve to death."

"Not with you sneaking him food. Yes, I saw you."

"A growing boy has to eat."

"I can't go out there. Please don't make me," I pleaded, peering through the Venetian blinds. Manny hadn't moved from the spot under my window. I was mortified. I lived in fear that Joel or my mother would let him in the house and he'd find his way into to my bedroom, and then I'd have no choice but to deal with him.

Sunday night came and he was gone. I was so relieved I walked outside and around the block to stretch my legs, careful to avoid the Gellars' house. It was awkward being around him after that. He was in almost every one of my classes, and we rode the bus to school together. Arranging to arrive late to class and leave early, I made my mother drive me to and from school in an attempt to dodge him.

After about a week, we fell back into our old easy

friendship. I had missed that. But we never talked about that incident and nothing was ever quite the same between us after that. The timing was off. By the time I realized I was ready for whatever he had in mind, it was too late. He never showed me his vulnerable side again. He remained friendly, but aloof. I had ruined my one chance with him, and I was sick about it.

From that point on, he seemed determined to pay me back for my rejection of him. Whatever Manny's true feelings were for me, it didn't stop him from taking every opportunity to make me jealous.

When we walked down the hall together, he made a point of looking at other girls and leaning down to whisper, "*¡Caramba!* What a set of *castañetas* on that one."

I wanted to disappear, it hurt so much. My cheeks flamed, and I tried to hold back the tears.

During his "cheerleader phase," Manny only seemed to be interested in being seen with the popular girls—Veronica "Ronnie Su" Lopez with her perfectly bobbed black hair, which matched her perfectly shaped figure and perky personality, and tiny Alexandra Renka, the coach's daughter, with her white-blonde pageboy.

Sometimes he could be so cruel. Always maintaining the upper hand like he was trying to conquer me—acting as if he didn't really care.

Right after my eighteenth birthday, when we were at his house studying for our American Lit final, I tried to test his true feelings for me in the language of love.

"You're chattering, Julie." Manny sounded annoyed as I continued reciting Emily Dickinson aloud.

"*Por tu vida, cállate*," he hissed. Then he turned on

the radio. "More rockin', less talkin'."

I laughed. My nerves were showing.

"Would you stop fooling around and put a lid on the laughing? I'm in the middle of something here."

He bounced over and took the book from my hands, grabbed my shoulders, and guided me back toward the couch. Then he gently sat me down and started kissing me until I went limp in his arms. His tongue was hungry. I had never been French-kissed before. But I responded. It was our first real kiss, and it felt delicious. His hands were tight around me, and I responded by reaching out for him. I wanted to cling to him and never let him go. He was anxiously pulling me down on the couch and moving against me in a burst of passion.

"Julie, I want you," he said, stroking me.

"No," I answered firmly, unsure if his feelings for me were genuine. At the same time, I was involuntarily responding to his touch. I could hardly breathe, and I was spinning out of control. His body was so tan and firm. And tonight, at least, he was all mine. It was a delicious feeling.

He was on top of me, doing his best to launch an all-out invasion. I could feel his excitement build. Then he kissed my mouth again, hungrily, and probed it with his tongue.

"Are you ready for me, *amada*?" he asked.

I moaned but came to my senses just in time.

"Manny, you know we can't. Not that…"

"*¡Maldita sea!*" he groaned. "Don't keep me waiting too long." I didn't have anything to say for a change.

"It's only a matter of time, you know," he

promised.

"That kind of talk went out with the cavemen," I retorted, rolling my eyes. "Are you going to club me over the head, drag me off to your lair by my roots, and have your way with me?"

"Look around. You're already in my lair. But I will, if that's what it takes. I'm betting I won't have to, and you'll come to me."

"I see your big ego is still intact," I said furiously, throwing a pillow at him. "You're about as subtle as a brick, Manny Gellar. And you're such a Neanderthal. What am I going to do with you?"

He laughed. "Do you really want me to answer that question?"

He entwined his hand in mine and kissed me slowly.

"I am crazy about you, you know," he said, sounding sincere.

"Yes, when we're alone together," I said flatly.

"No, all the time," he insisted.

Later that evening I pretended to fall asleep on the couch. His parents weren't home yet, and I wanted to see if he would try anything else or if he really respected me.

First, he kissed me lightly on the lips, and I wanted to kiss him back. When he began to glide his hand up under my T-shirt and tried to touch one of my breasts, I thought I was going to give it all away by giggling. Things were starting to get out of hand, so I yawned and stretched, and turned over so his hand slipped away from my shirt. Then he started to move his hands lightly inside my jeans. I tensed but waited a few seconds more to see if he would really go any further. I didn't have long to wait for my answer. I bolted up from the couch.

"I can't believe you, Manolo Gellar," I screamed. "How far would you have gone if I hadn't stopped you?"

He was laughing hysterically.

"Was this some kind of a test?" he wanted to know. "It was, wasn't it?"

"Yes, and you failed miserably."

"Yeah, right. I knew it all along. I was just seeing how far you'd let me go. You want me, you know you do, Julie. You are so ready for me. Well, the game is over. You win."

He grabbed me roughly by the shoulders, pulled me toward him, and kissed me long and hard, slipping his tongue into my mouth. Then he pushed me down gently on the couch and kissed me slowly and thoroughly. I got a funny, tingly sensation between my legs I had never felt before. Then he moved his body over mine again.

Shaken, I tried to push him away, but he leaned down and kissed me wetly, softly, then insistently, probing my mouth with his tongue again. I managed to break free, but my mouth was open in surprise. I wanted to get up, but my knees were too weak. I couldn't let him know, but I wanted him to do that again.

"How was that, Jewels?" He smiled. "Did I pass that time?"

"You're an over-sexed jerk," I replied indignantly, making a big show of tucking my T-shirt back into my jeans, trying to regain at least a shred of composure.

"If you think that's sex, then you've got a lot to

learn," he teased. "And I'm a great teacher."

I glared at him. That's when our relationship moved to the next level, from friendship to something more. I knew I was hooked on him, but I couldn't let him know it, not until he made it clear that I was more to him than just a girl to fool around with. Although I was inexperienced, I knew instinctively that once I revealed how I felt, the thrill of the chase would be gone for him.

I wished Manny would finally come to his senses and realize it was really me he was in love with. Manny could be maddening like that, always wanting what he couldn't have. And then when he got it… Well, that was a different story.

Manny almost always got what he wanted because he could charm the skin off a snake. A chameleon who could change colors to fit his surroundings, his appeal transcended cliques. He could move comfortably between the popular crowd, the jocks, and the brainy crowd. Even teachers loved him. He was the funniest boy in school, and he knew all the right words to keep me hanging on his every word.

I thought he was practically perfect. He thought I was "predictable" and much too practical. I was as reserved as he was gregarious, as steadfast as he was restless. He was always "on" for everyone else he encountered. He could be himself with me. With the exception of his indulgent mother, Elena, and perhaps his twin sister, Estrellita, I was the one constant in his life. I was the only person he could count on to distract him when he was dark and moody, a side he rarely showed to anyone but me.

On the dark side, he was a moving target—

impatient, egotistical, with the attention span of a gnat. Holding on to what was there was as elusive as touching a rainbow or grabbing the hot brightness of a shooting star. If you couldn't spark his interest immediately, he was on to the next kick. However, when the entire package weighed in, the scales tipped in his favor. I thought he was definitely worth taking on. Somehow I managed to hold his interest and keep him coming back for more.

Which was remarkable, because anyone brave or crazy enough to risk dating me had to go through my father first. The boys in the neighborhood called my father "The Blue Demon" behind his back, because he was built rock-solid, with a professional wrestler's body. He had been a boxer in the U.S. Army Air Force during the war. No one dared disrespect him to his face. My father kept a bow and a quiver of arrows in the laundry room, leftover from the days when he and my Uncle Arnie operated an archery range on the side of our house. If that didn't frighten off the boys, my father's arsenal of World War II weapons did. And whenever another boy tried to get close, Manny would flex his muscles and stake out a claim on what he considered his territory—me.

Manny was a favorite of my father's because he showed respect when he walked through the "gate without a fence" in front of my house. Cars passing through the neighborhood typically slowed down just to gawk at that chain-link swing gate. My mother had once planted a hedge there. One winter, when the bushes died, my father cut them down, and left only the gate standing to "keep out the riffraff."

Some of the neighborhood kids would swing on the

gate, just for spite, causing my father to do a slow burn. Manny always made a great ceremony of opening and closing the latch and walking through the gate, under two facing palm trees, and onto the short concrete walkway leading to our house, when he could have just as easily walked around it.

I lived in constant fear that a coconut would fall on my head every time I passed between those two giant palms. Maybe if I *had* been hit by a falling coconut, it would have knocked some sense into me where Manny Gellar was concerned.

Chapter Nine:
The Waiting Game

The College Years

It didn't take a knot on the head from a flying coconut to predict what would happen next. Just when I thought things might finally work out between us, Manny blindsided me, again.

In his sophomore year of college, he became obsessed with a golden-skinned, dark-haired beauty named Harmony Weiss. But there was a problem. Harmony Weiss was lavaliered to Tony Abrams, the most popular senior in the house and Manny's big brother in the fraternity. Sweet and beautiful, Harmony's features were a lethal combination of perfection with which I could never hope to compete. I knew I could never match Harmony's tiny frame and ingrained sense of style. Manny followed Harmony around hopelessly, a little lost lamb. Tony was tolerant. He saw it for the harmless crush it was.

When Manny asked me out on a double date with Tony and Harmony, I accepted, although I suspected I was just a front—an excuse for him to gaze dreamily at Harmony from a safe distance. Now that I was actually going out with Manny on an official college date, I was rattled and full of doubts. *Harmony is so beautiful. They could make beautiful music together. Manny is obsessed with Harmony. And I'm not Harmony.* Vowing to be as Harmony-like as possible, I sat out on the rooftop sunroom at the dorm in an attempt to tan to perfection. But since it was almost the dead of winter, the only thing I got was a bad case of windburn. I never even came close to my rival's natural tan. And I couldn't wear high heels because I didn't want to tower over Harmony.

During our double date, I chattered away, while Manny looked at Harmony with bare-naked longing.

"Doesn't Harmony have tiny feet?" Manny whispered in a trancelike state as he stared unabashedly at the object of his affection on the bleachers next to us. Harmony's size-four shoes had somehow slipped off, leaving her perfectly shaped, perfectly pedicured, slender, delicate, stockinged feet exposed.

While Manny gazed at Harmony, there I was, an ungainly giant, with my size-eight-and-a-half shoes, which I didn't dare remove, though my blistered feet were aching from the long walk from the parking lot.

"Yes," I had to admit, trying to change the subject. "Harmony is beautiful and so are her feet."

When Manny dropped me off at my dorm, he didn't seem to be concentrating on me. I suspected he had a lingering hard-on for Harmony and was somehow subconsciously trying to fashion me into his ideal. But when he kissed me softly on the lips he was kissing me, not Harmony, and I responded, melting into his arms.

He put his arms around me and tilted my face toward his. He kissed me so softly I could barely breathe. Then he probed my mouth with his honey-flavored tongue. My tears blended the salty-sweet taste. I waited for him to say he loved me, but he never did. I knew he must have strong feelings for me from the way he was kissing me.

Unfortunately, those *strong feelings* only lasted until his next crush. When Harmony was history, Manny had a brief fling with Anna Ruby Robicheaux, Miss Mississippi State. Miss Mississippi State proceeded to break Manny's heart when she dumped him for Robbie Bazemore, editor of the *Florida Law Review*. I was left to pick up the pieces in the latest of Manny's long line of failed relationships.

Eventually, Manny latched on to a tall, big-boned, loud, rich, sorority girl from Savannah, Georgia, named Bonita Weinstein. Mackie and I nicknamed her "the White Witch of the South," because of her long frosted white-blond hair, her even frostier demeanor, and her trademark year-round winter white wardrobe.

I was furious. I had been waiting years for Manny Gellar and trying too hard to get him. I had wasted my whole life on that boy, and I was finally coming to the conclusion that it was never going to work out for us. Even when he played Romeo to my Juliet in high school, we didn't end up together. In fact, we both ended up dead. Did he think I was going to wait around forever, always at his beck and call? Was I supposed to put my life on hold while he worked his way through every other girl at the university? It was becoming clear that I was going to have to get a life of my own, apart from Manny, or die a frustrated old maid.

Ironically, it was Manny who solved my dilemma by introducing me to one of his fraternity brothers, and that's how I met my future husband, Matt. I don't know if we would have managed to find each other on our own, or if fate meant us to find each other, or if it was only Manny trying to mastermind my life to suit his purposes.

Chapter Ten:
Matt Sightings

DoubleMac@aol.com: Remember the time right before my wedding when I found out Little Jon was holed up in that hotel room with a nineteen-year-old bimbo waitress during their fraternity pledge class reunion and you told me to forgive him if I really loved him?

Jewels@aol.com: If I really thought he was cheating, I would have helped you throw him out on his long, lanky ass. I still think the White Witch was just blowing smoke when she ratted him out.

DoubleMac@aol.com: Well now I'm returning the favor. Forgive Matt for whatever it is you think he's done, which for the life of me I can't figure out. He's one of the good ones, Julie. Your parents don't call him The Prince for nothing. He worships the ground you walk on. No matter how much shit you shovel, he just keeps coming back for more. You don't know how lucky you are.

Jewels@aol.com: I used to be able to count on Matt. He's all but deserted me. He's always working.

DoubleMac@aol.com: Julie, it's called making a living. Why do you think Matt works so hard?

Jewels@aol.com: Why don't you tell me?

DoubleMac@aol.com: He sees how successful Manny's business is and he wants to do better. He's been competing with the man since college.

Jewels@aol.com: Competing?

DoubleMac@aol.com: For you.

Jewels@aol.com: It's not a competition.

DoubleMac@aol.com: In his mind it is. Now with this new deal, he feels he's finally made it.

Jewels@aol.com: Did he tell you that?

DoubleMac@aol.com: He doesn't have to.

Jewels@aol.com: Oh, so just because you're married to a shrink, you feel you have the right to psychoanalyze me? Have you and Little Jon been talking about me behind my back?

DoubleMac@aol.com: I have my own opinions apart from my husband's. You need to be more understanding.

Jewels@aol.com: Whose side are you on?

DoubleMac@aol.com: Yours, always. And if you still love him...

Jewels@aol.com: That's the thing, Mackie. I'm not sure I still do. And I'm not sure I ever did.

A serious silence ensued.

DoubleMac@aol.com: Didn't you love him when you made Natalie Rose?

Jewels@aol.com: Yes. Then I did.

DoubleMac@aol.com: All those years with Matt—were you just faking it? Pretending to be happy?

I didn't have an adequate answer.

DoubleMac@aol.com: There was a time in college when you were so hot for him you practically followed him around like a stalker. Don't you remember?

****

The Matt I remembered was not the same Matt I was now married to. The old Matt was edgy and a little wild and dangerous. A rule breaker.

I tried to remember back to the time when Matt and I couldn't get enough of each other, but it seemed impossibly far away.

I first saw Matthew Paver at an Alpha Tau Epsilon party on Fraternity Row. After we met, I kept my eye on him the rest of the evening. Although Matthew wasn't much taller than me, he was very solid and muscular. Offsetting his dark hair was a milky complexion. His brothers called him the Black Sheep because he had a thick dark head of curly hair on his head, his chin and—it was reputed—in another more private spot—a theory I often daydreamed about confirming for myself.

There was a longstanding story going around the ATE house that one night, in a moment of madness or in a stoned haze, the Black Sheep had set his hidden black thicket on fire as he ran stark naked through the fraternity house. The brothers referred to that as the "Burning Bush" incident. Then there was the story about the "Slip and Slide," where Matt's fraternity brothers reportedly propelled him across a soaped-down terrazzo floor in the house, slamming him into a wall, when he was wearing nothing but a football helmet and the top of a wet suit.

Matt was different from the other boys I met at college. He was a year older, which might have explained some of the attraction. Dressed in his signature long-sleeve khaki Army Surplus shirt, he was involved in a near-riot at an anti-war demonstration in front of the administration building after the student shootings at Kent State. I didn't even know where Vietnam was.

He drew an unlucky 21 in the draft lottery but had injured his knee running track in high school. Armed with a note from his doctor, Matt was coded 4F—not qualified for military service.

Manny, on the other hand, managed to skate through those turbulent times relatively unscathed. The Vietnam War, the civil rights movement, Roe v. Wade, presidential politics, and the feminist movement didn't even register as blips on his radar screen. With no strong opinions and no apparent convictions, Manny's unspoken motto—Don't Rock the Boat—had served him well. Moved by nothing but the music of those decades, the only high Manny got was his draft number.

I spent the first three weeks after we met dreaming of Matthew Paver and looking for his white Volkswagen Beetle all over campus.

"There it is," I said, pointing out the car to Mackie, who tried to look properly interested. Not that I was stalking him or anything, but I found out where his classes were and arranged to "accidentally" bump into Matt outside of class or at least catch a glimpse of him as his white VW bug drove by. There were "Matt sightings" all over campus. I waited for him under the shade of the magnolia trees and the moss-draped oaks on the grass outside the library. I watched him walk by Memorial Tower in the center of campus and heard the carillon bells chime the hour when he changed classes. I saw him frequently at fraternity parties, and, as much as I contrived to talk to him, nothing I did seemed to make any inroads. Finally, Manny took pity on me and agreed to speak to the Black Sheep on my behalf.

When I got back to my dorm one evening, the phone was ringing, and it was Matt. "Hello, this is Matt

Paver, Manny Gellar's fraternity brother." I started to choke on my own surprise.

"Matthew," was all I could manage. I could hardly speak.

"Winter Frolics is next week. The Four Seasons are coming, and I was wondering if you'd like to go with me." Dead silence.

"Julie, are you there?" He laughed. "Cat got your tongue?" I could tell he was enjoying my awkwardness immensely. "Aren't you going to say anything?"

Of course I said yes.

Our first date wasn't a big success. Matt told me he liked sports and he liked to work out. I didn't tell him sports bored me to tears and that I wasn't remotely interested in anything athletic. We were perfectly mismatched, only I couldn't see it then. I did enjoy watching him play touch football in the field across from the fraternity house, but mostly because it gave me an excuse to drool over his buff body and the bulging muscles that were on prominent display under his sleeveless T-shirt and cutoffs. And a chance *not* to concentrate on Manny Gellar.

The second date was a marked improvement. We went to a movie and afterward up to his fraternity room—a small space crowded with books and record albums stacked on concrete block shelves.

"You want to smoke?" asked Matt. In the sheltered existence I led, smoking meant cigarettes.

"No thanks, but you go ahead," I said politely. Normally, I would have been repelled by his behavior, but nothing about Matthew Paver repelled me. I didn't need grass. I was high on Matt and the idea of him.

I was so hopelessly infatuated with Matt I couldn't

see straight. *When had that glorious infatuation ended? Where was that wild and reckless man who couldn't keep his hands off me? And when had he been replaced by the buttoned-up, straight-laced man who would no longer share my bed?*

Down the hall from Manny's room in the fraternity house, my relationship with Matthew Paver was beginning to blossom. The evenings we spent in Matt's smoke-filled room after the movies or parties were exciting. I was falling harder and harder for him, and he returned my affection. Matthew Paver was a great kisser. I loved to run my fingers through his wiry black hair. I loved the way his piercing green eyes smiled and his nose crinkled when he laughed. The way our bodies seemed to fit so perfectly together when we kissed. But I wouldn't let it go much further than that. I had learned the hard way that making yourself too available to the object of your affection was not a smart move.

It was nice to be in a relationship where my feelings were finally reciprocated. Now that I thought I might be falling in love with Matthew Paver, Manny was beginning to view me in a new, more proprietary light, although his time was mostly occupied by the wealthy and well-connected Nita.

My growing relationship with Matt somehow made my hopeless involvement with Manny seem bearable. The more confident and in control I became about my relationship with Matt, the less Manny's cavalier attitude had the power to hurt me.

But then Manny threw me for a loop, in the fall of my senior year, when he asked me to be his date for Opal Weekend, his annual fraternity party in Jacksonville Beach. What I later found out was that he would have asked Nita but they had argued and she was going to another fraternity weekend with another boy. And *not* going was *not* an option for Manny.

"It'll be a lot of fun," he promised.

I suspected what he had in mind. But I thought I could handle him.

"Oh, my God," said Mackie when she found out. "Manny really is a snake. He only pays attention when some other guy is hanging around you. It's a pattern with him. Now that Matt is interested in you, Manny wants to protect his territory. He's done it with every guy who's ever looked twice at you. You know I'm right."

"Yes, but this is what I've wanted forever, isn't it?" I reasoned. "Maybe this will be a new start for us."

Chapter Eleven:
Opal Weekend

TheBigMan@GellarGroup.com: Remember Opal Weekend?

Jewels@aol.com: That was a long time ago.

TheBigMan@GellarGroup.com: We could have that again.

****

In the end, all my memories of Manny Gellar culminated in a single event—Opal Weekend—the defining moment in my life. My early frame of reference was forever compartmentalized into tracts of time before Jacksonville Beach or measured after Jacksonville Beach, which was where all my problems started.

We arrived at the Holiday Inn at Jacksonville Beach on a cold Friday night in November. The thought of being alone with Manny Gellar all weekend had my pulse racing. My only regret was that seeing us together would hurt Matt.

We were bundled up in front of a big bonfire for a cookout. Mackie's date, Jonathan Shack, parked his car on the beach, and he was doing his best to keep Mackie's engine warm. Jonathan was affectionately known as "Little Jon," although his nickname belied his considerable height. He and Mackie always drew stares because physically they were such an unlikely couple.

The average observer would have pegged me as more Little Jon's type and Mackie more of Matt's. But the mysteries of attraction are unfathomable.

Little Jon was a mile high, and he towered over Mackie, who was so tiny she was barely visible next to him. But you could tell he was really into her. He called her his "Little Bit." He was a proverbial flirt, so his fraternity brothers sometimes referred to him as "Jon Juan" or "Love Shack." When Jon and Mackie finally joined the others, Jon turned off the ignition and left the car on the hard sand.

We roasted hot dogs, drank, and talked. Some of the brothers passed around joints and got wasted on weed and wine. The band was playing something romantic. I was nestled with Manny under his blue mohair fraternity blanket, and he was nibbling on my lips affectionately.

"Stop it," I said, not wanting Matt or anyone else to get the wrong idea. "Get a hold of yourself."

"I don't want to hold *myself*," he whispered. "I have big plans for us."

"Yes, I kind of figured," I said. "But can't you control yourself out here?"

"I'll try," he said. "But how about another kiss to tide me over?" I looked around. Matt was sitting nearby with his date, a friend from his marketing class he had invited at the last minute. He had been sneaking furtive, furious glances at the two of us the entire evening. I hesitated. At that moment, Matt roughly grabbed his date's hand and practically dragged her back toward the hotel. In midstream, he changed his mind, turned around and stomped over to where I was cuddled up with Manny.

"Gellar, let's have this out now," Matt growled. "You'd better watch yourself around my girl." Things were about to get out of hand.

Little Jon left Mackie and got between Manny and Matt as they circled each other menacingly.

"All right, you two. Time out. That's enough. Both of you get out of here and cool off for a while." He motioned to me.

"Julie, over here with me. They just need to blow off some steam."

I followed Little Jon to a picnic table out of the moonlight and out of sight of the rest of the group.

When I turned to look back at the campfire, Little Jon snuck up behind me, brushed my shoulders and wrapped his arms around me, pressing me against him. An erection the size of Texas signaled that I had interrupted something big between Little Jon and Mackie. Kilauea was about to erupt. Hot lava would soon flow into the cool sea, forming new parts of the island.

"Little Jon," I admonished, trying to slip inconspicuously out of his powerful grasp. Little Jon was lethally charming. Mackie was going to have her hands full with this one.

"Hey, Julie girl, why don't you ditch those two bozos and switch to a real man?" Little Jon said, pulling me back against him.

"Get serious." I laughed. "You're wasted, and Mackie's waiting for you. She's probably watching us now."

"I am serious, baby. Dead serious."

I laughed nervously and pushed him away again.

"Okay," he relented, finally getting the message,

"but you don't know what you're missing."

"I don't think Mackie likes to share," I said.

"There's enough of me to go around, Julie girl."

I rolled my eyes and walked off. Little Jon's ego was off the charts.

When he was gone, I turned around, and Manny was standing there. He told me Matt had gone back to the hotel. Manny led me back to our place by the fire. I relaxed and allowed him to kiss me softly on the lips. I shivered as he stroked me gently. The wind, the wine, and the music blurred, and we fell asleep in each other's arms on the beach. When we awoke the next morning, the tide had come in and swept Little Jon's car away.

That afternoon was the Florida-Georgia football game—that legendary arch-rivalry between the Florida Gators and the Georgia Bulldogs—the world's largest outdoor cocktail party. The Gator Bowl had been filling steadily since noon. It was bone-chillingly cold, unseasonably so for Florida. I shivered and asked to borrow Manny's orange and blue jacket. It stood out against the sea of red and black as we sang the Florida Alma Mater.

The excitement in the stadium built to a fevered pitch as the announcer remarked on the impressive opening drive for the Georgia Bulldogs. The roar in the stadium was deafening, but the crush of the crowd was exhilarating.

"The Bulldogs of Georgia have handled everybody this season, except the Gators," the announcer commented as the referee signaled a personal foul against the Georgia team.

"I'll be gentle when I handle you tonight," said

Manny, putting his arm around me possessively, tightening his hold and drawing me closer. *His idea of foreplay?*

"Well played by the Gators," commented the announcer about a later play. "John Reaves to Carlos Alvarez. Nice hands."

That's exactly what I was thinking about Manny.

In the end, the Gators shut out the Bulldogs in the second half. When the game was over, Florida fans stormed the field and tore down the goalposts.

Saturday evening was a formal dance at the hotel, and I spent a long time in Mackie's room getting dressed and fixing my hair.

"Did you find a ride back?" I asked.

"Yes, Matt Paver is taking us," Mackie said pointedly. "He'll probably be pining away for you the entire time. You're mean to do this to him. You're driving him crazy, you know, making him watch you and Manny together. Manny can't seem to keep his hands off you when Matt's around."

"I'm not doing it on purpose," I said honestly. "I hate that he has to see us."

At the dance, Manny was unusually attentive all evening. The treasured emerald medallion Manny's mother had given me for my Sweet Sixteen complemented my floor-length apple-green taffeta gown and blazed brilliantly in the artificial light of the room, blinding everyone who looked at it.

We danced every dance together, all but one, when Matt, who couldn't stand it any longer, walked over in an obvious huff.

Glaring at Manny as he had been doing all evening, he said, "I hope you don't mind if I dance with *my* girlfriend," and whisked me off for the last slow dance.

I was really attracted to Matt, and it felt good to be back in his arms, but I had only been dating him on and off since my junior year in college. Manny was someone I'd wanted for as long as I could remember. Circumstances had put us together this weekend, and I knew I had to play the evening out, to see if we might have a chance. Matt pulled me close. After the dance was over, he gave me a long, tender kiss.

"Don't forget you're still my girl," he whispered. I looked into his green eyes and was about to cry when Manny came up and grabbed my arm.

"She's already forgotten you, 'DoorMatt,' " he said as he put his arm around me and started to lead me away. Then he turned back to Matt and said, "Let's go up to our room, Julie. I can't wait to get you alone," leaving Matt standing humiliated and frustrated on the dance floor.

Manny had thought of everything. He'd brought his record player and the Johnny Mathis album, the one we studied by. He'd even ordered my favorite flowers, yellow roses, from the front desk at the hotel. He could be very romantic. Or at least he played a good game of it.

"The flowers are beautiful," I said.

"There's a card," Manny said, holding it out for me to open.

Jewels & Manny
Meant to be Together
Opal Weekend

"That's so sweet," I said, genuinely touched by the sentiment.

He locked the hotel room door, and we were finally

alone. He opened the window so the cool night air and the ocean breeze filled the room.

"Come to the window," he said, pulling me close as our hands locked and we looked out over the ocean together. The moon was full and shards of stars hung low in the heavens, sparkling like priceless jewels. The night enveloped me, fitting like a snug star-skin. I scanned the sky and identified Orion.

The sighting triggered memories of all the nights we had studied the constellations together at my house. I would spread a blanket out on the grass and we would lie down head to head. I'd point to the sky, easily locating my favorite constellation, Orion, by the row of three stars forming his belt and the row of faint stars forming his sword.

"There's Orion the Hunter," I would tell Manny. "He has two of the brightest stars in the sky. That blue-white star called Rigel marks his right foot. And Betelgeuse is the red star marking Orion's left shoulder."

My head was always in the stars. When I was younger, I wanted to be an astronaut. Manny and I had converted an old clothes dryer into our spaceship and actually tried to launch it from the side of my yard.

We had known each other almost all our lives, but I was still a little nervous around him, even though being here with him in Jacksonville Beach felt so right. I focused on the steady sound of the waves crashing against the shore outside our window.

It reminded me of the classic seduction scenes I had seen in the movies, and I thought I knew what was coming next. Manny looked at me with his dreamy brown eyes and reached out to embrace me. He caressed my face, kissed me long and sweet on the mouth, and led me over to the bed. He undressed me slowly, pulling down the zipper in the back of my dress, fumbling with the clasps on my bra, before he removed his clothes. He couldn't stop looking at me, and I didn't want him to stop.

His hand outlined the space around the medallion and traced the rest of my body. I shuddered, perhaps from anticipation or perhaps from the cold November air.

"Are you cold, Jewels?" he asked. "Come here. I'll make you warm."

He wrapped me in his arms and kissed me heatedly, pressing our bodies against each other. He laid me down on the bed and traced his fingers lightly over my breasts and along my stomach, and kissed me again. I couldn't believe how tender he was. I couldn't believe this was happening to me. He cupped my breasts in his hands and kissed them, then licked the nipples lightly with his tongue.

"Beautiful, so beautiful," he said.

Then he touched me between my legs until I was moist. I groaned. He kissed me again on the lips, and I responded to his touch.

"Are you ready for me, *amada*?" he asked gently.

I wanted him, but I whispered hesitantly, turning my face away, "You know this…will be my first time."

He sat up abruptly, breaking the mood. "You're kidding, right?"

"No," I said. "It's okay. It doesn't matter. I want to." I sounded tentative, but my body was aching for him and I didn't want to ruin the moment.

"But I thought… I mean, you and Matt… Didn't

you two…" he tried uncertainly.

"No," I said.

"But the way Matt talks, it's like he owns you. You never…?" Manny left the words hanging. Manny knew I hadn't slept with Matt. He had made a specific point of asking me earlier.

"Manny, of course not. I already told you that. Didn't you believe me?"

"Then I'm really the first?" he said, a big smile breaking out on his face. He seemed genuinely pleased. "I'm glad. Are you sure about this?" he asked again. I nodded, as if I could really stop this runaway train.

He kissed me hungrily everywhere, examining every part of my body. I was burning for him, although the room was sweet and cool. I wanted to be closer to him. Needed to be.

We were lost in each other to the strains of "Wonderful, Wonderful" and "Chances Are." When I thought I couldn't stand it any more, he entered me, gently at first, then insistently. I bit my lip for a moment, but I was so excited I didn't really notice the discomfort. It was the most perfect moment I'd ever experienced.

When it was over we both sat back, held hands, and stared up at the ceiling grinning. We focused on the steady whir of the fan. Then we looked at each other. Manny was staring at me like he was seeing me for the very first time.

"That was worth the wait." Manny smiled. "You don't know how long I've thought about us…you know, together like this."

I started crying.

"Jewels, I didn't hurt you, did I, *amada*?" he asked,

suddenly alarmed. "Was it okay for you?"

"It was wonderful…just wonderful," was all I could say, echoing the lyrics to the song I had just heard. I held more tightly onto his hand while he reached over and kissed me gently. Something inside me stirred. I wanted to be with him again, and sensed it.

"You're so sexy," he said, running his hands all over my body appreciatively, murmuring softly in Spanish, trying to drive me wild. He touched me gently between my legs while he kissed me until I was ready to climax. Then he climbed on top of me and was inside me again. I held onto him tightly. We remained that way until he rolled off me and we fell asleep, still in each other's arms.

Once during the night I woke up with a start and found him staring down at me. Something was troubling me, but I couldn't put a finger on it.

I could see his face in the moonlight. Such a beautiful face, I thought.

"I love the way your nose crinkles when you're worried," he said touching my nose. "Is everything okay?"

"Did you use anything, protection, I mean?" I asked, unsure of what that really meant. "I'm not on the Pill." Mackie was, but I didn't have the nerve to go to the infirmary for a prescription.

"Sssh," he whispered. "Don't worry. Everything will be okay." Risky behavior was part of Manny's repertoire.

"I'll protect you," he assured me. I was so naïve that I stupidly believed him. On the field that afternoon, the announcer had reported that the Gator defense gave their players great protection. But, cocooned inside our hotel room, I wondered about the level of protection Manny was providing.

Manny had always been my protector. As I began to drift off to sleep again, my mind raced back in time.

When we were in the fifth grade, Manny protected me during the air-raid drills at school. Miamians had gone crazy back then, building fallout shelters to safeguard themselves and their families against the threat of a nuclear attack from the tiny island of Cuba.

Sylvia Goldsmith, Elena Gellar, and Mackie's mother, Muriel, attended a community preparedness course at the local school, "How to Prepare for a Nuclear Attack," and learned about stocking up on canned goods, water, and matches.

Cuban missile crisis fever was rampant. With menacing Russian ships only ninety miles away from Miami, the women took the whole thing very seriously. Relations between the two countries were strained.

"It's all about the power," Elena pronounced in broken English, speaking with conviction. "Who has it, who wants it, who takes it!"

When the women returned from their classes, my mother went right out to tend her garden, as if flowers would really matter when the end of the world came. Sylvia watered her hydrangeas, and Elena pampered her petunias. My mother corralled my brother Joel and me and marched us single file down the long, dark hall in the middle of our house to wait for the all-clear siren. My mother hadn't wanted to scare us. "This is only a hurricane drill, children," she had insisted. But I wasn't fooled.

At school, twice a day, we were instructed to hide

under our wooden desks—scant protection against the blast—in preparation for the nuclear meltdown that mercifully never came.

It was during one of those duck-and-cover air raid drills that Manny and I huddled under our school desks. Our desks were always together because our last names—Gellar and Goldsmith—were as close as the two of us. The siren's piercing sound was deafening, and my hands flew to my ears. Instinctively, he reached out and grabbed my hand tightly, possessively in his. "Don't worry, Jewels, I'll protect you," he mouthed. Even back then, I desperately wanted to believe him.

At the hotel on Jacksonville Beach, I fell asleep, contentedly clutching the emerald medallion, which bound us to each other.

Manny's mother had given me the medallion at a swim party at West End Pool to celebrate my Sweet Sixteen. Lifting the emerald medallion from where it was nestled against my heart, I closed my hand around the precious stone and thought of the moment when Elena had bestowed the priceless gift on me.

"The best, most important thing is family," Elena had said. "You've always been like a daughter to me, Julie."

What Elena was essentially saying was that she had handpicked me, the daughter of her best friend, Sylvia, to marry her son. When I unwrapped the small but heavy package, I was shocked.

"But this is too much. Mrs. Gellar, I can't take this."

"I know if my sister were here, she would want you to have this." Elena placed the chain around my neck and hugged me. Tears clouded my eyes. And I knew that Elena had transferred all the love and affection she had felt for her sister to my mother, her best friend, and in turn, to me. Now maybe her dreams and my dreams were finally about to come true.

Manny and I slept in late the next morning and made love again. I felt free to be honest with him for the first time in our relationship. We explored each other playfully and talked about everything and nothing.

If things could only stay this way, I thought, the way they were in this room, on this morning. I thought Manny must truly love me, and there was now no doubt I was in love with him. I even let myself believe we had a future together.

"Jewels, you're beautiful," he told me as we walked along the beach together that morning, hand in hand, our bare feet—his large dark brown ones and my smaller pale ones—lined up in the surf and sand.

"So are you," I said, and meant it. He laughed, easily accepting the compliment. *He was*, I thought, his face so beautiful and exotic next to my ordinary one. That he might love me was almost beyond belief.

When we were younger, we were inseparable. Wherever I went, Manny was never far behind. There was nothing I couldn't tell him, except the way I really felt.

After what had just happened between us last night, I wanted him more than ever. But I didn't want to pressure him. This might be a momentary feeling that for him would pass. For me, I knew it never would. But he would have to take the lead in the relationship if it was ever going to progress.

We went back into our hotel room, took a long,

luxurious shower together, exploring each other playfully, before we packed and joined the others for breakfast. I didn't really want to see other people right now. I didn't want to break the spell, destroy the perfection we had shared, share him with anyone. I hoped Matt wouldn't be there, for he could certainly see that something had changed. I felt like the whole world was watching, like I was lit like some enormous neon sign, flashing, "Julie Slept With Manny." I hoped it wasn't that obvious.

We each took a plate, wound our way through the buffet line, and sat outside on the patio facing the ocean. It was a bright, cool, sunny morning. Manny was looking at me intently, almost territorially, playing with the curl that fell on my forehead and trying to put it back into place, finding any excuse to touch me, born of our new awareness of each other. Matt walked over to our table and pulled up a chair.

"Hey, Julie," he said trying to appear nonchalant, but I knew it had been difficult for him to come over. He was trying to read my emotions, which were transparent. Flushed, I turned away from him.

"Gellar…" He snarled the name. Manny was enjoying every minute of it. Matt swallowed hard. Manny put his arm around me protectively.

"Hey, Paver," Manny said. "Why don't you go find your date?"

Matt had probably guessed what had happened between Manny and me in our room last night. He was probably sick imagining us together like that. I felt bad about what he must be going through. I didn't want to hurt Matt. And what did I really have with Manny? Did he return my feelings? I wanted desperately to believe it, but I wasn't at all certain.

"We'd better head back," Manny said. "I had a great time." He put his arm around me and kissed me slowly, tracing my lips with his tongue, making it last for Matt's benefit. I hoped this wasn't just a macho competition between two fraternity brothers. Another notch on Manny's belt. It was obvious Manny had been with other women. He was very experienced. I could only hope that our time together meant something significant to him. We were silent, but content, on the drive back. We didn't need words between us. We never had.

When Manny brought me back to my apartment in Gainesville after the short drive from Jacksonville, he carried my luggage inside, took both of my hands in his, and pressed me up against the living room wall.

"I'll see *you* later," he said with a long, suggestive look and a deep kiss. "We have a study date before finals, don't forget." I looked up, unsure of what emotion I was seeing in his eyes.

I couldn't concentrate on studying, so I paced the apartment until Mackie returned. A few minutes later I heard my roommate at the door when Little Jon was dropping her off. That meant Matt was outside, too. I didn't want to think about that, and I hoped he hadn't seen Manny leave.

"Mackie, thank God you're here," I said and grabbed her arm, pulling her inside, leaving Little Jon out on the front step.

"She'll call you later," I said, making my apologies.

"So tell me everything. Did you two finally do it?" Mackie wanted to know.

"Yes, couldn't you tell?" I asked, beaming. "It was everything I've waited for. I just can't describe it."

"Sounds almost like a religious experience," Mackie said.

"Now you're making fun of me," I said. "It wasn't like that, but it *was* beautiful," I tried to explain, to make my friend understand.

"Did the earth move?"

"Yeah, it kind of did."

"You sound as if you experienced the second coming," Mackie said. "Or the third?"

I blushed.

"I can see that shit-eating grin all over your face," Mackie continued. "It was all over his face, too, but are you absolutely crazy? Giving up a great guy like Matt, who adores you for...what?"

"I thought Manny was your friend too," I accused.

"Yes, but he'll charm the pants off of you." Mackie giggled. "Too late. Apparently he already has. He's a louse where women are concerned. You knew that going in. I tried to warn you, and you wouldn't listen."

"But I love him. You know that. I can't help myself."

"Haven't you ever heard of free will?"

"He didn't do anything I didn't want him to," I admitted. "And we shared something really special. I think he feels it too, finally."

"I hope so," Mackie said sincerely. "For your sake, I hope this relationship has finally turned the corner. He's always had a thing for you, but I could never figure out whether it was lust or love."

"Don't be cruel," I said. "Just be happy for me."

Mackie hugged me. "You know I am. Well, what's

next?"

"I don't know. He said he wanted to see me over Christmas. I think that's a good sign."

"What about next weekend?" Mackie pointedly raised her eyebrows.

"We have a study date on Friday," I answered.

"Saturday is the last big fraternity party before winter break. Little Jon just asked me to go with him." When she got no response, Mackie looked down, avoiding my eyes.

"You know something," I insisted. "Don't you? Because if you do, you'd better tell me now."

"Well, Little Jon asked me what was going on between you and Manny. He said Manny was taking Nita Weinstein to the party."

I was sure I hadn't heard correctly.

"Are you sure?" I asked, even as I knew the answer.

"Yes. I'm sorry to have to be the one to tell you."

"Well, Manny probably already had the date before this weekend and can't break it now." I tried hard to fight back the tears. I was always making excuses for his bad behavior toward me.

"Maybe," Mackie admitted. "But he should have been man enough to admit that to you after he…"

I ran from the room. I was sure that was all it was—a previous engagement. But I wasn't going to call him. I knew we would be studying for finals this week. He'd tell me then. Maybe I shouldn't even keep the study date.

A short while later, the phone rang.

"Julie, it's for you," Mackie called out, cupping her hand over the mouthpiece. "It's Matt." I picked up the phone.

"Julie," Matt said almost in a whisper. He must have called the moment he got back to the fraternity house. There was an uncomfortable silence between us. He didn't want to ask and I didn't want to answer. "Can I talk to you?"

I was afraid my voice might betray me, so I said nothing.

"Whatever happened, I don't care," he began, his voice breaking. "It doesn't change a thing for me. Do you hear me, Julie?" He was in love with me. I was sure of that. I could almost hear his love for me pouring over the telephone line. And I didn't want to lose him if it turned out the experience at Opal Weekend had meant nothing to Manny. "We're having a fraternity party next weekend at the house," he said, and hesitated. "Will you—go with me?" Before Opal Weekend he had been so sure of me. Now he couldn't be certain of anything where I was concerned.

I impulsively accepted his invitation, thinking I couldn't assume anything with Manny. He had known about the party and he hadn't asked me. In fact, he already had another date lined up. When had that happened? I hated myself for being so possessive and feeling so betrayed. Maybe sleeping with someone didn't give me any rights. Maybe I was reading too much into the weekend. All the signs pointed to that.

Chapter Twelve:
Most Likely to Conceive

Miami

For someone supposedly so perceptive, I completely missed the signs. When I missed my first period, I attributed it to nerves. Mackie assured me that a menstrual cycle could be delayed because of a shock or traumatic experience. And I was beginning to think of Opal Weekend as the biggest shock my system had ever withstood, at least a 6.0 on the Richter scale. I worried myself sick about whether Manny's feelings for me were genuine. Or whether he had any feelings for me at all.

Mackie kept a close eye on me because I was beginning to show serious signs of disintegration and distress.

"God, Mackie. I couldn't be pregnant, could I?"

"It's a real possibility," Mackie had to admit.

"After only one time?"

"That's all it takes."

"But I don't have any of the signs," I protested. Almost as soon as the words came out of my mouth, so did the remains of my breakfast. I barely made it to the toilet in time.

Mackie dampened a washcloth and wiped my face.

"Let's wait," I said. "For another sign."

"Don't put your head in the sand," Mackie said.

I sat down on the bed and cried. "What have I done?"

"Just followed your heart," Mackie was instantly contrite and suddenly sympathetic. "Remember, it takes two. Manny's just as responsible."

"We still don't even know if it's true," I reasoned.

It was my first day back at Goldsmith's during winter break. The moment I arrived, I suddenly felt queasy. Running to the bathroom. I vomited again. Either I was coming down with something or the pressure was taking its toll.

Something was clearly wrong, I thought, as I glanced at my desk calendar. I ruffled through the pages, staring at the calendar for something that I couldn't or wouldn't fathom. Finally, I checked the dates. Normally, I was as regular as clockwork. I knew I was fooling myself if I thought it was simple stress. I had missed my second period, and I was on the verge of hysteria.

How could this have happened? I panicked. I knew exactly how it had happened. I wasn't on the Pill and Manny didn't use any protection when we were together. He said he thought it cramped his style, and he told me he would feel "closer" to me if he didn't wear a condom. Typical Latin macho male.

I avoided Manny for the next few weeks. I couldn't possibly face him after I had confirmed my worst suspicions.

"My mother will freak out," I cried to Mackie.

"And let's not forget about your father," Mackie pointed out. "If you weren't Jewish, he'd stick you in a convent. If he doesn't kill you, he'll never let you leave the house again, and then he'll go after Manny with one of his handguns or the bow and arrow."

It hardly seemed fair. For years I had resisted considerable pressure to sleep with Manny Gellar, who I truly believed was the love of my life. And the first time I had, he'd gotten me pregnant.

The situation shouldn't have surprised me. The evidence was right there in our high school yearbook next to the picture of Manny and me, labeled, "Most Likely to Succeed." It should have read "Most Likely to Conceive."

My mother would be disappointed in me, of course, but she would be more disappointed if she knew the identity of the father. In her wildest imaginings, Sylvia never would have suspected Manny. My parents and Manny's parents hoped that one day Manny and I would end up together. But not this way.

In the beginning, I protected the identity of my baby's father as staunchly as a journalist protecting a source. All the coaxing or screaming in the world wasn't going to make me betray Manny. In the end, I was so scared and alone I finally did confide in my mother, but only if she promised to keep the pregnancy a secret from my father and especially from Manny and Elena.

At first, my mother insisted that I tell Manny about the pregnancy. She and Mackie were both convinced he would do the right thing and marry me, that he would accept the responsibility. I think my mother was secretly excited about the baby. But I didn't want him to marry me because he felt responsible. I was unsure of Manny's feelings for me and didn't want to force him into such a big commitment while we were still both in college.

"I just can't tell him," I pleaded with my mother. "He doesn't think of me in that way."

"And exactly what way was he thinking of you when he slept with you and got you pregnant?" Sylvia asked, her anger almost palpable.

Then there was Matt. How was I ever going to tell him?

That's when my mother came up with the idea of sending me to Italy. She assumed total control of the situation. Locating a one-year study abroad program through the university, she enrolled me immediately.

Arrangements were made for me to visit one of my mother's good friends in England before I arrived in Florence, purportedly on a jewelry-buying trip to Europe. Ostensibly I would be living in the heart of Italy for the purpose of studying Italian and art history. But I knew my mother was sending me to Europe for one reason and one reason only. To explore the possibility of removing all traces of Manny Gellar from my life forever and to recover from the mess he had made of it.

But Sylvia Goldsmith hadn't sent her weak-willed, sexually active daughter out of the country to repeat her mistakes. This time my mother made sure I was armed with protection. She secured a prescription for the Pill with strict instructions to begin taking them as soon as I had "The Procedure."

"My mother refers to it as 'The Procedure,'" I lamented to Mackie about the first alternative. "Zip, zap, and it's over. It sounds so cold and heartless. She can't come with me now because if she leaves the shop at Christmas my father will get suspicious. Mackie, I wish you were coming with me. I don't think I can handle this alone. I'm not sure I can go through with it. I know it's impossible, but I wish there was some way I could have this baby."

Chapter Thirteen:
The Great Escape

Florence, Italy, by way of London

When I arrived in England, close family friend and business associate Richard Westphalen and his dark, handsome partner, Franklin Ingersoll Constable, affectionately known as "FIC," pampered and fussed over me in their London flat.

I had been hearing about Richard and FIC for years. My parents told tales of the terrific times the four of them had had in the Greek Isles, cruising the Mediterranean—to Athens, Santorini, Rhodes, and Kusadasi, through the Dardanelles Strait, and into Istanbul.

Richard and FIC afforded me the same courtesy as my parents did the lovers, asking no questions, making no judgments. To the rest of the world I would be seen as weak for giving in to temptation. The outside world would unjustly brand me, just like they branded Richard and FIC. But I was learning that life didn't always fit into some neat little package defined by the world's current standard of morality.

They lavished so much attention on me and took such fine care of their houseguest that I fairly smothered. But it was just what I needed. I was nurturing a new life inside me. But I feared that my spirit would never soar again.

London was a dreary, cold, wet place, draped in fog, and the atmosphere matched my melancholy mood. My pregnancy was as shrouded in secrecy as the city was shrouded in mist, which I thought was fitting. If I was miserable, it was only fair that everyone else should be too.

For the first two weeks, I refused to leave the flat. I lay still as a stone, weighed down by quilts and profound guilt over what I was proposing to do. I kept my hand on my stomach in a move to protect my baby—from myself. I wrestled with my decision over and over again in my head. Was I doing the wrong thing? How would I feel when I no longer had the baby? The procedure was irreversible. Once it was done, there was no going back. If I had told Manny about the baby, would things have been any different? Would he love me and protect me like I so desperately wanted him to?

Then I wept and couldn't be comforted. I spent most of the time on an emotional tightrope, my feelings alternating between disbelief that I was even contemplating taking the life of my unborn child and misplaced anger at Manny, although he never even knew about the pregnancy. I was angry with myself and angry with my mother, although her reasons for not keeping the baby seemed to make sense. I was too young, I wanted to finish college, and I wasn't ready to raise a baby by myself. But she had seemed as upset as I was about the whole prospect.

The bottom line was I had a hole in my heart that was eating away at me like battery acid, and I was convinced that if I went ahead with the procedure, I would never recover from the loss. In the end, I agreed to visit the clinic for a discussion.

"I'll make the appointment," Richard said. "I'll take you, and I'll be there every step of the way." I turned away so he couldn't see the hurt in my eyes. I was numb and could barely function. I was living a nightmare.

When the time came, Richard was very sweet and supportive. My most vivid memory was in the clinic waiting room. I remembered letting out a primal scream that came from the depths of my soul. I looked at Richard and whispered, "I'm sorry."

"For what?" he said, puzzled, never letting go of my hand.

"For screaming," I answered. I looked around the waiting room. No one had lifted a head from their magazines or their own contemplations. In reality, I hadn't made a sound.

Suddenly, I felt as if I were suffocating. All the memories I had tried to dam up, of Manny and the night we had spent together, came flooding back. How could something so beautiful be so wrong? I didn't see how I could sever this precious connection with the love of my life. I had to get out of there. Breaking free from Richard's grip, I bolted from the chair and escaped from the waiting room. Richard followed close behind.

"I can't do this," I said flatly.

"I understand. Let's go home, then." Solicitously, he bundled me up in my coat, and we walked out of the sterile room from hell. I never told my mother, and I never looked back.

Richard and FIC personally escorted me to Florence to join the school group. Most of the students had flown in to the town of Pisa from New York and taken a bus to Firenze, some thirty miles away.

My school group was staying at the Hotel Palermo on the Via della Scala, a few blocks from the train station, near the Church of Santa Maria Novella, right in the middle of the Red Light District and across the street from the police headquarters—the Carabinieri.

On the evening of our arrival, everyone was ushered into the hotel and settled down in the dining room in front of big platefuls of spaghetti. I finished my plate of pasta and got up to go to my room.

"Signorina, no, that is only the primo course," said our *primo* waiter Lucca. I soon learned, many meals and many pounds later, that in Italy pasta came before everything, and it came often and in large portions. *All tortellini, all the time.*

My new roommate Dana was beautiful, with a pale complexion, the face of a Botticelli angel, and luxurious, thick black hair that covered her like rich mink. She resembled a young Sophia Loren, with luscious curves in all the right places. I couldn't believe my luck when I discovered that Dana could speak Italian. We soon became fast friends. Which was lucky for her, because most of the students were hesitant to approach the porcelain-faced beauty that everyone on the program referred to as the Italian Ice Queen.

As we unpacked on that first day, I stared through the window. I had arrived a day earlier and picked out a large corner room—the best in the hotel. With windows on three sides, the third-floor room came with spectacular views of the city at sunset. I marveled at the cathedrals, the cupolas, and the architectural treasures of Florence. Pigeons fluttered overhead, lending the city character. The hotel surrounded an outdoor piazza, with a lovely garden in the center, under a beautiful arched, plate-glass ceiling.

One of our bedroom windows faced the Arno River, which bisected the city. Even with the windows closed I could hear church bells pealing the hour as Dana and I hung up our dresses in the closet and laid out the rest of our clothes in the drawers of the heavy wooden armoires we had each selected.

Another window overlooked a narrow cobblestone alley and the peeling, ochre-colored side of the building next door. Clothes hung out on a line to dry and couples intermittently streamed through, like ants, hurrying in and out on their way to and from their destinations. Tourists busily scurried about on quests to discover the treasures of the "Birthplace of the Renaissance," while fashionable Florentines strolled arm in arm on their way to dinners at charming trattorias. Gypsy women with babies were everywhere begging for coins, garbed in their multi-colored finery, trying to trap unsuspecting tourists and spouting life-curdling curses when they came up empty-handed.

Exhausted, I threw open all the shutters of my room and looked out on an ocean of cascading red tile rooftops for as far as I could see. I imagined the palazzos out in the country, the stucco buildings on the other side of the Arno, the Oltrarno or south bank. Florence was perfectly situated between the seaside, the countryside hills, and the Apennines mountain range that crossed Italy.

"Great choice of accommodations, roomie," Dana called out from the black-and-white-tiled bathroom. "There's even a bidet here." I had seen bidets on buying trips to Europe with my mother but wasn't sure exactly what they were used for. However, I was reluctant to admit that to the sophisticated Dana.

"We can use these for our hand-washables," Dana pronounced in her typical take-charge fashion. Dana literally took charge of me, which was fortunate for me because Dana seemed to know her way around every situation.

She finally coaxed me out of my doldrums with promises of shopping. I could hardly wait for daylight to begin exploring the quaint silversmith and goldsmith shops and jewelry stores that lined the Ponte Vecchio where the Old Bridge stretched across the Arno River.

I sat at the open window at twilight, facing the courtyard opposite a window at the far end of the garden plaza. Still dazed, groggy, and half asleep, I could see the moon rising, full and beautiful, over the terracotta rooftops. The night was warm, but it offered a gentle breeze, and I was happy to be here in such a new and exciting place. Tonight, Manny Gellar seemed a million miles away.

Noise coming from the room across the courtyard caught my attention. A crowd of students had gathered, and a party was in progress. The students were tasting true freedom in a city tantalizingly far from home. I was about to close the curtain when a tall, skinny, pasty-faced boy—I vaguely recognized him from the dining room the first night—sailed through the window opposite me. As I gaped in horror and tried to call out Dana's name, he glided in slow motion right past me and down through the plate glass ceiling. He landed with an unceremonious thud in the garden below, the glass shattering into a million shards. It was a picture I couldn't get out of my mind.

The next time I saw Todd Singleton, he was bandaged from head to toe, a mummy tucked away in the American Hospital, where no one spoke English and where he remained for the duration of the program. People soon forgot what Todd used to look like under those bandages. For me, Todd would always be frozen in time, billowing through space at the Hotel Palermo. In fact, I almost wished I could trade places with Todd Singleton and stay safely cocooned until it was time to go home. Right now, though, I couldn't imagine facing home.

Manny's letters started coming two weeks after I arrived in Florence, and they kept coming in a steady flow. When the first one was delivered, my initial instinct was to throw it away, but I fought the urge and opened it.

Dear Jewels,

I miss you very much and I spend a lot of time thinking about us. Why didn't you tell me you were leaving? Were you upset about what happened in Jacksonville Beach? I don't want you to be scared by any of the things I said or did, and if you would rather me not mention that night, please tell me and we can have a carefree, no-obligation relationship. The only hassle is that I care for you and I don't think I can stand being without you for a whole year. Please write as soon as possible and let me know how you're feeling. I'm looking forward to seeing you again more than anything else.

Love Always, Manny

I burst into tears. Why was he sounding so sweet

like this now, when we were an ocean apart? Why couldn't he admit his feelings before? Why had he asked Nita to that final fraternity weekend? Was anything he said in the letter real? How would I ever be able to tell? When the next letter came, I placed it in a pocket of my hanging shoebag, unopened. By the time I left Florence, there was no room for my shoes.

It drove Dana crazy.

"Roomie, if you don't open those letters, I will."

But I was adamant. "I can't. I don't want to know what's in them. It's too painful."

To this day I have no idea what the rest of the letters said. I doubt reading them would have made any difference. Before I left Florence, I stuffed the unopened letters behind the armoire in the hotel room.

Despite my state of mind, I adored Italy and felt right at home with the romantic cadence of the language, the fast-flowing Arno, the warmth of the people. I loved to wander down the narrow medieval streets and the wide Renaissance piazzas to explore the masterpieces of art and architecture. I studied Italian, religion, art history, mythology, and English. I loved the romantic and sentimental sonnets of the runaway lover-poets Robert and Elizabeth Browning, who sought refuge in Florence after their 1846 marriage. I visited the villa of Casa Guidi, overlooking the city, and wondered if anyone would ever love me the way Robert loved his "little Portuguese."

I spent the next four months living in Italy away from inquiring eyes and suspicions and as far away from Manny Gellar as I could get. I saw every piece of art in every church and every museum in the city. My favorite work of art in the city was Botticelli's masterpiece "The Birth of Venus" at the Uffizi Gallery. The first time I laid eyes on Venus, the goddess of beauty, in all her nakedness, splendid and seductive, yet innocent, it shook my emotions and spoke to my heart. I loved the pastel colors and the way the wind seemed to blow Venus to shore. But it just brought to mind that I myself was no longer innocent. I was also no longer skinny.

It was no wonder. I ate gelato at Vivoli's, and calzone, pizza, and spaghetti at Bruno's near the train station. Everyone attributed my weight gain to having given in to the tasty temptations of Florence. I never revealed my secret to anyone. I took long walks along the Arno, bought luscious fresh peaches at the public market, and listened to music at the Piazza della Signoria while sipping cioccolata.

I crowded myself with new experiences and new places in hopes of losing myself along the way. But nothing had changed except the scenery. Instead of forgetting Manny, much of my time overseas was spent dwelling on him, mired in memories.

When I was supposed to be studying Italian, I found myself writing my imaginary new name in cursive across the pages in my notebook: *Julie Gellar, Mrs. Manny Gellar, Julie Goldsmith Gellar.* The letters were so familiar I could even see them in my sleep. And I couldn't stop the fat tears that slipped down the side of my face and plopped onto the paper, blurring my vision and soaking my signature.

Mackie wrote that Manny asked about me all the time and wondered why I never answered his letters.

"I truly think he's lost without you. He mopes about like a hurt little boy, with no one to laugh at his jokes." But I had sworn my friend to secrecy. Under no circumstances was Manny to learn about the pregnancy.

Mackie's latest letter arrived in a package with a book about pregnancy and childbirth. "Julie, from what I'm reading between the lines, I'm afraid you're in denial. I don't think you've really faced up to the fact that you're pregnant. You're an ostrich with her head stuck in the sand. Eventually, this child is going to come out the other end and then what will you do?"

Was that what I was doing? Denying my child?

Time went by in a blur. Mostly I remember scarfing down pasta and barfing it back up. Instead of snacking on saltines, I nibbled on biscotti. Other than that, I guess that being pregnant was pretty much the same in any language. My stomach was still expanding at an alarming rate.

I was definitely *not* looking for any romantic entanglements. I was hardly in any position to be thinking in that direction, no matter how lonely I was. Even in my condition, I knew I still looked good in my brown cotton jeans, short-sleeved beige ribbed shirt, and clogs that clickety-clacked against the cobblestones. The familiar Italian pick-up line, the eternal male call, "*Ciao, bella*," still greeted me on my walks to and from class. It wouldn't have made any difference if I were wearing a potato sack. Italian boys weren't that discriminating. They would have loved to practice more than their Italian on me, but after what I had been through, the barriers I had built up were too strong for anyone to break down. My emotions were buried as deep as the layers of stone in Pompeii. It would take a long time to peel back those layers, and I doubted even a top-notch archaeological team could crack the surface.

Homesick and lonely, I spent a lot of time sitting in the disco—the hotel cellar—every night with the rest of the students on my program, listening to soulful American songs and watching everyone get mind-numbingly drunk on cheap Chianti. Drinking was something I couldn't indulge in because of my pregnancy. But Italy was another place, and I was a different girl. So one night I made an exception. When I was about to be sick, I stumbled back upstairs to find Dana was gone for the evening, again.

Dana, I discovered, was a serial dater. Four months into the program, she had graduated from the world of immature Italian boys to older, more sophisticated men, and my roommate and I had become somewhat estranged.

When I saw her leave the hotel that evening in her tight red dress, tottering on matching red heels and encased in a full-length fur, she was on the way to a fancy party, escorted by her latest handsome Italian gentleman friend. I couldn't quite see the difference between my roommate and the women of the night who plied their wares on the streets outside our hotel door. I didn't expect her back until the early hours of the morning.

When Dana returned from her date, I was throwing up in the bidet. *I knew that contraption would come in handy.* I didn't remember much else about the rest of the evening, except Dana cleaning up my mess and helping me into my flannel pajamas. There was a spreading stain on her tight red dress. I had ruined it, but she didn't seem to mind.

"Would you please tell me what's wrong with

you?" she insisted. "You're barfing your guts out and you don't even drink. You've been acting absolutely hormonal since you arrived, and I can't figure it out."

"I'm pregnant, okay?" I finally admitted. "Is that what you wanted to hear?"

"It's not what I expected," she answered quietly.

"You mean from Miss Goody Two Shoes?"

"I didn't say that. We don't know each other well enough for me to judge you. Even though sometimes I think you judge me. I'd like to help."

"Promise me you won't tell anyone, especially not the director. He'll ship me back home early, and I can't go home just yet."

"I won't tell. But ultimately someone is going to notice, don't you think?"

"Maybe. I'll just say I'm getting fat."

"That might work. What can I do for you?"

"Do you know any OB-GYNs by any chance? I need to get checked out, I think."

"As a matter of fact, I'm dating a gynecologist. His name is Roberto, and he's delicious."

"I don't need a meal, just some vitamins," I remarked.

"Very funny. Trust me. You'll like him. He's very discreet. Great hands, too. I'll take you to his office on Monday, and we'll work everything out."

I started crying and hugged Dana.

"Thank you," I said. "I've missed you."

"I know," Dana said. "Me too. I guess I don't have to ask whose it is."

"It's the Letter Writer's." That's what Dana called him.

"Does he even know?"

"No, and he's never going to."

"He's not going to hear it from me. I don't even know the guy. You'd better get some sleep now. All these late nights are bad for the baby."

How did Dana get to be so wise?

As I drifted off to sleep I thought how nice it was that someone over here on this side of my world shared my secret, and that I no longer had to shoulder that burden by myself. I wasn't alone, and the baby was somehow finally beginning to feel real. It was time to stop hiding out in Italy and get on with my life.

Chapter Fourteen:
I'm Not Fat, I'm Pregnant

Miami

Matt wasn't much of a writer, but whenever he did drop me a line, I answered his letters, purposely leaving out the part about my pregnancy. I got my hair cut in a stylish Italian shag and sent him a picture of me taken in an auto photo booth. I thought I looked pretty good—from the waist up. Matt wrote back that he couldn't wait to see me. Thrilled that I had come home early from Italy, it was obvious he was anxious to pick up our relationship where it left off. Although I suspected Matt was in love with me, he had never said the words to me, and I wasn't ready to say the words to him.

I went back to work for my parents at Goldsmith's Jewelers. My favorite part of working at Goldsmith's was helping young couples select their diamond engagement rings. The jewelry shop did a brisk and profitable wedding business, which kept my view of the world unnaturally rosy. All I ever saw, day in and day out, were people in love starting out together on an open road, focused only on each other, their new lives opening up in front of them, nothing but big dreams ahead of them.

I was determined to make my own mark in the

business. Media, marketing, advertising, dealing with customers, and anticipating trends were my areas of expertise. I had an eye for quality and style and knew what would sell. I designed ads and planned promotions that brought customers into the store and, once there, few failed to leave without a purchase.

Matt landed a position with a small freight expediter that provided shipping services from the United States to Latin America. They had a network of agents scattered in cities throughout the Americas, so considerable travel was involved. The company offered a generous compensation package with an opportunity for Matt to buy into the business if he proved himself. Meanwhile, he was trying to prove how much he'd missed me.

Parking his car by the lake near his house, he pulled me close and began kissing me. I responded instinctively.

"Julie, I'm going crazy. Did you miss me as much as I missed you?"

I didn't answer because I was confused about how I really felt. We had never made love before, and from the way we were fogging up the windows, it was evident that he wanted to tonight. I was definitely not ready to give myself to him completely, especially not in a cramped car. Maybe I would never be ready. I had given up any hope of ever getting together with Manny. That was a fantasy.

Matt was my reality, and he was here now, kissing me softly on the lips and telling me how much he loved me. But Manny was right there between us as surely as if he were flesh and blood, he was so much a part of me.

"Julie, I want to make love to you. Please can we?"

"No, Matt. I can't now. I'm sorry."

"Well, when then?" he said impatiently, touching me, trying his best to arouse me. "Doesn't it feel good when we're together like this, honey?" he asked, pushing me into a prone position with my head wedged uncomfortably against the door handle. Well, not exactly. My neck was getting stiff, and I was losing all feeling in my legs.

"I want more, Julie. I need more."

"I understand, Matt. That's why I—"

"No, I don't think you do. I have something for you. He reached into the pocket of his khaki slacks and stunned me when he pulled out a small green Goldsmith's box wrapped in a green ribbon.

Was this what I thought it was? I opened the box to find a beautiful diamond ring. The stone was very fine, at least a carat in size, with a wonderful antique platinum setting, something I might have picked out for myself. Matt was pleased when he saw me admiring the ring.

"Your mother helped me pick it out." He smiled proudly.

"My mother?" I asked, flabbergasted. "She knew about this? She never said a word to me." Sylvia Goldsmith strikes again.

"Well, I wanted to surprise you."

"You certainly did." I was furious at my mother. How could she conspire against her own daughter and blindside me like this? I didn't even know what I wanted, and now Matt and my mother had presented me with a *fait accompli*. The last thing I wanted to do was hurt Matt.

Then I realized this was my mother's contribution to the campaign to marry off her single, pregnant daughter. My mother had been shocked when I showed up at home as pregnant as the day I left for London. This was her not-so-subtle way of trying to arrange my life, again.

"You haven't said anything," Matt said.

I had traveled to Italy to uncomplicate my life, and when I decided to keep my baby, I could hardly tell Matt something so important in a letter. It never seemed to be the perfect time. I had planned to tell him the truth tonight. Now that we were face-to-face, it was time, way past time, to level with him.

"Matt," I said calmly, placing his hand on my stomach. "There's something I have to tell you. Something that I should have told you before. You're either incredibly unobservant or quite a gentleman. You never even commented about how much I've porked out in the past four months. I'm hardly the same girl you knew before I went away to Italy."

"I don't care how much you weigh, Julie. I love you."

"Matt, that's sweet, but you're not listening." I paused briefly. "I'm not fat, I'm pregnant."

Matt reeled and dropped my hand.

"You're pregnant? Julie, how could that have happened? We haven't, I mean we never…"

Exactamente.

"That's exactly my point. Now do you see what I'm trying to tell you? I'm so sorry."

"But who? Did it happen in Italy?"

"That's not important." If I told Matt the truth, he would confront Manny, and that was the last thing I wanted.

"It is to me."

"Matt, I know I've hurt you. I really wish I could…take the whole thing back, do it over, but it's done. I think you'd better take me home."

The silence between us was intense. Finally Matt spoke.

"But you haven't answered my question."

"Well, you haven't asked me anything," I pointed out, trying to stall for time, growing increasingly agitated.

"Julie," said Matt taking my hand in his. He brushed his lips against mine so softly that the sensation barely registered. "I love you. Will you marry me?"

I felt the tears stream down my cheeks. The man was some kind of a saint. I certainly didn't deserve him. How could he ever get past something as huge as this? How could he possibly want someone as huge as me? I did care for him a great deal, and I thought I could even grow to love him. It wasn't the passionate, all-consuming love I felt for Manny. But it also wasn't a destructive love. With Matt there was no pretense. He always gave a hundred percent. He never held back. And I knew he would never hurt or disappoint me. I also knew it would be a long time before I found anybody else to fill that empty space inside my heart.

Maybe it wasn't fair to compare him to Manny. Maybe nobody would ever measure up. Manny had spoiled me for anyone else. Matt's only fault was not being Manny. I wanted things to be good between us. I wanted to love him the way he loved me.

"The ring is beautiful, but it's such an important decision, I need some time to think," I stalled. "If we did get married, when did you have in mind?"

"As soon as possible, Julie. Tomorrow if we could. With my salary, I can support you—and the baby. I don't want to live without you one more minute."

It was one of the biggest decisions I'd ever make in my life. Selfishly, I knew that Matt could solve all my problems. But I needed to solve my own problems. At the same time, I knew I might not ever get another chance for happiness. Mackie would tell me to take that chance. And so would my parents. But when I thought about who I wanted to spend the rest of my life with, I knew it wasn't Matt. Hands down, no contest. There always was only one man for me. I doubted that would ever change.

"Manny came by the store yesterday and said he wants to see me again," I told Mackie the morning after the proposal.

"He's trying to break down your defenses," Mackie said.

"The trouble is I can't make up my mind about us. I love who I am with him and at the same time, I hate who I am with him."

"Manny Gellar is your biggest weakness," Mackie sympathized.

"How can love be a weakness?" I reasoned, dejected.

It was easy for Mackie to give advice. She was about to marry Little Jon and her life was falling nicely into place. Mine was still up in the air.

"You know how Manny is," Mackie said. "He doesn't want you, but he doesn't want anyone else to have you. He's still living in the past and he likes it there. He'll never let you go. He'll keep you hanging on until one of you dies. So you're going to have to be the strong one and put him completely out of your mind, once and for all, unless he makes some kind of commitment to you."

"There's still a connection between us on some level. I think there always will be. We'll probably grow old together—and not together. But we can't be just friends anymore. It's gone way beyond that. But whatever this thing we have is, the relationship is not moving forward."

"You don't see his flaws," Mackie said. "You deserve better. You deserve someone like Matt. At least you know where you stand with him."

"But I don't love Matt," I said, suddenly struck by the simple truth of it.

****

Matt was disappointed and hurt when I told him I couldn't marry him.

"Do you think there will ever be a chance for us?" he asked hopefully.

"I'm sorry, Matt," I apologized, giving him all the reasons but the real one.

"I'm going to hold on to the ring for a while, in case you, you know, change your mind." He looked away, but not before I saw how devastated he was. He didn't get the answer he had expected, and he was trying his best to deal with that.

Jeez Maheez! I hoped I wasn't making the biggest mistake of my life turning my back in the face of such a fierce love.

Chapter Fifteen:
Memory Lane

Jewels@aol.com: What do you know about sexy lingerie?

DoubleMac@aol.com: What's wrong with your regular underwear?

Jewels@aol.com: Jockeys are practical and comfortable, but boring.

DoubleMac@aol.com: Are these for Matt or for your trip to Palm Coast?

Jewels@aol.com: No, they're for me.

DoubleMac@aol.com: Okay, you're going to want satin or silk. No flannel, cotton or spandex. A sheer nightgown with spaghetti straps would be nice.

Jewels@aol.com: I like spaghetti.

DoubleMac@aol.com: You're busty. I have the opposite problem. Real women like you might have to shop at an alternative store.

Jewels@aol.com: Department stores are more convenient. They feature lingerie on the same floor as flip-flops.

DoubleMac@aol.com: Probably because they're both easy to slip off.

Jewels@aol.com: What would I wear under a naughty negligee?

DoubleMac@aol.com: As little as possible.

****

"My parents have given Joel and me the green light on our plans for the shop," I told my assistant Mercedes. "In fact, I'm meeting with my realtor this afternoon and we're going to discuss some possible locations over lunch."

"Oh, you got that new dress for your *realtor?* I can only imagine what you have on under that outfit." Mercedes knew too much for her own good, but I could trust her not to tell my mother anything about my lunch plans.

I had scoured the racks for the perfect dress. Businesslike, but sexy. I'd rejected the rows of slacks. I wanted to look foxy, not boxy. Finally I found it. The yellow silk dress was soft and flattering and did a passable job of hiding my stomach. A pair of expensive silk stockings and gunmetal-gray stacked heels promised to torture my feet but nicely complement the outfit. New French lingerie completed the package. My mother always told me never to leave the house without clean underwear. But she never said anything about wearing underwear the size of the Gross National Product. Besides, I wasn't buying new underwear for my mother. What if the business lunch turned into more? I couldn't let Manny see me in my ratty old cotton things that spread out like a billowing ship's sail.

A sheer ivory bra accented my best assets. I had a black fishnet negligee in my purse. Not even a Girl Scout could have been better prepared.

"I *needed* a new dress," I fibbed. "And my undergarments are nobody's business but mine." Mercedes rolled her eyes, but she knew better than to argue with me.

I went to my desk to collect the paperwork I

planned to show Manny during our meeting. I wanted to showcase the jewels Manny's mother had brought over from Cuba, using them to highlight the opening of the new boutique, which I would name Stones. The pieces weren't doing anybody any good locked away in the dustproof vault at Goldsmith's. They deserved to be seen and appreciated. We would build a special display and present the jewels as The Estrella Collection, named after Elena's sister. After I researched the provenance and history of the gems, I would prepare a color catalog, which would feature Manny's sister Estrellita on the cover. Each of the pieces alone was priceless, and as a collection they would be spectacular.

I could already visualize the shop—from interior to exterior, right down to the bougainvillea I would plant outside the storefront, similar to vines I'd seen adorning the facades of shops and homes on the Mediterranean coast.

I had it all worked out. I would spend the next few months closing on the new location, working with the interior designer to remodel, going on buying trips to find new merchandise to stock the store, and planning the gala grand opening. All the intense work would have to be done before the baby came.

I didn't let myself believe that my final decision had anything to do with Manny's sudden reappearance in my life. I had never felt so alive, and I didn't know whether that feeling came from the new life that was growing inside of me, from the excitement I felt about launching Stones, or from seeing Manny again.

I placed the designer's preliminary sketches of Stones with several other documents in a manila folder. As Manny's brand-new blue BMW sports car pulled up to the front of the shop, I grabbed my purse and went out to meet him.

My heart was pounding, just like it always did when I was around him.

"You look beautiful," Manny said when he saw me.

I was secretly delighted that the clothes had the desired effect.

"I'm really glad you could come," he said sincerely as he helped me into the passenger seat. "I wasn't sure if you would."

He drove without talking for a while. It was unlike him to be so quiet. I could tell he was nervous.

"I made us a reservation at Bellagio's," he began. "It's very private."

"I brought along some papers for you to look at," I said, trying to turn the subject to business. I was anxious to tell him my news about Stones and my idea for his mother's collection.

"We have plenty of time for that," said Manny. "Let's just relax and talk."

The restaurant was lovely, the service discreet. The view of the bay was breathtaking.

"Why don't you start with a drink," he suggested. "You used to like Singapore Slings, as I remember."

"Things change. Now it's Amaretto Sours. Besides, I don't think it's a good idea for me to drink." All it took was one drink to get me a little lightheaded, and he knew that. I needed to keep my wits about me, but the prospect of an entire afternoon stretching out in front of me without some support seemed a little daunting. I was going to need some kind of fortification for this encounter. Maybe just a sip, or one small drink.

We enjoyed a lunch of Caesar salad and my favorite—spaghetti *alla carbonara.*

"She'll have another drink." Manny signaled to the waiter.

"Are you trying to get me drunk?" I laughed.

"Too late for that, I see," he joked, but I declined the offer.

We had a great time, talking about my plans for the new store and reminiscing.

"You know I haven't laughed like this in so long," Manny said. Was that honesty I detected creeping into his voice? Unfamiliar territory for him. It was quite intoxicating. Or was it just that I was already intoxicated from my drink?

"I wonder what DoubleMac would think if she knew we were together now?" he posed.

"Mackie would think I was a fool to even see you after what you did to me," I said, noting some of the old resentment swelling up. Then I remembered Manny didn't know he had anything to do with my pregnancy.

"What I did to *you?*" he asked. "What do you mean? *You* were the one who went off to Italy without a word. I thought we had something special. Why did you have to leave with no explanation? I opened myself up to you in my letters and got nothing in return. What happened to us?"

"Nita happened to us," I replied simply. I knew that Nita Weinstein had worked her dark magic on Manny while I was away. Apparently, our Opal Weekend encounter hadn't meant a thing to him.

"She has nothing to do with us," Manny said.

"How can you say that?"

"I don't want you to think about her now."

"How can I not? She's part of your life. You can't separate her from her father, and her father controls you."

"No one controls me," Manny answered stiffly.

"So how come you're so busy playing with Nita and kissing up to her father?" Bolstered by the liquor I was brutally honest. "What was I to you, really? I wish I could finally figure it out." All the old anger was back, but Manny had no idea of the source or depth of those feelings. "Admit it. You never really cared about me. You were just using me. It's an old story. I was a fool and I played right along with your games."

"I always cared about you," said Manny. "I still do. You were my best girl, Jewels. You know that, don't you?"

"That's not the way I remember it. You must be living in a parallel universe. And if I was your *best girl*, then why are you still with Nita now that I'm back from Italy?" What I didn't say was how much it tore me apart to think about the two of them together.

"You left *me*, remember," he said stubbornly. "You dated Matt before you left for Italy. Then when you returned you were pregnant and you went straight back to Matt. What was I supposed to think? I thought you were gone from me forever. Nita cares about me. No one has cared about me the way she has, not since you. I guess I needed that."

I knew this had been a bad idea. I was furious all over again, like it was yesterday. If I didn't get out of the restaurant I was going to explode.

"You're upset," he said. "I'm sorry. That's not how I wanted this to be." He took my hand and stroked it softly. "Please just relax."

"If you want to talk about Stones, I'll stay," I said, pulling away.

"I don't care about the damn shop," he barked. "We have plenty of time for that. Let's get out of here." He slapped down a stack of bills on the table, took my hand, and led me to the car.

"I...can't stay here." My voice faltered. This whole idea had been ridiculous. I thought I could correct the past, somehow make up for it, and make it right. But it would never be right.

When we were safely in the car he put his arms around me, drew me close, and kissed me urgently on the lips.

"Jewels, I've been wanting to do that all during lunch," he said. "I got a place for us."

"A place?" I was puzzled.

"A small, private hotel not too far from here. I've registered us as husband and wife. It'll be okay."

"I really don't think this is such a good..." I began.

"Come on, don't say you don't want to do this," he shot back angrily.

"Look, have you forgotten about Nita?" I asked.

"I'm trying to," he replied. "I'll be honest with you. My life is a mess right now. I'm under a lot of pressure. There's so much expected of me... I have so much to prove. Things aren't the same without you. Do you understand that I *need* you?"

There it was again. The need mantra. Same tune, different verse. I was on the verge of tears, and I couldn't stop them.

"Don't do this to me again, would you?" I fumed.

"Do what?" he whispered. "What are you talking about?" He reached over and kissed away my tears, in a nurturing gesture. "Just come with me, just this once. We don't have to do anything but talk, all right?"

I was silent, sulking. I didn't believe that for a minute. He pulled the car away from the restaurant parking lot and drove over to the Biscayne Terrace, a small, very elegant and private hotel. Stubbornly, I remained in the car. If I went in with him, I knew I would cross the line. I didn't have the slightest bit of will power where he was concerned. But wasn't that what I had expected? Why had I gone to the fancy French lingerie shop, then? I hadn't misread him after all.

"Come on, Julie, please," he coaxed. He reached for my hand and kissed the inside of my palm.

I bit my lip and nodded. I could no longer ignore the pull of the past. This particular walk down memory lane was going to cost me. I was as sure of that as I was powerless to stop it from happening. But was I ready to pay the price?

Chapter Sixteen:
Doing It *en Español*

Manny flashed his smile and helped me out of the car. He held my hand as we walked toward the lobby.

"Uh, reservation for Mr. and Mrs. Charles Shumaker?" Manny said to the desk clerk. I looked away as the clerk handed Manny the key.

"Yes, here's your room key, Mr. and Mrs. *Shumaker*. No luggage? Enjoy your stay with us." We weren't fooling anyone. I wondered how many other illicit couples had come to this hotel, or more to the point, if he'd brought the White Witch here.

The second-floor room was lovely. Very understated. Very European. It had a nice terrace overlooking the bay. The goose down comforter had a tasteful Delft-blue checked pattern, and the furniture was a spare antique pine.

"I wanted this time to be special for us," Manny said. "I came here to check out the room first."

So he *had* planned this. I didn't move from my spot by the door.

"Why don't you come over here and sit down next to me," said Manny, patting the bed. I followed him reluctantly.

"Do you feel better now?" he asked, as I settled into the plush mattress as far away from him as I could.

"I don't know," I said. "I'm really not comfortable

with this. I don't know what we're doing here." I walked over to the table and pulled the sheaf of papers out of my briefcase. I would talk to him and I wouldn't let it go any further than that.

"Can you just forget the papers for a minute?" he said, grabbing them from my hand. "I need you. Can't you see that? My life is falling apart. Things between Nita and me, well… I can never seem to please her. Nothing is ever good enough for her father. She's in too much of a hurry. And I can't talk to her like I used to be able to talk to you."

I looked past him and felt as if I were teetering at the edge of a precipice. I could feel myself falling but could do nothing to stop it. It was almost as if I were in the scene of a movie but watching someone else playing my part. I was drowning, and I desperately needed to hang on to this little bit of happiness, a refugee clinging to a dream of freedom.

"I'll tell you what," he said decisively. "I'm going to order us some room service.'' Always a man of action, Manny picked up the telephone receiver.

"This is Mr. Shumaker in Room 204," he said. "I'd like a bottle of Di Soronno Amaretto, and two glasses."

"Manny, I've already had way too much to drink," I protested, throwing up my hands.

"Don't worry, it will help you relax," Manny said. "And you won't be drinking it, I will," he promised, brandishing his trademark smile.

He was the same confident Manny, who always got what he wanted. At least from me.

We reminisced casually until the order arrived. I hadn't felt this much anticipation in a long time.

Manny was tipping the waiter. I was staring at his

large brown hands. I loved his hands.

"Thank you, Mr. Shumaker," the waiter said discreetly, as if he really believed we were who we pretended to be. Manny closed the door behind him.

We easily resumed our edgy banter. It was vintage Manny. He'd thought of everything, right down to the fresh flowers—yellow roses—he had ordered for the room. I half-expected him to produce his stereo. Instead, he excused himself and got up to make a brief business call on the phone in the bathroom. There was a card with the flowers, with my name on the envelope. I tore it open.

Jewels and Manny
Meant to be Together
Happy Birthday

I felt the sting of tears in my eyes as I placed the card in my purse. Then he came out and turned on the radio.

"And now we have a special dedication. This Johnny Mathis classic goes out from Charles Shumaker to his wife on the occasion of her birthday," read the disc jockey over the air waves, and they began playing "Chances Are." That's when I stopped fighting him and myself.

"Let's get out of our clothes and into these robes first, *Mrs. Shumaker*," Manny suggested. He walked over to the closet, slipped the hotel's thick, white, signature terrycloth robes off their satin-covered hangers, and brought them over to the bed.

"Let me undress you," he said.

I nodded, breathless. I was already beginning to get moist, reacting like some pre-programmed Pavlovian dog. Although the memory was far away, the nearness of him was still familiar, and my feelings for him hadn't changed. He removed his clothes and put on the robe, but left it half open. And there he was in all his nakedness. He was never modest about his body, and he had no reason to be. He was already hard. But he was also very patient. If I remembered correctly, he had a lot of staying power and I had a very high threshold for pleasure. He held my face in his hands, stroked my cheek, and then pulled me toward him for a long kiss.

"You smell great. Are you wearing a new perfume?"

"It's only been four months. How can you forget I don't have a sense of smell? I don't wear perfume. It's just plain me."

"There's nothing plain about you, Jewels," he said softly. "My Jewels. You're so beautiful. Your eyes… They're even bluer than I remembered them." Then he was kissing my eyes and my long lashes and my lips, and slipping off my high heels, rubbing my stocking feet, trying to arouse me. He removed my new lemon-colored jacket and threw it on a nearby chair. Then he looked at my emerald pendant in surprise.

"You're still wearing it?" he asked, smiling broadly.

"I always do."

Manny lifted the large, round, beautifully worked medallion that hung around my neck on a heavy braided chain. Fashioned of Spanish silver, it flashed in the light, and his thumb rubbed the magnificent emerald in the center like a talisman. Manny called it my breastplate. Mackie called it The Swinging Medallion. My mother called me crazy for wearing such an expensive piece of jewelry around my neck with the

Colombian gangs robbing jewelry stores every day in Miami.

It was a priceless piece. I thought again of the history of the medallion. It had belonged to Elena's family for generations, and it was one of the pieces sewn into her dress when she escaped from Cuba. It had great sentimental value to Manny's mother, and it must have been difficult for her to part with it. I knew she thought or hoped that one day I would be part of the family. But life doesn't always go as planned.

Putting the medallion aside, Manny began to rub my breasts through the yellow silk dress. Then he lifted up the dress and began to rub my panties through my stockings.

"Let's just get these stockings off," he said, gently slipping them off while he continued to kiss and caress me. Then he peeled off my dress and threw it carelessly on the chair. He looked at me with naked desire.

I pulled the crisp sheets up to my neck. He tried to slide them away.

"Don't hide from me."

"But I'm pregnant. I look... I don't want you to see me like this. At least turn off the lights, please."

"No. I want to see you. All of you. I've missed you so much. You don't know how much I've fantasized about this." He sounded sincere. He massaged the mound of my belly tenderly, erotically. "I think this is sexy."

He traced the outline of my bra and slipped his fingers inside for a slight touch. I shivered.

"I miss the feel of you in my hands," he said, his voice as slow and thick as syrup. "I miss the taste of you. I miss everything about you. Do you want me to

161

tell you just what I'm going to do to you? How I'm going to make love to you?"

Crap! And double crap, because I want him to.

This Manny had some new lines and some new moves that were even smoother than before.

"Oh, Jewels. You've missed this as much as I've missed it, haven't you?"

I couldn't speak, but huge tears were rolling down my cheeks. I had missed him too.

He unhooked my bra, and within seconds he had me gasping. All that was left to come off were my new silk panties. I tried to kiss him, but he drew away.

"Not yet, baby. Be patient."

He removed my panties and slowly, deliberately, rubbed me till I was practically panting. Then he stopped and reached for the amaretto. Lifting the medallion to one side, he poured the amaretto onto one of my breasts and licked the sweet brown liquid off slowly.

"I said you wouldn't have to drink a drop," Manny said.

"Oh, God, Manny, please," I begged.

"Not just yet. I've waited so long for you. Let's don't hurry this," he whispered.

He moved the medallion to cover one of my breasts. The sensation was cold against my naked body. He poured the amaretto over my other breast. Then he barely touched my belly as he tipped the bottle lower, following the trail with his tongue.

He sensed that I needed to kiss him, so just as I was about to climax, he thrust his tongue into my mouth. Swollen and desperate, he pushed me down onto the bed and exploded into me with a primitive fierce jungle rhythm, until we both came together.

Satisfied, we lay back on the bed, hands clasped, and listened to the steady whir of the ceiling fan until our hearts regained their regular rhythm. I still had all my jewelry on, but nothing else. My brand-new French panties were lost somewhere in the cool sheets.

"C'mere," he said softly.

"I am here," I whispered, tugging on his hand.

"No, closer to me, *amada*," he said, leaning over and kissing me sweetly on the lips. "That was great. It's been a long time since I've felt this way," he said, echoing my thoughts.

I wanted to know how I compared to Nita, but I didn't feel secure enough to ask. He'd told me he wasn't sleeping with her. Could I trust that?

He rolled over to the side of the bed, leaned over the end table, and poured some more of the almond-flavored liqueur into a glass. He sipped some, licking his lips slowly, suggestively. Then he reached over and kissed my mouth again so I could taste the rich sweetness on his tongue. His mouth moved down to my nipples and he wet them with his tongue, licking them in a circular motion till they were erect. Then he blew on them.

"How does that feel?" he asked.

I groaned.

"Well, that's just the beginning, *amada*," he said softly, starting to kiss me again, long and deep. A new wave of desire swept over me. He moved his hands between my legs and touched me gently, moving his fingers expertly the way he knew I liked.

"You're all ready for me, again," he marveled, and whispered, "You were made for love, Jewels, made for me. Let me love you."

"Manny, please," I moaned.

Then he moved into me again, first softly, then insistently, with a hunger I found surprising. When we were lost in each other, I thought I heard him grunt an almost imperceptible, "I love you."

"You don't have to say that," I whispered faintly about the one thing I'd craved hearing from him. "If it's not the way you feel."

I don't think he even remembered the words coming out of his mouth. At least he didn't acknowledge them.

"I think I got carried away," he said instead. "I didn't hurt you, did I?" he asked sheepishly. "The baby, I mean."

I shook my head. *I won't ever let you hurt me again.*

"You know we've got to keep seeing each other—"

"I don't think…" I protested weakly, as the waves of excitement began to recede.

"Sssh," he whispered, and quieted me with long, sensuous kisses, stroking me all over. "Let me do the thinking." He cupped my breasts in his hands and fondled them. He didn't say so, but I was sure he was comparing me with Nita, whose breasts were as flat as the Serengeti Plains. He made me feel treasured, even though I knew I was bloated and unattractive. I wanted to ask him about Nita, but I didn't want the thought of that woman to intrude on our time together.

"I need you so much," he said simply. "You're so good for me. Isn't it good for you? I can't stop seeing you now. I could stay here all night with you like this. Something is missing in my life. And I think it's you."

He reached for me and held me close. "Jewels, I can't get enough of you."

"Where is this going?" I wanted to know. "Are you going to tell Nita about us?"

"I don't want to talk about her now," he answered. "I want to talk about us. How do you feel about me?"

"Are you fishing for compliments?"

"Always."

"Well, I guess I like you."

"Admit it, you still love me."

"I never said that."

"When can we see each other again?" he asked tentatively.

"I'm not sure that would be a good idea," I said, shaking my head at the inane dating banter. Although "dating" really wouldn't have exactly described our nontraditional relationship.

Being with Manny again seemed right. All my loneliness was melting away. The regrets and the pain he had caused me were being crowded out by the good memories that suddenly came flooding back. It was no use pretending or playing coy. I was hooked on him, and he knew it.

"Julie, what do you want from me?"

"I don't know." I sighed.

What exactly did I want from him? If I was honest with myself, I'd want him to say he'd stop seeing Nita, quit his job at her father's company, marry me, really want our baby, and solve all my problems.

Short of a permanent commitment, I needed to break off our relationship—this time for good. I would finally let him go, body and soul. And this time, I wouldn't waver or give in to him. I would make him realize I was serious. I doubted he would put up much of a fight. His career was obviously more important to him than I was. The trouble was that when I imagined myself growing old, it was with Manny. Deep inside, I knew I still believed we were meant to be together.

But I was through wanting what I couldn't have. And I was tired of this one-sided relationship. I was ready to move on. I couldn't help who I fell in love with, but if I ever let myself trust enough to fall in love again, I would look for somebody who was sure and steady and safe and real. Someone like Matt. But I had given up a sure thing once for a master showman. Manny was always playing games. Stringing me along to boost his ego. And I was finally ready to get off the merry-go-round. The baby and I would be fine on our own.

Despite my reservations, I desperately wanted to trust Manny. Seeing him again proved that I still loved him. And that I missed him. But I knew something was missing in the core of our relationship. I needed a sincere commitment from him that he just couldn't make. A commitment he could make if he truly loved me, if what he felt for me was real. I didn't want to come second in his life. I deserved more, and so did our baby. But I invariably delayed a decision about our relationship with a variety of excuses.

Facing the overwhelming prospect of launching Stones, I knew I would never be able to focus if I went back to the office. How could I concentrate on anything else? I wanted to stay here forever, reliving the afternoon. It was everything I had ever dreamed of. The most satisfying sex—well, the only sex—since the last time I had slept with Manny. He was a sensitive lover who always considered my needs first, at least physically. He delighted in my sensuality and loved giving me pleasure. And I couldn't deny I wanted to see him again, be with him like this again.

If we could be together just one more time to see what would happen... What did I think would happen? We'd tumble back into bed again and again, but beyond that, what more could come of it?

How much would my pregnancy complicate our high-stakes relationship? How much would it change what was happening between us? And what in the hell was I doing here?

I yawned and stretched. Manny took my hands. I could tell he didn't want to leave me. I felt tired. Maybe the baby was sapping my strength.

"Julie...you are so beautiful, soft as a kitten, but such a tiger in bed," he said, stroking me lightly, arousing me all over again and eyeing me like some prey he was about to devour. The power he held over me was complete. His eyes never left mine as he moved over me again and we came together. But now I was taking back some of the power.

Just hearing his voice and feeling him so near was intoxicating, addicting. We couldn't get enough of each other. And we had a lot of lost months to make up for.

"Come here," he ordered, filling his hands and mouth with my breasts. His tongue was doing wonderful things to my body. Then he moved his hands slowly up and down, from breasts to stomach, then lower, until he was driving his fingers into me and driving me crazy. I was totally ready for him.

"I want you inside of me," I said.

"And I want to be inside of you, Jewels, but not

until you're ready for me."

"I'm ready," I protested, feeling his arousal.

"No, baby, I'll know when you're ready," he whispered, stroking me and kissing me all over until I was throbbing and slick and ready to combust.

"Manny, please," I pleaded, wondering why he was torturing me. "Now."

He moved my legs apart as I shuddered and yelled out for him. He flashed his smile as he lifted himself on top of me and thrust himself forcefully inside of me, moaning my name.

I reached up for him and put my arms around him, and our bodies came together in a primal rhythm. I screamed out, "Oh, God, Manny, oh, God."

He continued his thrusting momentum until he came in a rush. If anything, this time was better than ever. For a few minutes neither of us said a word.

"Do you think I've changed much?" I wondered as I snuggled to get closer to him, settling into the familiar crook of his arm.

"We both have," he answered, fondling me absently.

"I mean, am I still, you know, attractive to you?" I asked tentatively.

"When we were first together, you were just a girl, Jewels. Now, you're a woman about to have a baby."

"And you're a man," I said and bit my lip shyly. We looked at each other admiringly.

"You still turn me on, if that's what you want to know."

"Practically everything does." I giggled.

"Everything about *you* does," he corrected. Manny was caressing me again. Every part of my body was awake now.

"Does this answer your question? Hell, yes, you're still attractive to me." And he proved it again. With his strong hands anchored on either side of me, he supported his weight and shifted his body quietly above mine, so as not to put any pressure on my stomach, moving ever so lightly without penetrating at first and then moving inside me in a steady vertical rhythm. Making love with Manny seemed so natural and right, and we fit perfectly together.

Spent, Manny relaxed and dozed off. Later that afternoon, I leaned over in the bed and watched him as he slept, a spoiled little boy, looking like he needed to be spanked.

I knew I shouldn't entangle myself in this relationship, but something was always pulling me back to Manny. I had no business being with him, because he refused to sever his connection to Nita. But whenever I tried to move away from him, my feet seemed cast in concrete.

I knew what he wanted and why he liked having me around. I was pliable and receptive. There was no real friction between us—just verbal foreplay and feeble protestations before I inevitably gave in to him. Harmless sparring he found enjoyable in a tableau that was always about him. At the same time, I didn't want to be without him.

His lips were so dangerously close that I could feel his hot breath on my face. I wrinkled my nose but couldn't smell him, though I tried hard to breathe in the taste of him so I could remember him like this when he was gone. Suddenly, he grabbed me by the wrist and pulled me down for a long kiss.

"Was this what you wanted, *amada*?"

"You're cruel," I said, trying to twist out of his grasp. But he was too strong. I doubted I would ever have the strength to leave him or stop loving him.

"Now let's do it *en español*," Manny whispered.

"You're a nut." I laughed. "How do you *do it* in Spanish?"

"Come here and I'll show you, my little *señorita*," he replied.

He pulled me down on top of him and smoothed his hand over my back and then lower around the rest of my body until I no longer tried to wriggle away.

"It didn't feel any different in Spanish," I smiled after we were done. "I guess it loses something in the translation."

"You look exhausted," he said.

"You wore me out, I think."

For a while neither of us said anything. I lay there listening to the slow ticking of the clock and the whirring of the fan overhead.

"Why don't you just get some sleep now, Jewels? I'll let you know when it's time to leave." Thoroughly satisfied, I snuggled up against Manny's body in the cozy king bed and folded my hand around the emerald medallion.

Chapter Seventeen:
The Curse of the White Witch

Jewels@aol.com: I've been feeling kind of lost lately and I need to talk to you.

TheBigMan@gellargroup.com: Can't talk now. I'm in the middle of something.

Jewels@aol.com: What?

TheBigMan@gellargroup.com: Nita and I are getting ready to play Taboo.

Jewels@aol.com: Oh, is that what they're calling it these days?

TheBigMan@gellargroup.com: I've got my clients to satisfy, and my wife to satisfy, and her father to satisfy, and now you to satisfy. I can't make you all come at once.

Jewels@aol.com: No one's asking you to.

****

A few weeks later, as I was walking in the door of Goldsmith's, Mercedes handed me the phone.

"It's your *realtor—again*," she said sarcastically.

I rolled my eyes at her.

"Hi," I said.

"We have to talk," Manny said insistently.

"We talked last night."

"I'm coming to the store."

"No, my mother will be here today. I'm not up for an inquisition. I thought we were meeting for lunch at the new shop space. We can talk then." Somehow I'd have to manage to get away.

Manny and I managed to "get away" at least three times a week. I wondered how he ever found time to work or spend time with Nita.

He'd located a lovely space for Stones in Coral Gables. He accompanied me to meetings with the interior designer and was totally involved in helping me implement the new concept for the store. He even made suggestions about what I could serve at the gala opening.

When Manny walked into the shop later that morning, I was just about to take a lunch break. I was anxious to get off my feet. The morning had been especially difficult. My pregnancy was exhausting me, and I couldn't wait to go home and curl up in bed with a good romance. There was always a happy ending in a romance.

"Hi, Jewels," Manny said. "You look beat. Why don't I take you to lunch, and then we can go back to my place. Are you up for that?"

"I'm not going anywhere near your place," I said stubbornly.

"Well, then, how about 'our place'?" he suggested.

"I'm not going to a hotel with you, either. I haven't been off my feet all morning, and I'm only going to take a short lunch so I can leave early."

"We can remedy that," he said, looking at me wickedly. "How about a foot massage?"

Actually, that sounded heavenly. "I'm drained. Mrs. Gottlieb was in, and I spent three hours with her. She's a great customer, but she wears me out. Why did you stop by?"

"You agreed to meet me for lunch, remember?" Manny said, eying me suspiciously. I was becoming more and more forgetful. "I wanted to see you again, and, well, I'm actually here on another errand."

His eyes met mine.

"Julie, if you could pick one ring from my mother's collection, which would it be? You always had great taste, and this is very important."

What a strange question, I thought, but I answered, "Well, that's easy. The emerald ring." The ring was magnificent, a five-carat Colombian emerald in an antique setting, flanked by two one-carat diamond trillions.

"Show me," he said.

I pulled the ring from the vault and placed it gingerly on a white velvet cloth before him.

"Is that your favorite?" he asked.

"I love it," I admitted. "It matches my medallion." He slipped it on my finger.

"It's beautiful," he agreed. "Perfect fit, too. Hey, wrap it up for me, would you? There's someone special I have in mind to give it to."

"Oh," I said, suddenly deflated. I didn't even have to ask him who that someone special was. The White Witch.

"Wedding wrap?" I asked, as my voice broke and my heart crushed at Manny's latest little cruelty.

"Perfect," he said, smiling. "I really think the girl I have in mind for this will love it."

What did he even know about love? My eyes blinked with tears, and I had to turn away.

"Okay, now let's go grab something to eat."

"I-I'm not very hungry," I said. "Let's skip lunch."

Several hours after he left, Nita Weinstein swept into the store. I bit my bottom lip as we circled each other warily. I wanted to tell her where she could park her broomstick. I had to admit she looked sleek in her signature white sweater set and flawless white pearls. She was perfectly put together, as usual, her long mane of white-blonde hair coiffed smoothly behind her head. She wasn't tired and exhausted and she wasn't porked out with pregnancy. But the total effect was ruined the moment she opened her mouth.

"Julie Goldsmith," she cackled.

"That's my name," I said blandly. "Can I help you?"

"Yes, I believe you can. My father's in town, and when he stopped by to give his regards to Manny, he noticed a Goldsmith's bag on his desk. He peeked inside and saw a small package that looked like a ring box. I want to know exactly what Manny purchased when he was in here."

"He didn't *purchase* anything," I answered carefully. "He chose a piece from his family's collection. Beyond that, I'm not at liberty to discuss my clients' transactions with you. I'm sure he'll tell you if he wants you to know."

"It wouldn't happen to be an engagement ring, would it?" Nita purred.

My cheeks reddened and I felt faint. Yes, the emerald could certainly be considered an engagement ring, but I wasn't going to give her the satisfaction of admitting it.

"I thought so. You know, your emotions are written all over your face, Julie. You're so obvious. You're just jealous because Manny is planning to give me an engagement ring, a ring you helped him pick out. Don't you think that's ironic?"

"I wouldn't know," I said, trying to maintain at least a semblance of composure.

Nita pulled out a large square envelope from her purse.

"I want to personally invite you to Manny's birthday party. I'm throwing it at the home of one of my father's friends, who lives on the Bay. It's going to be quite lavish. Let's just call it a pre-engagement party."

"I'm sure I already have plans."

"I haven't even told you when the party is. It's Friday night."

"I have plans to be sick that night," I said.

"This is one party I don't think you'll want to miss. Manny's whole family will be there. And I've invited Matt, as well."

"I'm not dating Matt anymore," I said. "I'm sure Manny told you that."

"Matt told me, in fact. And I told him not to give up hope, that you'd be available soon. And you're going to want someone there to cushion the blow when Manny and I make our big announcement. I thought that was rather considerate of me, to invite Matt for you. Now please say you'll come. And bring your little friend Mackie, too."

"Why would you even want me there? You and I have never been friends."

"Not since you tried to snake Manny away from me at Opal Weekend."

"I didn't snake him away. He asked me because you already had a date."

"He asked you because he wanted to get laid."

"How dare you," I fumed, reaching the boiling point, my eyes glistening. It wasn't true. I knew it wasn't. "I think you'd better leave now."

"The truth hurts, doesn't it? Well, I'll be expecting y'all at my party."

Before I could answer her, the White Witch swished out of the store and left me staring stupidly after her.

"Mercedes, I'll be in my office," I said, almost running into my safe haven and shutting the door behind me.

That explained why Manny was taking the ring out of storage. He was planning to give it to Nita at his birthday party. And I would have to watch him propose. I had given myself to him again, let him back into my heart, and this was my reward. I brushed away the tears that were spilling onto my desk.

But there was more than myself to consider now. I wasn't going to hand him over without a fight. I picked up the phone and dialed Manny's number. I honestly didn't know what I was going to say when I confronted him for the final time.

****

"I got home early," he said when I arrived at his apartment. "When you called you said it was important. Did something happen?" He looked worried.

"You could say that," I said, pulling him by the hand into the apartment, aware that I might be touching him for the last time. "I finally came to my senses."

I could barely speak. I was suffocating. Something unpleasant welled up in the pit of my stomach.

"Have you told Nita about us yet?" I demanded.

"I'm planning to tell Nita, and when I do she'll probably kill me. Then her father will ruin me. I really need that job, Julie, especially now."

"It's just a job. And you're good at what you do. I think they need you more than you need them."

"Julie, sometimes you can be so naïve," Manny said. "Beau Weinstein owns me. That's just the way the world works. He made me and he can break me. And to tell you the truth, I don't think he trusts me."

Manny tried to wind his arm around me. I inched away.

"Jewels, come on. This just hit me out of the blue."

"We've been sleeping together for months. That's hardly out of the blue. What I want to know is did you ever care about me? Really care? Or was this all a game to you?"

"I love what we have. It's the only good thing in my life now. And I intend to tell Nita, sooner than you think."

He reached for me again.

"Don't," I protested, pushing him away, tears threatening to spill over.

"Look, Jewels, as far as I'm concerned, nothing's changed."

"Are you crazy? Everything's changed. I'm telling you now that I can't go on this way anymore. It's not good for me or the baby."

"Jesus, Julie, please don't cry. We'll sort this out, I promise."

"I don't believe your promises," I said.

He reached over, kissing me softly on the lips as he brushed away my tears.

"I'm here for you. I don't want to lose you again."

"Manny, you're living in a dream world. We can't see each other again."

I tried to gauge what he was thinking, but I couldn't read him. Suddenly he grabbed me tightly to him and held on like he never wanted to let me go.

I was crying uncontrollably now, and I couldn't seem to get off this emotional roller coaster. My hormones were having a heyday knocking around in my brain. I knew leaving him was the right thing to do. It would all work out, I thought. I reached into my purse to grab a Kleenex, but I could hardly see, my eyes were so blurred with tears, and I was shaking.

"Don't worry," he soothed. "We're going to have the baby. I know that's what you want. Just don't cry."

"I'm having the baby regardless."

"What I meant was we can have it together."

"It isn't just about what I want. You should want it too. I'd never pressure you into anything. But you have to make a decision. Whether you want me and my baby. And you can't have us unless..."

Manny would have to decide if he was ready to give up his fancy job, his fabulous salary and everything that represented, specifically the White Witch. Reality began creeping in.

"The timing isn't the greatest," Manny lamented.

"It never was, for us."

But we were just making excuses, prolonging the inevitable.

"You *are* crazy. Go back to Nita. I'm going to walk out of here, and I don't want to see you again. Unless you're ready to make a commitment."

There, I'd put it on the table. I knew I shouldn't have given him an ultimatum. But I was fed up with the way things were going, or not going.

The words just hung there. I saw him struggling, but he couldn't bring himself to say or do the right thing. Sadly, I knew he wouldn't be there for me or the baby. Especially for a baby he didn't even think was his.

"You say you care about me," I said evenly, when I just wanted to scream. "I know that's a lie." I grabbed my purse, fished out my car keys, and closed the door in his face. If I didn't get out of there fast I knew I was going to be sick.

"I've got to go, and don't try to follow me." The steel in my tone and the rigidity in my body left no room for argument. The door opened.

When I looked back for the last time, Manny's head was sagging against the doorframe. He could sulk until the cows came home. I was not going back in there. I was through with the bastard forever.

When the telephone rang later that night, I knew who it was, but there was nothing left to say.

"Julie, have I lost you?" Manny asked when I finally ended the silence.

"I'm still here," I replied quietly.

"I just wanted to hear your voice again. You ran away so fast. I've been calling and calling you. We didn't get to finish talking."

"We're finished," I countered.

"Don't shut me out, Jewels. I have to see you."

"See me? Or sleep with me?" I corrected.

"Jewels, I'm serious," he said. "You can't mean you never want to see me again. I'm coming over so we can discuss this rationally."

"Don't," I said firmly, knowing that if he did come

over he would just make a mess of my resolve. I was a bundle of nerves, so stressed out I couldn't think straight. I wanted him to make things right, but dammit, I knew with certainty that he wouldn't.

"You're still coming to my party, aren't you?" Manny asked. "Promise me you'll come."

I didn't think he could be so cruel.

"I don't make promises I can't keep," I said.

"Things will work out for us," Manny said. "You'll see."

Chapter Eighteen:
Life Is Not a Pleasure Trip

The day of Manny's birthday party, I struggled out of bed with a colossal headache, courtesy of the river of tears I had cried the night before. But I wasn't going to let that witch intimidate me. Going to the party would be difficult, but I would have to face Manny and Nita again at some point. I could try my best to avoid them. But it was inevitable that I'd run into them at restaurants and in social situations, and I'd have to manage more than a polite hello. Even with millions of people, Miami was still a small town. Now I was about to see the White Witch in action making her dreams come true.

Halfway into the party, my resolve deserted me and I realized that going had been a big mistake. When I decided I'd had enough, I tugged on Mackie's sleeve, indicating I was ready to leave. Seeing Manny and Nita together was pure torture. It was uncomfortable enough seeing Matt again.

"He's over there in the corner mooning over you, Julie," Mackie noted, her eyes drifting over to where Matt was standing. "He asks about you all the time. He's still in love with you. He's pretty great, Julie, if you'd give him half a chance."

"He's wonderful," I agreed, "but he's not Manny."

"Please put him out of his misery and marry the

poor guy. You need a father for your baby, and he very definitely needs you. Can't you cut the guy a break? He still has the ring, you know. He showed it to me. He carries it around with him everywhere, hoping you'll change your mind."

"I'm sorry about that. We already talked tonight. Matt is sweet, but I don't love him. And I'm not going to use him just because it would be convenient to have a father for my baby. I'm leaving. Are you coming or not?"

Manny blocked my way.

"You can't leave yet," Manny pleaded. The White Witch flew to his side, apparently equipped with some kind of internal witch radar.

"I have other plans I can't cancel," I lied, pulling away, still feeling the heat of him on my body. I struggled to see past Manny's penetrating brown eyes.

"But you'll miss the best part," he said, suddenly earnest.

I gave him a venomous look. If he was intentionally trying to hurt me, he was succeeding. I felt nauseated and turned to leave.

"You'll do fine without me."

Manny tried to follow me to Mackie's car, but I slammed the door right in his two-timing face.

When Mackie dropped me off at my house after the party, I walked around to the back yard. I wasn't quite ready to face my parents. I'd seen them leave the party right after I did, and they were no doubt huddled in the house right now in a family conference, the subject of which was the plight of *poor Julie, the unwed mother-to-be.* I was actually surprised to see them at the party at all, but Elena must have convinced my mother to come for moral support.

I placed the silver chain of my evening bag around my shoulder, sat down on the rusty old swing set next to the pool, and began swinging and crying, confident that no one would see or hear me out here.

Just around the corner of the house was the place Manny and I had buried our treasure in elementary school. Manny had come to my house with some of his prized possessions in a cigar box. Inside was his father's old Navy ring with a missing stone, an Indian Head nickel, some baseball cards, and a five-dollar bill. I had contributed a photo my parents had snapped of the two of us out on our backyard swing, ten crisp one-dollar bills I had taken from my "Coral G Rangers" savings account from the small bank on Tamiami Trail—a small fortune—and a ring fashioned of nickel by my father's favorite brother.

We had each grabbed a rusty spade from my laundry room and dug a deep hole, marking the spot and sealing our hidden treasures in the battered old box beneath the dirt. We made a pact to return to that same spot on the side of my yard, under my parent's window, next to my mother's prize hydrangea bush, five years later.

We latched our pinkies together, and Manny leaned over and sealed the pact with a solemn kiss. I remembered how warm his lips felt on mine, and when we pulled away we just stared at each other in unspoken wonder.

On the exact day of the five-year anniversary, we walked home from the school bus hand in hand like two co-conspirators. In fact, we had each forgotten exactly what was inside the box, but the "buried treasure" as we referred to it, had taken on vast proportions in our minds. Manny was sure he had placed a 1913 Indian Head nickel in the box that must be very valuable. When we arrived at the spot, we excitedly dug up the earth, trying in vain to locate the cigar box. The only thing we dug up was my mother's hydrangea bush.

Disappointed, we just sat there in the grass in silence, hands clasped around our knees, absorbed in our loss. The sprinkler cycled on and, every few seconds, doused us until we were drenched. I was wishing Manny would kiss me again. But he didn't.

It was all over by now, I thought, jerking myself back to the present. The happy couple was probably toasting their engagement, sneaking a private kiss out on the boat dock under the moonlight, and planning their perfect new life together. The White Witch had won. I looked up to search for my favorite constellation.

"Did you know that Orion has two of the brightest stars in the sky?" boomed a voice behind me.

I almost jumped off the swing. "Manny, what are you doing here?" I could pick out his sensual features by the light of the moon, and I tried my best not to focus on them.

"I could ask you the same thing. You should be inside." He took off his sweater and wrapped it around my shoulders. "The cold isn't good for the baby."

I looked up at him, and even in the low light he could see I had been crying. He wiped off my tears with his thumb as they continued to splash onto my face.

"No tears, Jewels. I came to find you."

"Shouldn't you be with your fiancée?" I asked stubbornly.

"I hope I *am* with her," he said.

I was confused. "Did you bring that wicked bitch to my house?" I looked around for Nita, certain she was lurking somewhere in the shadows.

"No," he said patiently as if talking to a small child.

"Then what do you mean?" I sighed. "Tell me why you're here. To pull out my heart and stomp on it? Just go ahead then, because I'm ready for this whole thing to be over. I can't do it anymore."

"Do what?" he asked.

"You know...I'm not cut out for this."

"For what?"

He didn't seem to understand.

"Like I told you last night. I'm giving up." I started swinging again.

"You can't give up on us. Not now. I'm not here to hurt you, Julie. I came to ask you something. And I want you to take me very seriously."

I didn't even put up a fight as he stretched his arms to stop the movement of the swing. Then he enfolded me in them, pressing my back against his chest and whispered against my ear.

"Remember our buried treasure?" Manny began. "We lost my father's ring out here in the side yard. We never did find it. But I've dug up something else that I think you'll like."

I was still confused.

"Here, open it, Julie," he prodded, coming around to face me.

He handed me a small box wrapped in Goldsmith's paper. Was this a consolation prize, for coming in second in the Manny Marathon? Something he and my mother had cooked up to pacify me? I wasn't sure I could handle this.

Tearing away the wrapping paper, I just stared at the ring box. I lifted the lid cautiously. When I looked inside, I caught a glimpse of the ancient emerald, bathed in the moonlight, so pale and pure and square and fine. The fire and flash of diamonds brightened the darkness.

"T-this is the emerald ring that you p-picked out at the store?"

"No, that is the emerald ring you selected. I asked you to pick out your favorite."

"But I thought you were going to give it to Nita, as an engagement present tonight. I know she'd never have turned you down."

"Where did you get a crazy idea like that?"

"Right from the witch's mouth."

"Oh, God, Julie, I'm so sorry. I was trying to keep it a secret, trying to surprise you. That's why I couldn't tell you last night. I felt terrible about the way we left things, but I was hoping my surprise would make up for it. I had planned to give you the ring tonight and ask you to marry me at my birthday party in front of my family and yours. But then you left, so I had to come after you."

Was I hearing him correctly? "This ring is for me?"

"Yes, silly. Who else would it be for?"

"Well, I thought that..."

He took my face in his hands and kissed me then, a long slow, intimate kiss, and I flung my arms around his neck and kissed him back.

"I think we're doing this backwards, Jewels. I'm supposed to ask you first, remember, before we kiss."

"Okay," I said, beaming. "Let's do it right. I've been waiting for this for a long time."

Manny took the ring box, bent down on one knee before me on the swing, and took my left hand. My heart was beating rapidly, and I fought to control it. Were my dreams finally about to come true?

"Julie Goldsmith," Manny began, looking deep into my eyes. "My mother thinks it would be a good idea if we got married."

"Y-your mother?" I said, gasping as I jumped off the swing, shoving and knocking him off balance.

"Yes, you know how much she loves you. She's wanted me to marry you for years. She gave you the medallion at your Sweet Sixteen, and I think even back then she had her heart set on us."

"You knew about that?" My eyes widened.

"That my mother had an agenda where we were concerned? Living in that house, a person would have to be deaf, dumb, and blind not to have seen it. My mother has been trying to marry us off since second grade. Everyone was pushing you on me. My parents, your parents. Even you. You know I don't like to be pushed or crowded."

"I didn't mean to push you. That wasn't my intention. It was never a game to me. I cared for you, plain and simple. I didn't know any other way to behave. Well, now that I know how your *mother* feels, how do you feel?" I continued, trying to catch my breath and stem my anger.

"I'm here for you," Manny said helplessly. "Whatever you want to do. You know that. You need me. You can't have this baby by yourself."

"Are you planning to have it for me? That would

be a miracle of modern science. Let's get one thing clear. I'm going to have this baby, with or without you."

"What I mean to say is the baby will need a name."

"The baby will have a name," I shouted. "Mine!"

"But I thought you wanted to marry me?" Manny looked confused. "Don't you?"

"Give me one good reason why I should marry you." *Please*.

"With the baby coming, I thought you would want…"

That was not the reason I was looking for. I was sure if I told him the truth about the baby's paternity, he would marry me. But holding on to him that way wouldn't make either of us happy. He had to want to marry me for the right reasons.

"Maybe I'm not saying this right," Manny explained. "Julie, what I'm trying to say is, I have a good job now. I'm making a lot of lucrative deals. I can take care of you and the baby."

"Take care of me? What are you talking about? You have your job because you're dating Nita Weinstein, who hates me as much as I hate her. I don't need that kind of support. You know that having me in your life is an impossible complication for your career."

"Why don't you let me worry about that?" he said, urging me to take some time to think over his proposal and repeating his earlier admonition. "I'm serious."

"I can't take anything you say seriously. Why are you doing this to me?" He hadn't used the word love in connection with his marriage proposal. I knew I was really afraid that if I actually accepted his proposal, he'd suddenly laugh and withdraw it.

And if he thought I was a damsel in distress who needed rescuing, well, then, he had another think coming.

I placed my hands against his chest and pushed him.

"You can tell your *mother* that although I love her dearly, and as flattered as I am by *her* very touching and romantic proposal, and as much as I appreciate the lovely sentiment, I'm going to have to turn *her* down!"

"You're turning me down?"

"I never heard *you* ask me!" I shrieked.

"I may have said the words wrong, but you have to understand that…"

"Understand this, Manny Gellar. I wouldn't marry you if you were the last man on the face of the earth. Is that clear enough for you?" I stomped into the house leaving Manny with a flustered expression on his face, holding the ring box in his hand.

"But Julie…"

He followed me and pounded on the front door.

"Julie, come back out here. We're not through."

I was startled by a shriek coming from inside the house that sounded like a wild animal noise or the cry of a banshee. I realized it had come from me.

"Mr. Goldsmith, sir, I have to talk to you right away," said Manny, as my father ushered him into the living room.

"Well, come in then, son."

"If you let that vile person into my house, I'm leaving," I warned from the kitchen.

"Julie, just what did the boy do to upset you?"

"I asked her to marry me, sir," Manny said. "And she said no. I have a ring, too."

"The boy has a ring, Julie."

"I know that," I shouted, stomping my feet.

"Then why won't you marry him?"

"He very specifically *did not* ask me to marry him," I raged, banging the pots and pans around in the kitchen cabinet for maximum impact. "What he said was his *mother* wants him to marry me."

"Oh, well, that explains it. Why do you want to marry my daughter, son?"

"To protect her. She has the baby coming, and I don't think she should be alone."

"That's very commendable. But are you sure you know what you're getting yourself into? My daughter has a vicious temper, as you can very plainly hear. You're as close as a son to me, and I felt it only fair to warn you."

"Daddy!" I screamed and started to come at the two of them with a carving knife.

"Get back into the kitchen, Julie, before you hurt someone with that thing," my father said, shaking his head.

"Yes, she does have a temper, but I've also seen a softer side," Manny said. "She can be sweet."

"At times," my father countered.

"And she's very compassionate."

"And?"

"And passionate."

"Hmm," my father said, narrowing his eyes at Manny.

"And, she laughs at my jokes," Manny managed, maneuvering to safer territory.

"That's always helpful," Sid conceded. "But she can also be very obstinate. She always wants to get her way. And she's very moody."

"Whose side are you on, Daddy?" I screeched.

"True, but she has the ability to compromise," Manny pointed out.

"Well, if you think you can handle her, son, then she's all yours. Take her with my blessing."

"Daddy, you can't give me away like a piece of property. I don't want to marry him!"

"Well, son, I can't force her to marry you. You'll have to do better than that."

Suddenly there was another knock on the door. My father opened the door to Matt.

"I'm the father of her child," Manny announced as soon as Matt entered the room. Matt compressed his lips.

Sid turned on Manny, eyes blazing in full WWII mode, sporting a take-no-prisoners attitude.

"You're the sneaky son-of-a-bitch who did this to my daughter?" I guess the revelation put to bed any illusions my father had been operating under about the anonymous Italian bastard on the next continent and allowed him to redirect his anger closer to home.

"He's lying to you, Daddy!" I called out from the kitchen. "I never told him he was the father."

"But is there a possibility that he could be your baby's father?" Sid demanded.

There was only silence from the kitchen.

"He's not the father, Mr. Goldsmith, I am," Matt stated quietly.

"You too?" I could almost smell smoke coming out of my father's ears, which was pretty remarkable, since I don't have a sense of smell. "Tell me, is there anyone in this city who *hasn't* slept with my daughter? Julie

Goldsmith. Get out here, right now, where I can see your face. I want the truth. Which one of these two dead men did you sleep with? Or was it both of them?"

I had only slept with one man in my life. Those two losers were making me sound like the slut of the century, in front of my own father. I walked out with my hands clasped in front of me, agitated, and stuck out my bottom lip. I walked over to Matt.

"What are you doing?" I asked incredulously.

"Fighting for you and the baby," he said simply.

"You know this baby can't be yours," I whispered. "Why are you accepting responsibility?"

"I don't care whose baby this is," Matt whispered back miserably, caressing my cheek. "I love you, Julie. I want to marry you. I've made up my mind. I don't want to live without you. I can't."

"You slept with Matt?" Manny accused, shifting my attention and staring straight into my eyes with a look of anger and pain I'd never seen there before. "I thought that—" He took a deep shuddering breath, and it looked like he was going to be sick. He put the ring box back into his pocket. I'd never seen such a look of devastation on his face.

"Manny, please—" I sputtered, tears slowly rolling down my cheeks.

"Matt, tell him," I implored.

Things were getting out of hand.

"How could you do this to us, Julie?" Manny said, turning away to get control of his own emotions.

"Young lady, I'm tired of your theatrics," my father barked. "You're about to have a baby, and you're acting like one. It's about time you thought about someone other than yourself."

"Daddy! You don't mean that."

"The hell I don't," my father barked. "Life is not a pleasure trip! You *are* going to marry one of these boys if I have to shoot them both. Do you want to choose or shall I?"

"Daddy, that's archaic. That's not the way things are done."

"It's the way things are done in *my* house," my father insisted.

Tech Sergeant Sidney Goldsmith, who had enlisted in the Army Air Corps in 1941 and was a top turret gunner with the 533rd Squadron of the 381st Bomb Group, had killed from the anonymity of a top turret. He'd watched Forts blow apart, hurtling toward earth in a dozen flaming pieces, and ships go down in a flat spin and burst into a sheet of flame when they hit the ground. He'd fought nausea and broken out in a cold sweat when he saw his first flak, as thick as the soup he flew in over 30,000 feet up, vomiting in his mask and all over the floor-plate of the turret during the really rough missions. But I knew with certainty that he could kill here on the ground if anyone ever threatened his family.

Ever-vigilant, my father was prepared for any emergency. Deprived of vengeance on the unnamed hormonal Italian who had left his pregnant daughter high and dry, he was seriously itching for a stateside showdown. My father had trained for just such an occasion. His entire life had been a prelude to this moment. A survivor of the Great Depression, Sidney Goldsmith had remained on high alert throughout the Nazi threat and the Communist threat, armed and ready to defend his family against all enemies, foreign and domestic, real or imagined; prepared to protect us from the hordes, and all other lurking foes.

Rigid and cautious, my father threw a damper on anything spontaneous. His favorite part of the Passover Seder was reciting the ten plagues. My father saw to it that no risks were taken and that my life was regimented and safe. Joel and I were raised to follow orders and fall in line as if we were raw military recruits.

In this corner, we have our reigning heavyweight champion, "Big Sid Goldsmith," a.k.a. *The Blue Demon*. And in this corner are the contenders—Manny Gellar and Matthew Paver.

Manny was down for the count before my father had even delivered the knockout punch. "One, two, three, four…" *"Get up, you worthless weasel, and be a man,"* I pleaded silently. "Five, six, seven, eight..." *"Stand up for me, and our child, you slippery bastard, and do the right thing,"* I prayed to the heavens. "Nine, ten." *"Why aren't you even trying to fight for us?"* He didn't even last one round.

While Manny tried to slink away, Matt stepped up to the plate. "I guess this will have to be a shotgun wedding, then, sir," said the man who was there to clean up my mess.

"A shotgun wedding is when the groom is forced into a marriage, not when the bride is the unwilling partner," I explained to the clueless Matt, clenching my teeth. I had experienced my father's temper before, and I wasn't about to test him. He was seriously pissed. And Matt had no idea that my father was *not* joking.

"You want to see my gun? Sylvia, go get my magnum from the dresser drawer."

"Right away, dear," said my mother, who had been hiding in the hall, away from the fray and out of the line of fire.

"You think I don't know what goes on right under my own roof in my own house?" he shouted, looking directly at Manny. Then he seared me with his eyes. "I am your father. I am on top of everything."

"Except me," my mother laughed, trying to ease the tension in the room.

"I told you to get my gun, Sylvia!"

Sid turned back to face Manny and me.

"You kids have been tripping over each other since you were in grade school. You're crazy about each other, always have been, but you're both too damn foolish and stubborn to see it. You two were meant to be together," Sid raged. "Now, Manny, do you love my daughter?"

"I thought I did," he answered.

"Is that what you're looking for, Julie?" my father demanded, exasperated.

"Words!" I screamed. "I don't believe a word that comes out of that man's mouth. You think it's going to make me happy to listen to his lies?"

"Here's your magnum, dear," my mother said, coming in from the hall and gingerly handing my father the weapon and a fresh box of bullets.

"Then go ahead and shoot him full of holes, Daddy. I don't care whether he is or is not the father of my child, and I'm not saying that he is. I am not marrying Manny Gellar, and that's final. And you can't force me to."

Chapter Nineteen:
Take a Deep Breath and Say "I Do"

"Blessed are you who come in the name of God; may you be blessed this day and every day of your lives together," said the rabbi, as he began the hastily arranged wedding service at my temple. "May the One supreme in majesty, beyond all praise and infinitely great, bless this man and this woman who now enter into marriage.

"Do you, Julie Hannah Goldsmith, now affirm your marriage with Matthew Daniel Paver, and do you promise to love and honor him, to sustain and help him, and to keep faith with him always?"

I looked at my father, my eyes blazing, and he turned his head up, as if he were communing with God. I had almost fainted before the march down the aisle. My hands had shaken while I signed the Ketubah in front of two witnesses before the ceremony. My father had held my face to the water fountain and forced me to take a drink and compose myself. He and Matt had closed ranks. They were in lockstep where my future was concerned. My father had already secured the perimeter and there was no way out for me now. He had even given Matt a gun as a wedding present and taught him how to use it. That was his less than subtle way of handing over to my new husband the job of protecting me.

His final words to Matt when he handed me over after the walk down the aisle were, "Never give up your weapon, son."

If you're thinking that a shotgun wedding could never happen in this day and age, then you don't know my father. I'm living proof that it can and did happen on that day and at my age.

Right before the wedding, Matt checked in on me to see how I was holding up.

"Matt, we can't get married," I wailed miserably. "My wedding dress is too tight."

"That excuse is not going to work." He sighed and looked at me in my dress with longing, like he couldn't wait to get me out of it.

"First, know that I'd marry you even if you were wearing a burlap sack," Matt said calmly.

"I don't know who you think you're seeing when you look at me," I murmured, tears threatening to spill over. "I'm nowhere near the person you think I am."

"I know exactly who you are, Julie," Matt said tenderly, as if he didn't have a doubt in the world we were doing the right thing.

"I don't deserve you," I said, my voice breaking.

"You deserve to be happy," he said simply.

A few minutes later, when we were standing in front of the rabbi, I smiled weakly and clutched Estrella's medallion. It seemed to be weighing me down.

"Julie," Matt whispered, touching me delicately so I wouldn't startle. "Take a deep breath and say 'I do.' "

"I d-do." My assent was barely audible.

"Do you, Matthew Daniel Paver, now affirm your marriage with Julie Hannah Goldsmith, and do you promise to love and honor her, to sustain and help her, and to keep faith with her always?"

"I do," Matt answered strongly, as if to compensate for my uncertainty.

"Ha-rei at m'ku-deh-shet li b'ta-ba-at zo k'dat mo-sheh v'yis-ra-el," recited Matt, slipping the ring on my finger. "By this ring you are consecrated to me according to the tradition of Israel."

"Ha-rei a-ta m'ku-dash li b'ta-ba-at zo k'dat mo-sheh v'yis-ra-el," I mumbled, almost dropping the ring I held in my shaking hand before I managed to place it on Matt's finger. "By this ring you are consecrated to me according to the tradition of Israel."

I must have looked pale enough that Matt was afraid fainting was a definite possibility. So he grabbed my hand and squeezed it, bracing his other arm around my waist to hold me up and guarantee that I wouldn't bolt.

"We praise You, Eternal God, Sovereign of the universe: You sanctify Your people Israel under the sacred marriage canopy," said the rabbi, as he stood before us and continued to chant the benedictions.

"May God bless you and keep you. May God look kindly upon you, and be gracious unto you. May God reach out to You in tenderness, and give you peace."

Matt broke the traditional glass to conclude the service. Delighted that I'd remained conscious for the entire ceremony, he tried to sweep me up into a long and passionate kiss. But he couldn't manage to coax, persuade or even pry my lips apart. They were firmly shut, worse than a bad case of lockjaw.

"We did it," he said with a sheepish smile on his face. I stared back at him in shock. I wouldn't move at first, so he practically carried me back down the aisle.

"There," Matt said, still holding me up. "That wasn't so bad, was it?"

And then I fainted into his arms.

When I came to, I whispered, "I just dreamt that we got married."

"It wasn't a dream," Matt said softly.

"Did I faint?"

"Yes. You must have been overcome…with happiness."

"I need to sit down," I said woodenly, pleading, "Will you please get me some water?"

Matt helped me into a metal folding chair and walked over to the water pitcher to fill an empty paper cup. He wasn't worried about me bolting now; he could see that my legs couldn't even support my weight, which by this time in my pregnancy was considerable.

"Can you at least pretend you're happy?" Matt frowned. "We have to go back out there in a minute and thank everyone for coming on such short notice."

I was slowly regaining my color. The liquid felt cool going down.

"First, we're going to have to establish some ground rules," I insisted, still shaken.

"What kind of ground rules?"

"Sleeping arrangements. You know I was forced into this marriage."

"I love you, Julie. I wanted to marry you. I will love the baby, too. And I'll protect you."

"I didn't need you to ride to my rescue. I'm perfectly capable of providing for my baby and myself. I don't need anything from you."

"I'm your husband now. You and the baby are my

responsibility, part of my life."

"And don't think you can lay a hand on me, ever, unless I give you permission," I warned.

"I made a commitment to you. I'm taking those vows very seriously. This is a real marriage, Julie, in every sense of the word, and I won't tolerate anything less from you. I think I've been very patient."

"We'll just see about that."

Matt traced my lips deliberately with his thumb.

"I know you care for me. I think you could love me. I've wanted you for so long, Julie. Let's go home. I think we've waited long enough to consummate this marriage."

I shivered when Matt put his arm around me.

"We can't just leave our guests," I said. "As you pointed out, there's a hall full of people waiting out there at the reception. Let's worry about consummation later, much later."

We were greeted by a fanfare. There were people everywhere waiting to celebrate our first moment as man and wife. My first instinct as a bride was to run away and hide. I hadn't seen Manny during the ceremony. I noticed him now coming toward us.

"What are you doing here?" I hissed. "You shouldn't have come."

"Yeah, Gellar," Matt snarled. "I didn't invite you."

"Had to congratulate the bride, kiss the bride," he said, grabbing me and placing his lips firmly on mine until he forced them open, trying to weave his invisible sexual spell. Trying to make me respond to him.

He was hanging on to me to keep himself upright.

"You've been drinking." I was horrified at his behavior.

"Only way I could get through this," he said.

"I'm truly sorry," I said. "You should go." Matt pulled me away from his arms.

"I heard you and DoorMatt weren't taking a honeymoon," Manny said.

"Where did you hear that?" Matt demanded.

Manny smirked and I blushed. "So it's true."

Manny's face turned angry when he looked at my new husband and the way his arm wound possessively around my shoulders, the way his thumb stroked my cheek, the way he forced me to lean into him as if I would faint if he weren't standing there to support me.

He walked away toward his sister.

"Look at the way he's touching her," Manny growled to Estrellita, loud enough for me and everyone else in the room to hear. "He can't keep his damn hands off her."

Estrellita tried to sooth him. "She will be devoted to him now. They are married, after all."

Manny looked like he was in pain.

Mackie was already drinking heavily, a habit she had picked up since she and Little Jon broke up. I walked over to where my friend was sitting. I knew why Mackie was so unhappy. It was only a month before her wedding. She and Jon were still fighting about the weekend he'd spent with the curvaceous blonde waitress at his pledge class reunion. After he paraded her around at the cocktail party in front of his fraternity brothers, he was reportedly missing in action for the remainder of the weekend, as they were presumably occupied in Little Jon's hotel room. At least that was the story Nita Weinstein had spread. Little Jon denied it, but Mackie refused to forgive him.

"Little Jon is over there by the bar. He wants me to take him back. He denied the whole thing. What a crock. Julie, what am I going to do? We had so many plans."

"You're going to take him back. You love him and you two are perfect for each other. I can't believe you'd give any credence to anything the White Witch has to say. She's just using her Black Magic to stir the pot. You're going to go through with the wedding. I'm going to be your matron of honor, as planned, and you're going to walk down the aisle and live happily ever after with the man of your dreams."

"Like you did?" Mackie slurred the words.

"Not exactly. This was a forced march down the aisle."

"What's the difference how it happened? It's what you needed."

"Not what I wanted."

"You could have had the man you wanted. You were too stubborn."

"Not at my wedding. Don't do this to me."

I noticed Nita Weinstein out of the corner of my eye. "Dammit, Mackie, what is *she* doing here?"

"Well someone must have invited Manny, and I guess he brought her as his date."

"I didn't have anything to do with this guest list. It was all my mother's and Matt's doing. And Matt knew nothing about it."

Nita wore her white-blond hair down to her shoulders, like she was on her way to a virgin sacrifice where she was the guest of honor. I blinked when I realized what she was wearing.

"Tell me that's not a wedding gown," I whispered,

aghast, to Mackie.

"She always wears white," Mackie pointed out, "and I guess she's celebrating."

"That witch needs a major wardrobe readjustment," I lamented.

"What she *needs* is a best friend and a full-length mirror."

Nita was trying to corner Manny now and round him up in her dominating lasso. She sounded as if she were braying something in her annoying, nasal twang. Every opportunity he got, Manny glanced over in my direction and shrugged his shoulders helplessly as if to indicate he was trapped. But that was none of my concern now. He and Nita could have each other. He was out of my life forever.

When Manny finally managed to get away and walk over to the bar, Nita sashayed over to where Mackie and I were standing.

"Congratulations," Nita barked. "Next y'all will be congratulating me. Now that you're married, maybe you'll keep your hands off my boyfriend. I can make him happy, you know. He'll get over you. I'll make sure of it."

I walked over to the bar to order an orange juice and confront Manny about Nita's nasty remarks. He brushed up against me. "I'll have an amaretto," he said to the bartender, holding my eyes meaningfully. As I reached for my glass I found my hands trembling and my knees about to buckle.

"Did you have to invite her?" I implored. "She said the most hateful things to me."

"I know. Just ignore her," Manny said. "She's a loose cannon. I owe her father a lot. You understand, don't you? I had to invite her."

"To *my* wedding?" I hurried away before he could see my tears.

Manny's parents were seated a safe distance from Nita. There was no love lost between Elena Gellar and Nita Weinstein. The two women would never get along. Elena was from Havana and Nita from Savannah, worlds apart.

Manny was conversing with the DJ. When "Chances Are" started playing, Manny held my eyes from across the room and walked over as if in a trance. Right in front of Matt and Nita, he reached for my hand and pulled me to the dance floor for the sentimental slow song.

We were lost in the dance and in each other. When the song was through, he leaned over to kiss me. It took everything I had not to respond to him, and then we both snapped out of the spell and remembered where we were.

"I guess this is really goodbye, then, Jewels," Manny said with finality and regret.

"You have to let me go," I pleaded.

Visibly shaken, he led me back to my seat and looked deeply into my eyes. That look said everything. It spoke of love. I was beginning to believe that maybe he did love me, had always loved me. But that chapter of my life was over.

Tears were streaming down Elena Gellar's face, bittersweet tears spilled over what might have been.

"It's obvious," Elena whispered to her husband when she thought I couldn't hear. "Look at the way he looks at her, Sam. He's in love with her."

"He always has been," Sam agreed. "He just can't

see it."

The White Witch hadn't missed any of the spectacle. She fairly flew over to the head table, jaw clenched, eyes like daggers as she fixed her gaze on me and addressed Mackie.

"That was quite a performance," she cackled.

"That's not a performance," Mackie assured her. "Anyone can see the way they feel about each other."

Matt came over to me.

"I'm sorry," I said, ashamed of the way I had behaved.

"It's okay, because you're mine now," he said, gathering me protectively into his arms as he dropped a tender kiss on my forehead.

His generous show of forgiveness deserved a special gesture. I felt the baby move and placed Matt's hand on my belly so he could feel the signs of life for the first time.

"God, Julie, he's ours. It's amazing. I can feel him."

"Or her." I laughed lightly. "Do you care if it's a boy or a girl?"

"Not really," he said with certainty. "As long as the baby needs me."

"We'll both need you," I said, looking into his eyes. *And I'll try very hard to love you.*

"If I haven't said it before, thank you for marrying me," Matt said.

"I should be thanking you."

"No, I'm the lucky one," Matt said. "You won't regret it. I promise you that." And I knew that was one promise I could take seriously.

"Let's go home, Julie," Matt prodded. A single tear

slipped down my face. I nodded, subdued, even though home was the last place I wanted to go with Matt, who only had one thing on his mind.

As I said my goodbyes to my parents and the Gellars, I tried hard to close my heart to the man I had *not* married. I wondered what Elena would think if she knew my unborn child was really her grandson. But I was determined not to tell anyone. It was too late. But wasn't it lovely that these two families with their disparate histories and customs would soon be blended together forever in a crazy quilt with the birth of their grandchild. And it felt so right.

Chapter Twenty:
The End of a Dream

Minutes From the Colonoscopy Club—2014:

"What do you fantasize about when you and Matt are screwing?" Mackie wonders.

That's easy. I fantasize that Matt and I are screwing. "The usual," I answer evasively, rattling off the expected list of movie star hunks. "Brad. Russell. Ben. Pierce." *Manny.* "What about you?"

"I fantasize about the nephews. Little Jon's nephews are incredibly hot. The middle one is a real Studley Doright."

"Do you enjoy shocking me? You really fantasize about Little Jon's nephews?"

"Have you seen them? You're just jealous."

"You're probably right," I have to admit. Not only am I not getting any from Matt, but he doesn't even have any hot nephews for me to fantasize about.

"Do you ever fantasize about Little Jon?" Mackie asks, her voice turning serious.

"Gross," is the first thing that comes out of my mouth.

"You think Little Jon is gross?" Mackie probes.

"Of course not, but I can't even imagine what you're suggesting."

"I'm not *suggesting* anything."

****

Matt was driving me crazy trying to get me into bed when all I wanted was to get some sleep.

"I'm tired," I said, padding around in the living room of his apartment in my robe and slippers. All the wedding gifts were piled up in Matt's guest bedroom, which left me no choice but to share the master bedroom with my husband. "You honestly want to fool around?"

"I'd hardly call it fooling around," Matt countered. "We're married now. This is supposed to be our wedding night."

"I didn't ask for this wedding. I didn't want it." My nerves were frayed.

"Well, you're stuck with me. So why don't we try to make the best of it?"

I sulked. I was fresh out of excuses and time. Matt was trying his best to sweet-talk me out of the new nightgown he had purchased especially for this occasion. He pulled back my robe to reveal the black lace clinging to my body.

"For a start, why don't you take your robe off, and let me see what's underneath?" he suggested.

"You'll have to take it off if you want it off," I retorted, pouting.

"So this is the way you're going to play it. I think I've been patient long enough, don't you?"

"I guess," I said, my voice barely rising above a whisper.

"Is that a yes?"

"I guess."

"You're a difficult woman," Matt said.

"Then why did you marry me?" I asked petulantly.

"I hope I don't live to regret it." He laughed, trying

to maintain some levity.

"Such tender words from my loving husband," I said facetiously, trying to trigger his temper. But Matt didn't have a temper, which was even more infuriating because I was itching for a brawl.

"Come on, Julie, please be nice. I really do love you, and I want to be with you. Do I have your permission to touch you?"

I was confused.

"After the wedding. One of your ground rules, remember?"

I must have been in a state of shock. I didn't remember a thing about our wedding. I stared at Matt's hands as he pulled my robe off slowly and reached inside my nightgown to caress me. I trembled. I had not been with him this way before. I had only been with one man. And now, I had no choice but to submit—to my husband, who was looking at me like he had won the lottery. Then he kissed me gently, slowly, a deep drugging kiss that sent my world spinning, and moved his lips a hair's breadth away from mine for an agonizing moment, leaving me hungry for more. I suddenly remembered his kisses.

"Do you want me to stop?" he asked roughly, looking into my eyes to gauge my reaction.

I shook my head slowly. I was in a daze.

"Can we go into the bedroom?" he asked hoarsely.

He had every right. I was his now, and I felt powerless to do anything about it. He was carefully walking me backwards into the bedroom and removing my nightgown, trying to strip me of all my defenses, and more.

He placed me gently on the bed and looked at me

for a long time, his eyes roaming all over my body. I flushed and my breathing slowed.

"Where to start," he began.

He placed his hand over my heart and his fingers splayed out over my breast. My pulse was racing.

"Your heart is beating so fast," he whispered. "You don't have to be afraid of me. I would never hurt you or the baby." I struggled slightly, instinctively. I tried to shift away from him, thinking that this was wrong, that I was betraying my true love, but his hands were too strong.

"Please don't fight me, Julie." I shivered and sighed and was still.

He outlined the shape of my body, rubbing his hands up my sides, briefly moving to caress my breasts, where he didn't linger when I wanted him to, then slowly tugging off my panties. "There, now it's just you," he said. "That's right. Let me feel you, all of you." He lifted me into his arms and he kissed me, softly, wetly, on the mouth, and stroked my stomach, gently tracing the mound of my pregnancy. Then his smooth hands pressed my patch of hair, and his pale fingers crept lightly over a more sensitive spot. I imagined darker fingers touching me. My breath caught in the back of my throat as I gave myself over to my fantasy like some sacrifice as Matt tried to coax every last ounce of pleasure out of me. God, I didn't want to want this man, but my body betrayed me, and I couldn't resist this or him. I was so ready for him I was shuddering when he mounted me carefully and thrust himself into me.

It was—nice, nothing earth-shattering. He didn't fill me, didn't fit me perfectly, so I grabbed his bare white hips from behind and tried to help drive him into me. He mistook my disappointment and frustration for passion. When he made a move to get up, I kept him inside me and pressed my face against his neck so he couldn't see my tears. I wanted to try to make my marriage work. But our coupling somehow lacked completeness.

"You belong to *me*, now," Matt whispered, as if he had put his brand on me.

"I don't belong to anyone," I murmured.

"Only me," he repeated as he held me close, and tears continued to stream down my face.

"Please don't cry," he said sincerely when he felt the wetness on his neck. "Did I do something wrong?"

"No, it's just been a long day." I was anxious to put my wedding night far behind me.

My bottom lip quivered, and my shoulders began to heave. I tried, but I couldn't stop the tears from coming, again. I think I needed a serious tear duct adjustment.

"Julie," Matt whispered, folding me into his arms. "Julie, honey, what's wrong?"

Matt was holding me close, but I crossed my arms against my stomach in a defensive move.

"I have to go to sleep," I said stubbornly, untangling myself from his arms and pulling the covers over my head, like an ostrich. "So just leave me alone, please."

I knew that I was merely postponing the inevitable, putting off a number of unresolved complications—mainly doubts about my marriage. Was I secretly trying to put distance between myself and my new husband? I knew I was avoiding the biggest issue of all—how was

I going to be able to cope with a new baby? And the loss of the one man I truly loved.

As I drifted off to sleep, all I could think about was the way I felt in Manny's arms on that night so long ago in Jacksonville Beach and, more recently, in the hotel room on Key Biscayne, replaying every moment we had spent with each other. I was a horrible wife. I hoped I would make a better mother.

****

When I finally returned to the shop, I reluctantly took a call from Manny at the end of an exhausting day.

"I miss you," he announced in a rush.

"This is not an appropriate conversation," I cautioned. "I'm married now."

"Don't pretend you're offended," he mumbled.

"You're a vulture," I accused.

"I really am sorry for the way things worked out between us," Manny said, genuinely apologetic.

"It's too late for regrets, don't you think? Goodbye. And stop calling me."

I held the phone and listened to the dial tone before I placed the receiver gingerly back in the cradle. When I did, Matt called. He sounded intense and possessive. He was crowding me when what I needed was some space to think about my life.

"When are you coming home?" he asked anxiously. "I can leave work now and pick you up."

"I have my car here. I'll drive home. To tell you the truth, I'm really swamped. I have a lot of paperwork to catch up on before the opening." I wondered if Matt could tell I was stalling. Mercedes was already turning off the lights.

"Technically we're still on our honeymoon," Matt

pleaded. "We never really got a honeymoon, Julie. Please don't shut me out."

"Okay," I relented, realizing that marriage was all about compromise.

When I walked in the door of our apartment, Matt welcomed me home and wrapped me in his arms.

"Did you miss me today?" he asked.

"I just saw you this morning."

"Julie, honey, I missed *you*, so much," he said, trying to steer me into the bedroom and obviously hoping I would say it back.

"And now that you're home, you can show me just how much," he added, lowering his voice and staring at me longingly with his piercing green eyes.

Matt shut the bedroom door behind me, giving me a long, slow kiss.

"God, Julie, you look good enough to eat, but I brought dinner in for us," he said. "I think dinner will have to keep until we've had a chance to catch up."

His kiss heated up, and I kissed him back. He slipped out of his clothes and stood before me in front of the bed.

I looked into his eyes to steady myself as he reached out to pull me into bed with him. He removed my dress and kissed me hungrily, moving me onto the bed. Slowing the pace a little, he pulled off my panties and began to touch me gently, slowly, methodically, until I was aroused, gasping in delight. He kissed me greedily again and entered me firmly, almost roughly, until he came inside me in a rush of passion. Being married would take some getting used to, but it wasn't turning out to be so bad.

Matt and I began our marriage together trying to

work out a rhythm we could live with. I knew I would be fine as long as I stayed away from Manny and focused on letting go of the memories. There were several times I was tempted to take his calls, but I knew that if I heard his voice again I would capitulate. I was still that vulnerable.

The next afternoon the insistent ringing of the telephone distracted me. It was Manny. He sounded agitated and preoccupied. He definitely had something on his mind. Was he thinking about the baby growing inside of me and wondering, maybe wishing, that it had been his? Or was that just wishful thinking on my part?

Over the past eight and a half months, I had often fantasized about telling Manny the baby was his and imagined his reaction, wondered how different things would be if only I had.

"I have to see you, Julie."

"No," I said, trying to fight back my desire to see him again. "Can't stop. Can't talk. Too busy. Not today."

"Make time for me, Julie," he ordered, with his typical dramatic sense of urgency. "I'm standing at the pay phone right outside the shop. I'm coming in."

I gripped the counter of my desk and twisted the telephone cord. I couldn't leave the shop. I was alone there and about to close up. I had no choice but to face him.

As soon as I saw him, I could tell there was something very wrong. And, married or not, the urge to tell him what I had been keeping from him was clawing at my insides to get out. Spilling my secret would have dangerous consequences, but I couldn't fight it any more. I hadn't gotten pregnant by myself. I couldn't keep it from him any longer. It was time. If I didn't speak up now, and clear my conscience, I'd wonder about it for the rest of my life.

"There's something I need to tell you," I said in a rush.

"Good, because I have something to tell you, too," Manny said, wiping the perspiration from his brow with his long-sleeved white shirt.

"You'd better go first," I said, starting to lose my nerve.

"I went to look at a house yesterday," he began. "It has a beautiful view of the Bay. Plenty of rooms. Very upscale."

"A fancy mansion, then," I said, offering him only a shadow of a smile. "But why do you need so much room?" And suddenly I knew why, and the bottom dropped out of my stomach.

"Julie, Nita and I are getting married. I didn't want you to hear it from anyone else."

I was stunned, but I shouldn't have been so shocked when the announcement knocked the breath out of me with the unexpected force of a one-two punch to the gut.

"She wants to have a baby right away," he said miserably, staring at my stomach. Nita wanted everything I had, and everything I didn't have.

I was already busy imagining Manny and Nita together, tumbling naked in their bed, the White Witch slithering under him and his lips coaxing her lips apart and tangling with her serpent's tongue, his brown eyes searing hers. And then a smiling Manny holding his child, their child. I couldn't get the distressing pictures out of my mind. I had to get out of the store before I became ill. I rushed toward the door, and then my tears started flowing.

"Julie, wait," he said getting up to follow me. "I'm sorry, really."

"Don't. Come. After. Me. Don't try to see me. It's over." Was I insane? Of course it was over. It had ended the day I got married. Was I ever going to come to grips with that fact?

"What is it you wanted to tell me?" he asked, suddenly remembering.

I choked on my bitter laughter, and I could feel the bile rising in my throat. I wasn't going to make it to the car in time. I ran for the bathroom, locked myself in, and vomited.

"Nothing," I called out. "Nothing at all." I composed myself. "Just go away."

I watched from the tiny bathroom window as Manny's car crawled out of the parking lot. I lingered in my office, not quite ready to go home and face Matt. I was so exhausted I sat down in my comfortable chair, clutching my medallion, crying, and aching inside. It was the end of an impossible dream. Now that there was no hope at all, I was resigned to going home to Matt and making my marriage work. I rubbed my swollen belly, whispering repeatedly, "It will be okay, baby, we'll be okay."

Chapter Twenty-One:
A Fresh Beginning

Coral Gables, Florida

I was singing along with the salsa band warming up in the corner as I surveyed the room for a final time. Everything was ready for the opening. The mood was set. I had achieved the perfect balance between hot and cold. The music was pulsing. In contrast, the room was lit to glow like moonlight, for a cool and elegant effect. The jewels in the Estrella Collection glinted in their specially designed display cases in the center of the room, heralded by the alternating vertical Estrella Collection flags and jade-green Stones banners.

Models wearing fashions from some of the trendiest boutiques in the city and accessorized in the latest jewelry creations from Stones were already circulating. Heavy hors d'oeuvres featuring spicy food with Cuban and Spanish flavors were being passed. The bars were set up and already serving the early arrivals. The massive ice sculpture spelling out Stones was attracting attention.

I was most proud of the way the Estrella Collection brochures had turned out. They were neatly stacked near the display case. I'd spent weeks researching the pieces in the collection and supplementing the descriptions with a bit of Spanish history from the period. Interviewing Elena for personal stories was really a labor of love. I wrote the copy and supervised the photo shoot with Manny's sister Estrellita in the gardens at Vizcaya. Estrellita's photo graced the cover, and she modeled most of the signature pieces on the inside pages. Some of the pieces were displayed in the gardens. The full-color catalog was destined to become a collector's item. Antonio, one of the hottest photographers in the city, had done a fabulous job. Tonight he only had eyes for Estrellita. He never let her out of his sight the entire evening, and she was blossoming under his attention, shedding some of her shyness.

Elena was surrounded by reporters curious about the collection. I was overwhelmed by the media response. Cameras and reporters from local, national, even the international fashion press were on hand to cover the event. The sales staff couldn't take the orders fast enough.

The décor was understated and dynamic. The selection of jewelry was the best we'd ever offered—collection quality gems, spectacular stones with the best color and clarity, from international jewelry designers and dealers.

The counter at the front of the store displayed trends of the season and the most coveted jewels in the shop. White gold and platinum pieces were housed in one case and yellow gold in another. The shop carried all the contemporary styles with clean, classic lines as well as antiques. A trunk show featuring a popular jewelry designer displayed more modern lines and newer looks that I predicted would outpace the old-fashioned, traditional ones in sales.

We offered just the right assortment of merchandise, a good value, and excellent service to ensure that customers could always find what they wanted at Stones.

"So, Mrs. Gottlieb, what do you think of the new Stones," I prompted, cornering my best customer. "Is it up to your expectations? Or do you miss Goldsmith's?"

"The shop is fabulous. I've already seen several pieces I have to have. But don't tell my husband. I'm going to buy them and introduce them gradually over a six-month period. Then when he asks me if what I'm wearing is new I can honestly say, 'This old thing? I've had it forever.' "

"That's the way to handle Harvey, Mrs. Gottlieb." I laughed. It was a ruse many of my female customers used, and their husbands fell for it every time. I had used it myself on Matt, who had never understood my fascination with jewelry.

Mrs. Gottlieb had her eye on an exceptional, absolutely breathtaking ten-carat canary diamond I was featuring in one of the display cases at the front of the store. The rare, emerald-cut, flawless stone was magnificently set, with baguette sides in platinum. I took the key out of my handbag and opened the case. First, I put the ring on my finger. I held my hand up so the jewel reflected the artificial light in the room. It was elegant and cool. This rock would have glowed in the dark.

"It's absolutely gorgeous," Mrs. Gottlieb breathed.

"Would you like to take it off my hands?"

The cut was marvelous. The stone sparkled like sun-kissed waves breaking on a beach. A million stars were captured in that stone; it glittered with the look and feel of luxurious bath beads. The piece would be unaffordable for most clients. But not for Mrs. Gottlieb.

"Why don't you try it on?"

I gingerly lifted the ring off my finger and slipped it on Mrs. Gottlieb's hand.

"It looks great on you. Why don't you wear it around the party for a while and get the feel of it?"

"You wouldn't mind?"

"No, of course not. I have to admit, I'd like to own that stone myself. But I don't think Matt would be able to afford it."

"By the way, where is that handsome husband of yours?" Mrs. Gottlieb asked.

"Matt?"

"Is he the one standing over there with the beautiful cover girl in the brochure?"

I gazed at Manny in his tuxedo.

"He is handsome, isn't he?" He looked over at me and smiled, displaying his dimples, and I involuntarily blushed at the sight of him.

"No, he's not my husband. We're just good friends."

"I thought, I mean the way he's been looking at you all evening…"

I directed her to Matt. "That's my husband."

"He's a nice-looking boy too," she said, trying to recover gracefully.

I smiled.

"And now you're about to have a baby. My, how time flies," Mrs. Gottlieb fussed. "I remember when you were just a little girl yourself, coming into the shop in Westchester to help your mother. Soon maybe you'll have a daughter to follow in your footsteps."

"That would be nice, wouldn't it?"

"When is the baby due?"

"In two weeks, but it feels like it may be any day now," I said, shifting my feet and placing my hand behind my back for support. Matt noticed my discomfort and came right over to rub my back in a gloriously soothing motion.

"Honey, are you okay? I think you should sit down now. You've been on your feet all day. It's not good for the baby."

"You worry too much." I smiled. Things had been much better between us lately, now that I had given myself more than half a chance to care for him.

"I do worry about you, Julie. You have to take it easy. After the opening, that's it. Maggie can help Joel in the shop for a while. You'll have to hire some extra help, from the look of tonight's turnout."

I looked over at my sister-in-law with appreciation. Maggie was a jewel. Joel was a graduate gemologist and a gifted jewelry designer. He knew almost everything there was to know about the design and production of precious gems. So he'd had no trouble recognizing one when Mary Margaret Monteleone walked into Goldsmith's one Saturday.

After she eyed every piece of jewelry in the store, my brother asked, "Did you find anything you just can't live without?" As it turned out, the one thing Maggie couldn't live without was Joel.

At that moment Manny came over to join us.

"You should be proud of yourself. Stones is going to be an overnight success."

"You made quite a contribution," I said, crediting Manny. "If it weren't for you we wouldn't even have this space. You helped me with every aspect of the concept and design. You were with me every step of the way. Thank you."

"And I will be with you from now on," Matt said, planting a possessive kiss firmly on my lips. He enjoyed watching Manny squirm.

"Estrellita is really enjoying the spotlight," Manny said, trying to ignore the obvious display of affection between Matt and me. "But I think that photographer is monopolizing all her time. Is that a good idea? She thinks she's in love. But she practically just met the guy."

"Did you ever stop and think that maybe they really are in love?" I ventured.

"She's too young to know anything about love. Too innocent."

I laughed.

"You think it's funny?" Manny asked, and I could tell he was struggling to keep his cool.

"No, it's just that she's your *twin* sister. She's exactly your age, and maybe she *does* know something about love. Haven't you ever been in love?" I speared him with my eyes, waiting for his answer.

"That's different. I've been around."

"Ah, yes, we all know that," I said, rolling my eyes. "What's good for the gander isn't good for the goose, is that what you're saying?"

"You're talking about my sister."

"She's also a grown woman, Manny. Or hadn't you noticed?"

"Well I'm going to start keeping a closer eye on her from now on, I can tell you that. He's nothing but a Latin lover."

"And he would be different from you, how?" I laughed, finally comfortable joking with him about our past. "Look at the guy, Manny. He's a hunk," I said. "Yes, it's a good idea. And he's very successful and actually a pretty great man."

"And what about me?" Matt said, fishing for a compliment. "Am I a hunk?"

"God, yes," I laughed and ruffled my fingers through Matt's wiry hair. "You are to me. I can hardly keep my eyes off you. I was just saying as much to Mrs. Gottlieb."

Matt beamed. "And I can hardly keep my hands off my sexy wife. I just want to make sure you're satisfied."

Manny looked like he was going to be sick. Watching the two of them reminded me of their jealous bickering at Opal Weekend. It seemed like a lifetime ago.

"Matt," I chided. "I'm hardly sexy. I'll be happy when this baby finally makes an appearance. I don't think I could get any bigger. As it is, I'm as huge as a house."

"You never looked more beautiful to me," Matt said, patting my stomach and rubbing it in a seductive, circular motion. Manny's eyes were fixed on Matt's hand on my stomach as if he were watching a train wreck and couldn't look away.

"That's sweet, but I know I'm a cow."

"Lucky for you, I'm a carnivore."

Elena wandered up and kissed Manny, then me. I threw my arms around her.

"Julie, you look beautiful in that dress," Elena said. "I love that color on you. And the shop is wonderful.

You've put together such a nice tribute to my family." Her eyes began to water. "It's so nice to see all the pieces displayed like this. My sister Estrella would have loved this. And my mother, too."

"I sincerely hope so. I tried to honor their memories. I'm afraid such valuable pieces will have to be put back into the vault after everyone goes home. The collection has attracted international attention. We've had some impressive offers. I've been approached by buyers regarding a number of the pieces. Are you interested in selling any of them?"

"I might be. We can talk about it. How are you feeling?"

"I'm fine," I said, "just anxious for it to be over. Nothing fits me anymore. I'll be glad to get out of these maternity clothes."

"I'm so excited about the baby, for both of you." Elena started crying again. I could tell she was wishing it were Manny and I preparing for this special time in our lives. Maybe my mother had told her the truth?

"Don't worry, Mrs. Gellar," Matt assured her. "Everything will be fine. Julie already has her overnight bag packed and waiting here in the office. She takes it home with her every night and brings it back. Since she practically lives here at Stones, it's more likely she'll go into labor here."

"I think you're overdoing it, Julie," Elena said. "You have been working such long hours getting ready for the opening."

"This is my last night at the store until after the baby is born. I promise. Oh, wait, I see a reporter from *Sparkle* magazine. I've got to go over and talk to him. He's promised us the cover of the Christmas issue." I squeezed Elena's hand, kissed Matt, and slid by Manny as I waddled over to where the reporter was standing at the door.

"Julie," Mercedes said, walking with me toward the door. "We've broken all sales records. This is our best day ever, including last Christmas."

"That's great, Mercedes. You're doing a fantastic job. And thanks for agreeing to pick up the slack for me while I'm out on maternity leave."

"I'm flattered that you asked me. What are friends for?"

After I talked to the reporter and made some suggestions to the magazine's photographer, I walked over to my mother.

"So, Mom, what do you think?"

"You were right. Stones is first-class. It's something to be proud of. And it was all your vision. The design, the pieces we brought back from Europe, and the Estrella Collection was a stroke of genius."

"I'm so glad you're pleased."

"And I've taken so many orders tonight. I'm afraid we're going to run out of jewelry."

"I doubt that."

"I'm serious. I've never seen so many customers. And once all the buzz about the shop gets out, we're going to have a great Christmas season."

"Yes, and have you seen Mrs. Gottlieb?" I asked wistfully. "I think she might be the lucky woman to walk away with the yellow diamond tonight. I'll be sorry to see it go."

"Let's keep our fingers crossed," Sylvia replied.

My mother excitedly rushed off to help another customer.

After the last guest left the shop, I allowed myself the luxury of propping my feet up on my desk for a brief respite. Antonio had taken Estrellita out to celebrate, and Manny was dropping his parents off at their house.

Matt wanted to drive me home, but I told him I had too much to do to close the shop. I had my own car in the lot and convinced him I could manage to get home by myself. I was only pregnant, not incapacitated.

He finally relented, not wanting to cause friction on what he knew was one of the most important nights of my life.

I wriggled out of my shoes. My feet were sore, and I longed to soak them in a hot tub or have Matt massage them in the privacy of our bedroom. Mmm. That would be nice. Matt gave great massages. Perhaps I had overdone it this evening. I hadn't accepted much help. I had wanted to do everything myself because I'd wanted everything to be perfect. Trying to achieve perfection was a habit I'd have to break, or it would break me first.

Once the baby was born, I would have my hands full. And less time to worry over every detail at Stones. Truthfully, I hadn't done much to prepare for the birth. Matt had been the one to turn the second bedroom in our apartment into a nursery. I had been too busy with the opening to be involved. I had promised myself I would devote the next two weeks to the project. That's how I thought of the baby right now, as a project. I hadn't had the time to really think through what was about to happen to me and how my life would change once the baby made its appearance as a living breathing little person. A person I suddenly couldn't wait to meet. A sweet little girl or a precious little boy.

I was singing along to a song on the radio in my office as I began to lock away the pieces from the Estrella Collection in the vault. I had placed my overnight bag, shoes, and my beaded evening bag and wrap on the desk in my office so I'd remember to turn off the radio before I left. I needed those reminders because pregnancy was definitely making my mind wander. I supposed I was singing because I was so happy lately. Matt had been wonderful, and I was beginning to get comfortable with thinking of Manny as just a good friend. I still couldn't quite warm up to the White Witch, but I was determined to remain civil to her. Thankfully, Manny'd had the decency to prevent her from coming to the opening.

I walked to the back of the shop to place the jewels in the vault. I examined the emerald medallion. It sparkled in the beam of artificial light as I turned it over in my fingers for the last time. The silver and emerald and the memories weighed heavily on my mind. Now that I was no longer wearing the stone, I felt a huge weight had been lifted from my heart. It had been a millstone around my neck. Once it had brought me such joy, but it was also the cause of a lot of pain and bad memories. I flexed the hand that held it. I decided I'd put the medallion in the vault and save it for my daughter, if I had a girl, to wear when she became a bride. Perhaps that would close the circle and give Elena's tragic story a happy ending.

I locked the necklace carefully away in the safe. It was part of my past now. It had been my connection to Manny, but I no longer needed it because he was no longer part of my life. He had been my best friend, my first love, my first lover, my best lover. The father of my child. But somehow that hadn't been enough for us, and I was going to have to make a fresh beginning without him.

I felt something wet between my thighs, and a stream of liquid soaked the carpet. That's when the sharp pain hit, and I doubled over from the intensity of it. I had to get to a phone. The baby was coming. Suddenly I felt dizzy, and I slumped against the wall and onto the floor.

The beam of headlights blinded me. I squinted to see who was here. Maybe Matt had decided to come back. I prayed it was Matt.

There was a loud knock at the door.

"Julie, are you in there?"

"Manny," I screamed. "I'm in the vault. The door is open." I gestured to him, somehow making him understand.

He was beside me in a matter of seconds. When he saw me on the floor, he came undone. I didn't ask how he knew I needed him, and he offered no explanations.

"My God, Julie! What's wrong?"

"I think the baby's coming," I said.

"I'm going to call the hospital and have them send an ambulance. I don't want to move you now."

"No, don't leave me," I pleaded. I was clutching his arm, and he had to lean down to hear me speak.

"Julie, I'm not going anywhere, count on it," Manny said, and squeezed my hand. "I'll be right here. Let me just make this one call." He eased away gently.

I held his eyes and had trouble turning away from the raw emotion I saw there. Jealousy, desire, and real regret. I hadn't realized the intensity of his feelings for me or that he was capable of such feelings, and it seemed to come as an even bigger surprise to him.

When he returned to my side, he kissed me tenderly on the forehead, held me, and stroked my sweat-soaked hair as I leaned into him.

"Everything will be all right," he promised.

"I'm glad you're here."

"I wouldn't want to be anywhere else."

"I was afraid I was going to have the baby alone right here in the shop."

"I'm with you now. You don't have to be afraid. I was driving by on the way home from my parents' house, and I saw the lights. You shouldn't have stayed so late."

I felt another pain, and I wanted to cry out again, but Manny held my hand tighter and spoke soothing words like one would use to calm a fussy child or a lover. I was bone tired and lacked the strength to play games, too weary to worry about my pride, what little pride I had left. I didn't want to open myself up to any more hurt, but I knew we were taking the last step in the tenuous tango we had been dancing since we'd met. Whenever I got closer, he pulled away. When I tried to move away, he pulled me back. I was all tapped out, too drained to do the dance any more. It was costing me too much.

"You know, I've been chasing you all my life," I sighed.

"I think I've been running away from you my whole life, when all I really wanted was to run toward you. I guess I thought you'd always be there for me."

"I've been here the whole time. All you had to do was reach out. But I didn't think you really wanted me."

"You were always so sure of what you wanted," Manny said. "I wasn't. Until now."

"Now is too late," I whispered softly as we waited for the ambulance to arrive.

When the vehicle screeched to a halt in front of the hospital emergency room, I was in pain and still clutching Manny's hand like a lifeline.

"Julie, what is it?" Manny said as he noticed my grimace.

"I think the baby's coming, right now."

"This woman is having a baby," Manny called out frantically to the attendant.

When I was settled in a private room, Manny called my mother and told her to notify Matt to come to the hospital. Then he vanished. It all happened so quickly that by the time everyone arrived, the baby was already on its way. There was no time for an epidural. It was past time for procrastination. I was going to have to face up to the fact that I was having this baby.

Matt arrived and stayed at my side throughout the delivery. What I really wasn't prepared for was how much I loved the new life Manny and I had created and that Matt and I would share. From the moment the baby was placed in my arms, I knew that being his mother was who I was meant to be.

When the nurse brought the baby into my room for his first feeding, Matt looked at his new son with amazement. Miraculously, the baby had a full head of dark hair, with one unmanageable curl that was beginning to wind its way down his forehead, just like mine.

Matt couldn't seem to get over his new family.

We had talked about Italian names, since Matt still

believed my son had been conceived in Italy.

"No, Matt, but I do want to tell you who the father is."

"I'd really rather not know. This baby is mine. I want to start with a clean slate. No baggage, no regrets."

"Are you sure?"

"Positive." We decided to name him Josh, after Matt's deceased grandfather.

Manny came into my room later that night, after visiting hours were over. I don't know how he managed it. He had probably charmed one of the night nurses. It was dark and quiet, and I was feeding Josh by lamplight. For a moment, as the artificial halo bathed the three of us, I envisioned that Manny and I were married and our little family was complete.

From force of habit, Manny leaned over to pull the curl back from my forehead and did the same to the baby's head, pressing a tender kiss against my brow. Then he dragged a chair close to my bed and sat down next to me so he could concentrate on watching me nurse. He seemed fascinated by the baby.

"He's absolutely perfect, isn't he?" I smiled.

"I can't see a single flaw," Manny agreed.

He has your dark coloring, I was thinking, and your beautiful brown eyes.

"He has your little pug nose," Manny said aloud, transfixed by the baby as he reached out tentatively to touch the baby's nose and every other feature on his tiny, angelic face.

"Hopefully not my sense of smell," I said, laughing foolishly as the baby curled his hand around Manny's finger.

"I think he knows me," Manny said.

"That's just what babies do." I began to cry silently.

"Julie, are you okay? What is it? Is it something I said?"

"I'm just so happy." This baby wouldn't know his father. And that was sad.

I never tired of hearing Manny talk. His voice lulled me into a trance; its steady rhythm rocked the baby and me into a deep slumber.

When I awoke, Manny was gone and Matt was by my side. It must have been a dream. I had made the biggest mistake of my life, I thought, right before I dozed off again.

PART THREE
THE ROAD HOME

PALM COAST, FLORIDA, LATE SUMMER 2014

Chapter Twenty-Two:
Out of Step

I'm afraid I am making the biggest mistake of my life, I think, the moment I lay eyes on Manny Gellar again. I know I'm about to do something I'm going to regret. So what is sex in the general scheme of things? My well-honed sense of right and wrong is in overdrive. But then Manny holds my hand as we walk toward the Crab Shack Café on AIA. That simple act of walking in tandem, in itself, is a minor miracle. Lately, wherever I go with Matt—to the grocery store, the Mall, or to a movie—he walks ahead of me, always in a hurry. Sometimes he gets all the way to his destination before he even notices I am missing in action. It's like when he's finished in the bathroom and he turns out the lights while I'm still brushing my teeth, as if I am not even in the room. That's how out of step we have become with each other. Warranted or not, my anger at Matt is still raw.

The seafood restaurant, not high on atmosphere to begin with, looks even less appetizing all boarded up.

"Do you think it's even open?" I ask.

Manny knocked loudly on the door.

"We're closed," the manager bellows. "Don't you folks know there's a dangerous hurricane coming?"

"Please," Manny pleads. "We just got into town. My wife is hungry, and we haven't had a chance to go to the grocery store yet. I'm not sure if the supermarket is even open."

I crinkle my nose at his improvised wife remark.

"Okay. I think we can scrape together something, but you two better evacuate as soon as you leave here. The bridge will be closing soon."

"Thanks," Manny says politely.

Lunch goes much better than I expect. I'm hardly nervous at all. Manny looks different, yet still the same to me. He has gained weight. His hair is turning gray. Somehow he has morphed into his father since the last time we've seen each other, maybe a year ago. I think it was at the Publix in Miami. His witchy wife was with him, of course, so we couldn't say more than a few impersonal words to each other. There was so much more I wanted to say.

But underneath the outward appearance I recognize my first love. After the first few awkward minutes, we get used to being around each other, and then things start to settle down.

"You look good, Jewels," he says sincerely, eying me appreciatively. I've taken off some weight since the last time I saw him. I could thank Matt for the days he forced me to work out. Working out bored me to tears, but it did have its benefits. And my hair is longer now, streaked with expensive blond highlights, courtesy of my overpriced salon, The Strand.

"Have you been on the Science Diet?" he asks.

"Nita is on that."

"No, my dog is on the Science Diet," I correct him. "I'm on the South Beach Diet."

"You haven't changed at all." He dispenses his customary charm out of an internal smoothie machine.

I ask him about work. He says he's under constant pressure to sell more, grow more, be more. Right in the middle of a potential real estate bust in South Florida. He looks depressed, miserable, really. I guess that's what success does to a person. And signs of his success are spreading like kudzu, literally. You can hardly drive a mile in Miami or Fort Lauderdale or up and down both coasts of Florida without seeing the familiar *Gellar Group* billboards or yard signs.

As we wait for our seafood order, Manny is in the mood to reminisce.

"We had some good times, didn't we, Jewels?" he says as he leans closer to me and takes my hand. I know I will cave the moment he touches me. I try to pull away, or at least mentally prepare myself, but I know resisting will be as futile as swimming against a rising storm surge. My reaction to his touch is immediate and obvious. My heart actually skips a beat.

"I don't think this is a good idea."

"Where did you think this was going?" he asks quietly.

"I honestly don't know," I reply nervously. Hesitant to break the connection, he doesn't let go of his death grip on my hand.

"Where do you want it to go?" he presses.

That's the way Manny is. He never answers first, never reveals his true feelings. And I'm not about to fall back into our old pattern and reveal mine only to get shot down again.

"I don't know," I repeat numbly, my emotions spinning out of control.

"Yes, you do, Jewels. Tell me what you want." He stares intently into my eyes and strokes my hand gently. I shiver, although it's not particularly cold in the restaurant or outside.

"I thought you wanted to explore our relationship," he challenges.

"This feels more like a seduction," I say, uncomfortable. "I'm in the market for sincerity."

"I want to give you whatever you need," he says.

"What if you don't have it to give?"

"Are you looking for a proposal or something?" he snaps, shifting into irritable-child mode.

"I didn't say that," I answer, attempting to repossess my hand. "Obviously we're both still married to different people. And don't worry, I'm not getting any ideas!"

"Julie, calm down. It's just that I can't stop thinking about you, about us," he states. "This thing between us, whatever it is, is not over."

I don't say anything.

"It's never going to end," he insists. He is probably right about that. Manny is such a big part of my past. That's why I'm here, isn't it? Because I can't let go of the past?

His thumb massages my palm in a circular motion, like a deadly spider, spinning its soothing, sensual spell around me. I pull my hand away and the sizzling sensation abates.

"Jewels?" he says expectantly. "Say something."

"What do you want from me? I don't honestly

know what you want me to say."

"I think you do. I need you, Julie. Can't you see that? Do you want me to beg here?"

"What do I really mean to you, anyway?" I ask.

"That's what we need to find out. What we mean to each other." He is saying all the right words. "Is there somewhere we can go, I mean, to be alone?"

He knows about my condo, then. I'm sure Mackie has given him all the details.

"Maybe the car," I suggest, wanting to slow things down because I am not quite ready to risk everything. At this point it's not too late to turn back.

Manny pays the bill, leaving a generous tip, thanks the manager profusely, and grabs my hand again as he leads me out to the parking lot.

We have been so engrossed in each other we haven't even noticed the weather has worsened, considerably. By the time we leave the restaurant, the rain is coming down in steady horizontal sheets. Bitter, blowing bands of wind, torrents so powerful they push us sideways, lash the sand and gusty rains, and sting our faces as we dash for his car. Covering my eyes, I hold on to Manny to keep myself upright. Churning relentlessly, the ocean across the narrow highway has grown surly in the space of only an hour and spits up monster waves, a surfer's wet dream.

Manny's flimsy forest green Gellar Group umbrella whips uselessly inside out in the roaring wind and driving rain. I can hardly see the parking lot; the steady rain is obscuring the view and the visibility. My throat constricts with fear. By the time we manage to negotiate our way to the car, locating it by touch, we are thoroughly drenched.

Note to God: If you let us live, I won't go through with this. I won't cheat.

"Get in," Manny yells, trying to make himself heard above the wind. "We've got to get out of this weather."

He opens the car door on the passenger side and helps me in, then goes around to the driver's seat. I sense he is also nervous about the storm, but his eyes signal his hurry to get closer.

In the end, my body and my mind betray me. I long for him; he leans towards me. I strain toward him; he shifts toward me, eager to close the space between us. He reaches over the console to pull me against him, and as he opens his arms, I slip back into them. The years fall away. My tears won't stop falling. We are both in the same place, finally, and we both want the same thing. Then he kisses me, tenderly at first, until we get the sense of each other again. Turning fierce and impatient, his cunning tongue tangles with mine, touching off a firestorm. Our wet clothes are stuck together, and I am suddenly hungry for his warmth. I want—no, need—to keep his lips against mine. The wind whines, and we answer its siren's call.

Shit, I thought, shit, shit, shit. Nothing's changed. I still want him. Even after all these years.

"Can we go somewhere, sweetheart?" Manny asks in a husky voice, sensing capitulation. I don't recall that he's ever called me sweetheart before, and I come undone. "This isn't going to be enough."

I bite my lip and pull back, but he grips me with his powerful arms. I am not sure I can go through with this.

"You have a condo here, don't you? We could go there and talk, just talk."

"I don't think…"

"Just tell me where," Manny says, reluctantly releasing his hold on me to start the engine. "Quickly." When I don't answer, he turns around. "You know we're going to do this. I came all this way."

Why does his selfishness surprise me? What did I *think* was going to happen? Well, I'm not going to let it happen.

"I think you'd better take me back to my car now," I say, although the last thing I want to do is ride out this ugly storm alone. "You need to fill up your tank before you get back on the road."

"I can't drive around in this, and neither should you," Manny argues. "It's dangerous."

"Being with you is more dangerous," I reply.

"Julie, be reasonable."

When we try to turn into the service station, two of Palm Coast's finest are blocking the entrance. The station is either out of gas or out of power to pump the gas. The city is locking down.

"Well, I don't have any food in the condo, so let's stop by the Publix first, before you take me to my car," I suggest, trying to postpone the intimacy. "I'm going to need some food in case I get stuck here."

"You're still practical."

"Well one of us has to be." I glare at him. "I can't believe I let you talk me into this, with a hurricane coming," I mutter, but I know I am partially responsible.

We finalized the plans to meet before the hurricane was even on the horizon, and I would have lost my nerve if we had rescheduled. He probably feels the same way. But I can tell he isn't ready to leave me.

"Okay, come with me to the Publix, if they're not already boarded up. I'll get you something for the road. I don't remember what you like."

"I remember what you like," he says, trying to put his arms around me again.

"I'm talking about food," I say, swatting him away.

The wind is fitful and angry, whipping the car around as Manny wrestles to keep the vehicle on the road. Windowpanes are already out in some of the stores in the strip shopping center on the left side of the road. As we approach the toll bridge, palm fronds are strewn on either side of the entrance to the causeway, and debris is flying all around us. We are stopped over the Intracoastal by a solidly built, brick wall of a police officer, a cocky troll who won't let us cross the waterway. His dark, beady eyes impale us.

"Sorry, folks, we've closed the bridge. It's not safe."

"But officer, we have to get to the Publix," I plead.

"This area has been under a mandatory evacuation all day. Where have you two been? Don't you watch TV? This bridge is too windy for traffic. You'll have to find another way out. You could try A1A, but the roads are pretty clogged, and some sections might be washed away. We already have reports of power lines down."

Outside, the wind and rain are picking up force. Conditions are worsening.

"There *is* no other way out except to drive right into the path of the hurricane," I begin nervously. "Please, just let us over, and—

"Can't do that," he interrupts.

"Can't or won't?" Manny snarls, starting to get out his wallet. I slap his hands.

"Don't do that," I implore.

"It's what he wants. It's what they all want."

The officer glares at Manny through the lowered window.

"I know I didn't just see you attempt to bribe an officer of the law," he begins, pulling out his ticket book. His other hand rests firmly on his weapon.

"No," I say, pressing my hand against Manny's. "My *friend* here was just looking for his driver's license."

"Let's go back," I say, resigned. "We can't make it to Publix or back to my car. We'll have to take our chances and ride out the storm at the condo. It'll probably be okay. It was built to the new hurricane code. The windows are designed to withstand winds of up to 130 miles per hour. And the store is probably out of milk and bread anyway."

By this time, Manny is growing restless. His face is sweating and his hands grip the steering wheel as he backs out of the toll lane and turns the car in the opposite direction. I give him directions to get to the condo through the back entrance on A1A.

"Is something wrong?" I ask. His face is losing enough color to concern me.

"This is Hurricane Andrew all over again," Manny says. "Is this a Category Five?"

"Honestly, I don't know. I haven't been watching the weather reports."

"Maybe we should both go, then," he says tentatively.

"I don't think we can get out now. You heard that officer. It's too late. But I'm sure we'll be okay." Growing up in Miami, hurricanes like Donna and Betsy were as familiar as school friends. But they weren't in the popular group. They were more like passing acquaintances, the kids nobody wanted to hang around with—the outcasts and the bullies.

"You weren't there in '92."

Matt and I had been out of the country when Andrew struck Miami, but I'd heard that Manny and Nita's house had been totally destroyed and they'd barely escaped with their lives. My mother said when it was over, rescuers found them in a state of shock, hunkered in a bathtub, covered by a mattress, which was all that was left of the former structure and their possessions. I'd seen the devastation firsthand when we returned to find South Dade in ruins. The area resembled a war zone, and its survivors thought they'd never recover from the swath of death and destruction in the aftermath of that killer storm. South Dade was literally a dead zone populated by the endless drone of helicopters overhead. The birds didn't return for months.

Were we about to experience another catastrophe? Like Andrew or Katrina? Our original plan was to have a leisurely lunch and see how the afternoon played out. Manny had intended to drive home later this afternoon. Spending the night was never in the cards.

"I've got to let Nita know I can't get home," Manny announces. "She's expecting me back tonight. She'll be worried."

"I've got a better idea," I suggest. "Let's start a telephone tree. You call Nita, and she can notify Matt."

"I see what you mean," Manny agrees. "Bad idea."

"Anyway, it's not a good idea to use our cell phones. If we lose power we won't be able to recharge them. We might need them in an emergency later on."

"You've gotten smarter," Manny says.

"I really miss your backhanded compliments. Now I'm remembering why I didn't like you very much." But as we drive toward my condo and the underground garage, what I'm really thinking is how much I still like him.

I remember feeling jealous when I first heard about Manny's storm story. Jealous that the crisis must have brought Nita and Manny closer together, cemented their relationship. I even imagined I had been the one huddling in that bathtub with him, and we had been fighting for our lives in *our* house, with *our* son. I could pretend that he never loved Nita before, but the storm surely changed all that, building an impenetrable bond between them. Instead of being terribly romantic, this experience is shaping up to be terrifyingly real.

"Are you and Nita happy?" I ask suddenly.

"The truth is she's turned into a shrew," Manny says.

News Flash! That witch was born a shrew. She was wicked in the womb.

But I decide to be charitable.

"Well, you're probably not exactly the easiest person to live with."

"Thanks," he says dryly, then smiles and smoothly steers the topic away from his wife as he steers into the parking garage underneath my building. The low lights of the deserted parking lot only add to the eerie feeling of isolation and give confirmation to the fact that we're the only two people left on the property.

Chapter Twenty-Three:
Living on Love and Water

"We're soaked," I exclaim as we step out of the elevator on the fifth floor and walk into the foyer of my condo, dripping water. At least the electricity still works.

"Give me your wet clothes and I'll give you some of Matt's clothes to put on while I dry ours." In the master bedroom, I find some clothes in the dresser I share with Matt. I come out and toss Manny an old gray T-shirt and a pair of beige shorts, then return to the bedroom to change into a body-hugging black T-shirt dress and dump our soggy clothes into the dryer down the hall. I walk into the middle bedroom, which opens out onto the golf course, and look through the sliding glass doors. Some of the streetlights are already twisted. I pull a fresh, folded towel from the linen closet, hand it to Manny, and watch while he dries his face and his hair.

"This place is great," Manny notes, as he surveys my condo. Grateful for the distraction, I proudly show him around my home-away-from-home. Anything to keep my mind off the storm. The kitchen features shiny stainless steel appliances and sleek granite countertops. Museum-white walls provide the perfect backdrop for paintings with just the right splash of color. My favorites are the windows and doors of Bermuda and the shot Matt took recently on our trip to Cinque Terre, Italy, of the island of Monterossa. The living room furniture is a serene shade of Scandinavian blue. A companion fabric covers the dining room chairs.

"It has that whitewashed look," Manny observes.

"I wanted it to look like Greece," I point out.

"The musical?"

"No, the country," I say, shaking my head. We are coming from opposite directions now. Has time severed our connection?

"Depressed wood," he notes.

"No. I'm depressed. The wood is distressed."

"What do you have to be depressed about?"

I just stare at him. The man is clueless. If he thinks this reunion has been easy for me...

"Three bedrooms, office, three and a half baths," he continues, switching into realtor gear. So much for compassion.

"I'm not interested in putting it on the market," I say dryly. "So stop playing realtor."

"Just assessing the property," he notes, smirking slyly. "You could get a fortune for it," he adds eagerly, looking out at floor-to-ceiling windows that cross the entire width of the condo. "Million-dollar view, I'll bet, if we could see it."

On the ocean side, the darkening sky has completely obliterated the sun, and the blinding rain creates a white-out.

"With this hurricane coming, you can hardly see the ocean, but I assure you it's out there," I answer. You can hear the sound of the surf from almost any room. And it is growing louder.

"I want to get a closer look at the master bedroom

and bath," he says pointedly, leading me down the hall.

"Why do we always end up in the bedroom, I wonder?" I ask.

"Because we're so good together there."

"We are definitely *not* going into the bedroom," I counter, pulling him back into the living room. He is thinking about sex. I am thinking about survival. Somebody has to be the adult, and right now I seem to be the only grownup in the room.

I walk into the kitchen and peek into the refrigerator. We have some Brie that is still good, leftover from my last visit. In the cabinet I find some fancy crackers, two unopened bottles of wine, a jar of crunchy peanut butter, a box of granola bars, some microwave popcorn, breakfast cereal, and a case of bottled water. At least if there is a hurricane and we aren't killed outright, we won't starve. If we lose power, we'll find out in a hurry that you can't live on love. Well, maybe we can survive on love and water, for a week anyway.

Used to taking direction, out of necessity I begin issuing orders like a drill sergeant, recalling the lessons I learned at Tech Sergeant Sidney Goldsmith's basic training camp during the frequent hurricanes that plagued Miami when I was growing up.

If Matt were here, he'd know exactly what to do. Matt can handle anything. He is good in a crisis. He considers the impossible a challenge. Manny has always been useless when called on to do anything practical. He has survived all this time on his charm alone.

While I gather the supplies we'll need, Manny is hunched over the coffee table in the living room. When

I come up behind him, he snaps to attention.

"What are you doing?" I bark. It looks like he is clipping his toenails into the drawer of my coffee table.

"Nothing," he denies, with a sheepish grin. "Just a nervous habit."

Holy Crapola, Cowabonga, and OMG don't even begin to describe my feelings. My Romeo has been reduced to a sniveling toe-clipper.

"That is disgustingly gross, Manny," I scold in my best fishwife imitation. "Stop it right now and clean up those clippings. Do you think I want to clone you for posterity*?" Too late. I've already done that, almost, with Josh.* "Does Nita know about your disturbing habit?"

"Yeah, she doesn't seem to mind." Maybe I am wrong about Nita. Maybe she's not a witch. Maybe she's really a saint.

Then I notice Manny is trembling, and we haven't even seen the worst of the bad weather. Perhaps he is still traumatized by his experience with Hurricane Andrew, still shell shocked and storm weary and suffering from Post Traumatic Stress or Hurricane Fatigue.

I place my hand on his arm and experience what amounts to an electric current that isn't coming from the lightning outside. Is the power flickering?

"It's okay." My voice is soothing, but I quickly remove my hand from the source of the shock.

"I need to get out of here now, Julie. I can't go through this again." And I know he is talking about the hurricane. But he is being irrational. We are trapped here. "It never goes away. It's not something you ever forget." The windows are rattling, and Manny is having difficulty breathing.

"Why don't you lie down and let me get things ready," I suggest, taking his hand and gently pushing him to a prone position on the couch. He pulls me down with him and holds me, and I can hear his great big bear of a heart beating under mine. He cradles me in his arms for a minute before I untangle myself from him.

I make a big show of gathering towels, a flashlight, and everything we need to outlast the storm. But it is all bluster. Inside, I am shaking too, and it has nothing to do with rattling windows, nothing to do with the hurricane at all.

Chapter Twenty-Four:
The Secret Lay Between Us,
a Living, Breathing Entity

I was an obedient daughter, never wanting to test my father's temper, and an obedient wife because that was how I was conditioned. Right now, I only want to obey my own thirst. Manny Gellar is still blowing smoke, and it is definitely getting in my eyes. My hormones are fissionable and seeking release. And I am on the verge of taking a big gulp of whatever drink he is serving up. The storm is just injecting another forbidden element into the dangerous mix.

"All right, here's your big chance to talk me out of it," I say to Mackie when I reach her on my portable phone while enclosed in the master bathroom, squandering my remaining precious minutes of power.

"What?" her voice comes back garbled and muted, distant, like it is surfacing from the bottom of the ocean, a million miles away instead of just hundreds.

"Listen to me, Julie," Mackie is saying in a steady, serious voice. "Absolutely *everyone* is calling wanting to know where you are. We're all *worried* about you. Matt is frantic."

"I'm going to turn my phone off again after this. You call him in New York and tell him I'm okay."

"What's it like outside?" she asks.

"Raining, windy, you know," I said. "It's doing

typical hurricane things."

"This is a very *dangerous* storm," Mackie warns evenly. "It's made a turn, and it's headed right for Palm Coast. It's out over the water, and it's building strength. I hope you two had the good sense to get out of there."

Silence.

"You have evacuated, haven't you?" she presses.

"We haven't, but my insides are about to. I'm caving. I want him, Mackie. I ache for him. I'm about to combust."

I can almost hear Mackie shaking her head over the phone and feel her wanting to shake some sense into me.

"Well, it's too late to get out now, anyway," Mackie mumbles. "Okay, what's he offering?"

"That's what I'm about to find out. Here he comes. I'd better go."

I think I hear her yell, "Be careful," before I break the connection. And I know she's talking about more than the impending storm.

"Why are you hiding in the bathroom?" Manny wonders, cornering me against the sink, maybe eager to get his hands on me, probably afraid to be alone.

"I'm not hiding, I'm thinking."

"About what?"

"Old memories."

"Good memories, I hope?"

"Mixed. What am I going to do with you, Manny Gellar? What do I really mean to you?" Here I am, fifty years old, fairly sophisticated, yet still capable of the same range of raw emotions I felt back in college—the love and the hurt and the vulnerability. I am still that same insecure girl, full of doubts, needs, and unfulfilled hopes. Still unable to resist Manny Gellar. Still defined by this particular man who should no longer even be a factor in my life.

"You have to ask?" he says. "You mean everything to me." Then he kisses me with all the passion he is capable of. I resist, but I want to return his kisses and pretend that things are still the way they were. I wonder if he can tell I'm trying to hold the hurricane at bay.

"I do love you, Julie," he coaxes. "It's okay to let me know how you feel."

He is so good at saying all the right words. So good with the kissing. So good at strumming on my fragile emotions. His lips inch up my face before he covers my mouth with his again. It is getting harder to fight my feelings. I don't know if it is true love or pure lust. I just know I am desperate to hang onto it, and he is hanging onto me like a shipwreck victim clinging to a piece of flotsam.

"Jewels. You haven't said it. You haven't told me how you feel."

"What do you want me to say?" I whisper, almost choking on the words.

"That you love me. You do love me, don't you?"

I won't say it, but I can't exactly deny it.

He whispers words of love into my mouth, his arms enfolding me. "You make me so crazy. I can't think straight when I'm around you."

We stand swaying in place, wrapped in each other's arms for what seems an eternity. I can hardly catch my breath. I want more, and he does too.

Outside, night is descending with loud noises and thumping. If we strain and look out the back windows, we can see that all the palm trees are moving in one direction. The pool area is beginning to flood, but we should be safe on the fifth floor. Sand is splattering against the windows, the wind is shrieking, and the building is beginning to shake. Manny tightens his grip on my hand.

"We belong together," he says, echoing my thoughts. "You know we do."

He leads me to the master bedroom.

"Manny, no, not in here," I protest. My knees are weak, and I lean on him for support as he leads me across the dining room into the guest bedroom. I stand outside the room and grab onto the doorknob, willing myself not to go in.

The guest bedroom is decorated almost entirely in white, Sherwin-Williams-Snowbound-white interior walls, a white ceiling fan, a pearl-encrusted white fabric lampshade, and a white-on-white striped satin comforter against a stark black, heavy iron bed frame. A bridal suite that will soon be visited by the devil. White for the wedding we never had. The honeymoon we never took.

"Please, no," I repeat, putting the brakes on. "Let's stay in the living room." Disappointed, irritated, but resigned, he leads me back there.

"Stop playing games, Julie."

"I'm not."

We sit on the couch next to each other, and he places his hand possessively on my knee, pushing up my dress slowly. He rubs my thigh and talks in that dangerous, mesmerizing voice of his. I push his hand away.

"This isn't right," I say. "I can't do this."

"Yes, you can," Manny says, continuing to

massage my thigh, stealing a kiss and sliding closer. "You know you want to."

What I want and what I am going to do are two different things. The bottom line is I definitely do not want to betray my husband. I know that what I *was* contemplating would be a breach of trust our marriage would never recover from. Matt might be cheating on me, but that doesn't mean I have to return the favor. If I do, I will hate myself forever. If our marriage is over, Matt is going to have to make the first move to end it. But there are still unanswered questions. I still need closure on my relationship with Manny.

"Look, if I had thought for one minute that you were really serious about me back then, things might have been so different for us," I say. "Why can't you just admit it now? You never were. Serious. It was all about sex. It still is."

Manny gets up and begins pacing the spacious room.

"Is that what you really think? That what I feel for you is casual? If you do, then you don't know me at all, Julie."

"Then I guess I don't," I answer warily. Manny rarely calls me Julie unless he is out of sorts or out of control.

"Sure, I love the way we were together," he admits, returning to sit beside me. "But my feelings for you are real. I loved you then and I love you now. I never got over you."

Wanting to believe his words, I eye him suspiciously.

"Do you mean that?" I say. "I need to know. There's a lot at stake here, for both of us."

"Damn right I mean that," he replies, moving his hands up to my breasts. When they slip inside the top of my dress, I nearly bolt from the couch, thinking lightning has struck inside the condo.

I try to get my emotions back under control. He isn't ready to break contact, so when I try to move his hand away, he clasps mine.

"I need someone I can count on," I say. "Someone who doesn't turn his feelings on and off the way you do. Who doesn't play games. I need to know where I stand."

Manny hesitates before he asks. "Is it better with Matt?"

"This isn't a contest."

"But I do turn you on, don't I?" he wonders.

"There it is again," I say. "Sex."

"I never heard you complain when we were together. And you didn't put up much resistance to Matt, either, in college."

"No matter what you think I did, you know I was never with Matt that way before we got married."

"Yet somehow you managed to get yourself pregnant," he challenges.

"I didn't get *myself* pregnant, you moron. I don't even know you anymore. I never know whether I'm getting you or some hyped-up image of you. I don't think I've ever heard an honest word come out of that mouth of yours." That incredibly sexy mouth that I want to sink my tongue and teeth into, I hear my bad self thinking.

"Julie," Manny pleads. "Are you listening to me at all? I'm pouring my heart out to you. Do you think this is easy for me? This is real, this is me. I came all the way up here to see you."

"To sleep with me, you mean," I argue. "Everything is sexmanship with you."

"Is that even a word? What will it take to convince you that I'm serious?" he insists.

"That word is not in your vocabulary," I counter, biting my lower lip. But I desperately want to believe him. I want to hold him, really hold him, not hold back, and, as if he senses victory is at hand, he pulls me tightly against his chest.

"Enough talking," he growls, as he slides my head onto the arm of the couch, and roughly pushes me down, barely cushioning the impact. When I push him away, he lets loose with a string of Spanish expletives.

"Why are you doing this?"

"You knew what would happen when you brought me here."

"If I did, I changed my mind. I don't want you now."

"Well I can't turn it on and off the way you can. I want you so bad I can taste it. I miss you. I need to feel you again, Julie. I need to love you again. I need you to love me. You're wrong if you think this is just about sex."

Somewhere in the corner of my mind I am thinking, isn't this what I've been missing? Maybe this "just about sex" thing is not such a bad deal.

Panting, his perspiration mingling with his tears, he gropes me blindly and kisses my lips hungrily, almost angrily, like he has to possess me totally. In the past, I had been his completely. He didn't have to take me by force. I would have gone anywhere with him, done anything for him, willingly. But instinctively I know he is exposing the true depth of his feelings.

So naturally I pick this most inopportune time to cry.

"I'm sorry, so sorry if I ever hurt you." He sounds properly remorseful. "But I really thought you knew I did love you. I wish I could go back and do it all over again from the start. Fix my mistakes. Make things right between us again."

When he holds me, time melts away. The past and present blur as my tears seem to flow into the ocean raging outside. I am in a different place, but in my mind we are back in that hotel room in Jacksonville Beach at Opal Weekend. I hug him fiercely, finally sure of his feelings for me.

"I do love you, Manny," I say, surprising even myself. Was this what I have been waiting for? Longing to say to him? I've kept my feelings so tightly corked for so many years; I no longer want to deny them. And it feels good to be honest with my emotions. But what outcome am I expecting?

He wipes away my tears with his thumb.

"But it's not real," I breathe softly.

"It's real, Julie," Manny promises. "You can believe it."

He kisses me again on my forehead. I don't care whether this is real. I want to hang onto this feeling, savor it, if only for a while longer.

Manny's honey-sweet, gravelly voice draws me like a magnet. I crave his large brown hands on my body again. I sigh as he cradles me in his arms. All my promises to be faithful threaten to leap out the window like traitorous lemmings. But I am determined not to let it go any further.

In that moment, the room grows dark and ominous, other worldly.

"I just wish…" Manny says wistfully.

"What do you wish?" I sigh, my eyes searing his meaningfully.

"That the baby had been mine."

He couldn't have surprised me more if he'd kicked me in the head. I'd imagined exactly this scenario in my mind at least a thousand times. And I am bursting to blurt out the truth.

"You know, Nita couldn't have children," he continues. "We tried for years, and it never happened for us."

A single tear slips down my face, and I wipe it off slowly but say nothing.

But here's how I am feeling. At the same time I am stealing something from Matt, I feel like I have also stolen something precious from Nita. Having Manny's child was the only thing she wanted but couldn't have. The one thing her money couldn't buy. Hating her had become a habit. Maybe I shouldn't hate her so much anymore.

"Well, you must enjoy Estrellita's and Antonio's brood then," I counter. "Two sets of twins."

"My sister's kids are great, but it's not the same," Manny admits with regret.

The secret lies dormant between us, a living, breathing entity, looming monstrously in front of me, waiting to break free. Right now, I don't want to focus on any insurmountable problems. I want to block out everything else in my life but this moment.

Chapter Twenty-Five:
The Emperor's New Clothes

The howling wind and rattling glass shake me out of my fantasy. The couch is directly in front of a set of sliding glass doors that lead out to the patio. Water is seeping in toward the furniture. Nature is intruding on our little love nest as a strange and sinister storm rocks Palm Coast. We are going to have to leave the couch soon. I want to stay cocooned here, under the soft, warm blanket, forever.

Outside, the wind viciously strains against the glass, a monster breaking out from under the bed in a child's nightmare. The Big Bad Wolf outside is refusing to be ignored as he does his best to huff and puff and blow my second house down. The Big Bad Wolf inside is also howling.

"Manny, could you help me put some towels in front of the sliding glass doors?" I rocket up from the couch and grab another handful of towels from the hall linen closet. I take charge of the situation again, since Manny doesn't seem inclined or capable of doing it.

"It sounds like the floodgates are opening. Help me move the couch and the chairs and end table and cover them with sheets. Let's move whatever food we have left into the guest bathroom so we can get to it more easily. And grab the flashlight sitting on the counter in the kitchen. Then we'd better move into the bathroom, close the door, and hope the windows in the back bedroom will hold."

I instruct Manny to take the duvet cover from the queen-sized bed in the guest bedroom and wrap it around himself to protect his body from flying glass. He takes another duvet cover for me from the twin bed in the second guest bedroom. Closing the bathroom door behind us, he blocks the shower entrance with the queen-sized mattress he has pulled off the bed. We sit next to each other on the shower seat, praying we will survive the night. He knows the drill. He's been through this before.

The wind takes its vengeance against the building. Outside, debris flies, more glass shatters. I'm on the precipice of a rollercoaster, right before the fall, my stomach about to lurch out of control.

The stream of rushing water won't be denied. It seeps beneath the back sliding glass doors, pushed by the force of the high winds and steady, slanting rain. The windows rattle and the condo shakes to the rock-and-roll beat.

Night is descending. Huge, powerful flashes of light glow and fade out my back window. The streetlights are out, and the lights that arc the causeway bridge are gone. Lights in the direction of St. Augustine have blinked out. Our power is gone. It's dark and beginning to get hot and stuffy with all the windows closed.

The palm trees splinter and crash outside to the sounds of roof shingles and fronds tossed against the windows. Glass shatters on the ocean side, blowing sharp splinters into the living room. We haven't listened to the radio, so we know nothing about the location or severity of the hurricane. But we can hear the storm strengthen ominously. Will it be another killer like Katrina?

As the train roars, we clutch each other to ride out the tornado. It sounds and feels like the roof is collapsing and caving in around us, like the condo is being ripped apart, chunk by chunk, by a vengeful God. My pulse races. I pray that we'll be safe in the shower.

"The bedroom door is going to blow in," Manny predicts, probably recalling his experience during Hurricane Andrew. "We've got to get out of here and put all our weight up against it." He helps me up and out of our safe place in the shower stall, and we stand shoulder to shoulder against the guest bedroom door, trying to hold it in place, to keep the wind out, while the building sways all around us. As we stand there for what seems like hours but is probably only minutes, our arms grow sore and my back aches.

A series of what-if scenarios swirl around my head. We could die. The building could collapse on us. We could get flattened by a flying palm frond. Anything could happen, and there is nothing I can do about it. It is out of my control completely. I am soaked with fear.

Suddenly, it is eerily quiet.

"I think it's stopped," I say. "Let's take a look out on the back balcony."

Stretching, we walk over to the sliding glass door. I pull up the shades and pull back the lock. From the balcony, the night sky spreads before us and we can see the stars. Unbelievable.

"That's a good sign, right?" I ask Manny, breathing in gulps of fresh air, letting the breeze cool down the perspiration that seems permanently stamped on my forehead and my chest.

"It's just the eye. We need to get back inside. It will be coming around again, soon, and stronger."

Standing in a pool of water, I fasten the lock on the sliding glass door and pull down the privacy shades. Fifteen minutes later, Manny's prediction comes true. The wind roars back, shifting direction, and the glass doors resume their incessant rattling.

More than anything, I wish Matt were here. I feel the safest with Matt. I have to face the fact that there is a more than even chance I am going to die in Palm Coast without ever seeing my husband or my children again, without telling them how much I love them, how happy they have made me. How much of my life would be missing without them. I desperately need to talk to Matt. I turn my cell phone back on. But there is no signal. I'm cut off.

There is nothing I can do about that now. But there is something I can do to correct my past mistakes, to make things right, to clear my conscience before it's too late. If I am going to die in Palm Coast, I need to make peace with my past by finally coming clean with Manny about Josh. I wonder if I can even trust him with the full explanation.

Restart. To give it a test drive, I imagine how the conversation will go.

"There was a reason I left to go to Italy," I'd begin. "There's something you didn't know then. That you still don't know. That I never wanted you to know."

"So tell me what it is I don't know about you. I used to know everything about you."

"Yes, I'm an open book where you're concerned," I'd say sarcastically. "Only some of the pages are missing."

"You're not making any sense," he'd reply, flustered.

"When I went to Italy," I'd say hurriedly, before I lost my courage, "when you lost touch with me, it wasn't accidental. My mother sent me out of the country to get me away from the baby's father, to erase that part of my life forever."

"Why didn't you just tell Matt about the baby to begin with?" Manny would reason, because of course he still believes the baby is Matt's.

"Are you totally dense?" I'd raise my voice above the din of the wind and the rushing water, exasperated. "I never slept with Matt. You were the first and only person I'd ever slept with before I married Matt." Then I'd look directly at him.

"But I thought you said that you—I mean all those Italian lovers you had," he'd sputter.

"Aren't you listening to me? There were no Italian lovers. It's only ever been you."

He'd just stare at me for a minute until he got it.

"You mean I'm Josh's father?" He'd look genuinely stunned. "Josh is my son?"

"Yes," I'd say quietly, folding my hands with the grace of an angel, carefully choreographing my tears to stream down the landscape of my face. "Matt doesn't even know. That's what I've been trying to tell you. It happened that night at Opal Weekend. Now do you finally understand?"

I'd listen for his answer but would hear only the sound of the wind slamming against the windows and more glass breaking. I'd huddle under my duvet cover, frightened to death. I envisioned Manny gathering me closer to him, but reluctantly, because he wouldn't trust himself to be near me right now.

"Say something," I'd coax.

"Damn you, Julie," he'd hiss, glaring into my eyes. "Why didn't you tell me? I would have married you. You didn't have to run away from me. I wanted to marry you."

"Because you would have *had* to, don't you see?" I'd finally have the opportunity to explain. "I didn't want to pressure you. I was too embarrassed to tell you. I didn't think you really wanted me. And we were so young. Besides, you were dating Nita after we—"

"There was never anything between us, then," he'd say defensively. "I had just finished college. I wasn't ready to get married, not to her anyway. You cheated us, Julie," he'd say. "Things could have been so different if you had only trusted me." Large tears would start streaming down his face. Embarrassed, he'd hide his head in his hands. He was right. I hadn't trusted him then and I didn't trust him now.

Reality check. In all the years I'd known him, I'd never seen Manny Gellar cry. Touched by his sincerity, I would smooth my hand over his head in calming strokes. At this point, we'd both be crying and clinging to each other.

Outside I could hear more glass breaking, what sounded like walls buckling, trees snapping, furniture crashing as the condo cracked and imploded around us, rain rushing through the outer rooms, stray rooftop tiles sailing through the "hurricane-proof" windows like deadly projectiles. But that was nothing compared to the storm brewing between the two of us.

Then he'd stop being mad and become, at once,

tender and protective.

"I'm so sorry I put you through that," he'd apologize.

"I wanted to keep your baby," I'd confess, trying to make him understand, and the tears would keep flowing. "It was so hard. I was so alone. I needed you so much. I wanted us to get married, but I couldn't hold on to you that way."

"Don't cry, all right?" he'd soothe, doing his best to calm me down. "It will be okay. It *is* okay. You know it means a lot that you kept our baby. You scored big points with me."

"Points?" I'd ask, confused through my tears. "This isn't a game." Something was seriously wrong with his reaction, like he wasn't firing on all cylinders. But I dismissed it. After all this was only a dream, my dream.

"A picture, do you have a picture of my son? Of Josh?" he'd ask and grab my hand. "He'd be about twenty-five now, right?"

I'd nod beatifically.

"What's he like? Tell me about him. Did he play sports? Is he smart? I hope he's smart. He'd have to be, wouldn't he? You're smart. What was his major? What are his favorite things to do? Does he have a girl? If he does, is she pretty and sweet, like you? Are they in love, really in love, really happy?"

I'd laugh and put my fingers across his lips to slow him down and keep them pressed there until his mouth stopped moving.

"I have twenty-five years' worth of things stored up to tell you if you'll just give me a chance," I'd say, smiling. And he'd answer, "I'm not going anywhere."

I'd try my best to close the gap, to tell him every

little thing I could think of about Josh. Important things, unimportant things. They'd all be significant to Manny. He'd want to learn everything he could about his son. He'd want to know if I thought Josh looked like him.

"You'd be so proud of him, Manny. He speaks fluent Spanish. I made sure he learned so he'd be comfortable with his heritage, even though he doesn't know about it. I can't believe you never noticed the resemblance. He looks exactly like you. He has all of your good qualities and none of the bad. He had a fantastic father."

Manny would flinch at the insult because he'd know I was referring to the man who raised Josh. But that would be the truth. If there was ever a time for honesty, this would be it. Did I want to punish him? Yes. While I did love Manny on one level and probably always would, I was beginning to realize that maybe a large part of his current charm's potency was a combination of my sexual frustration, my ever-present anger at Matt bubbling to the surface, nostalgia, and the enormous strain of the secret I'd been keeping from him and from Matt for so long.

When it came to the kind of man I wanted to raise my son, Matt had done a fine job. Better than fine. He had taken such good care of us. Admittedly, things hadn't been right between Matt and me for a long time, but despite the problems, I think we'd made a pretty good life for our children and ourselves. I had to admit I had been happy. Maybe the fact that Matt and I had the power to hurt and even annoy each other meant that some strong feelings still existed between us. Feelings we could build on if we could just communicate honestly with each other.

What did I seriously want? In the past, that question had always been defined by my feelings for Manny. But now I was sure of what I didn't want. I didn't want to tell Manny the truth about Josh.

Because here's what I knew would happen if I did.

"I don't want to tell Josh about you," I'd say slowly. "He thinks Matt is his father, and that's the way I want it to stay."

Manny would be visibly disappointed, and then he'd grow surly.

"Did you enjoy playing God with all of our lives?" he'd ask cruelly. "He's my son, too, Julie. I want to know him. I want him to know me. There are so many things I could give him, that I want to—"

"You didn't earn that right," I'd reply harshly, cutting him off.

"You didn't give me a chance to."

"You had plenty of opportunities, but you pissed them away," I'd say bitterly.

At the first sign blame was being laid at his door, Manny would be contrite.

"I'd like to see him."

"You can spend time with him, as a family friend. I don't want to upset him. He's about to get married."

Manny's eyes would light up.

"She's a beautiful girl," I'd say, my eyes filling with tears, my heart shining with pride. "Really beautiful inside and out. I already love her as if she were my own daughter. Her full name is Zenaida Suarez, but everyone calls her Zandy. She's Latina, so in the end I think it's so right. She's everything you'd ever want for him. She'll make him very happy."

That's the way it should have been. But that's not

the way it is going to be.

Love could be so simple. Josh had fallen in love with Zandy the moment they'd set eyes on each other, and there was never any doubt that he'd marry her, offer to share his life with her. There were no complications or problems with commitment. In that way Josh was not at all like his biological father, whose love affair with the remote won't even allow him to make a commitment to a TV channel. *Luckily, the recessive commitment gene that seems to have skipped a generation is deeply embedded in my son's DNA.*

Matt is Josh's real father in every way that counts. Remembering how proud Matt is of his son, all of the beautiful father-son moments come tumbling back.

"Matt, sweetheart, guess what? Fabio, Jr. made the highest grade in his math class. He's a genius."

"Julie, honey, isn't it great? Fabio, Jr. made quarterback on the football team."

"Matt, sweetie, you're not going to believe this. Fabio, Jr. is the high school valedictorian. He just got his acceptance letter from Johns Hopkins."

"Fabio, Jr. studies rocket science," I mused.

"Fabio, Jr. wins Nobel Peace Prize," Matt stated.

"Prince Fabio crowned king," I joked.

"Fabio, Jr. wins Olympic gold medal," Matt continued the illusion.

"Fabio, Jr. rules the world."

"Fabio, Jr. wins Academy Award."

"Fabio takes a bride." I laughed.

"Isn't that great about Josh and Zandy's engagement?" Matt glowed.

"You might want to remind The Leader of the Free World that he needs to take out the garbage."

"Hey, son, do your old man a favor and take out the garbage, would you?" Matt called out. "Your mother and I, uh, have to get busy on a project in the bedroom."

I remember just the way Matt looked at me then, before he pulled me into his arms and thanked me for Josh. God, I miss Matt and the way we were then.

"It seems inadequate to say after all this time, but thank you for keeping him, for having him, and for raising him," Matt said gratefully. Something Manny should have said to me. Is that what I've been waiting for all this time? To hear that gratitude, that sense of validation from Manny? Maybe that acknowledgment is all I really ever wanted from him. But I know enough to separate fantasy from reality. If we'd really had that conversation about Josh, all I would get from Manny would be recriminations.

"I want my son to know I'm his father," Manny would insist. "You can't stop me from seeing him."

"The bottom line is I don't trust you with my son," I'd answer.

"Then why did you tell me about him?" he'd say.

"For my own selfish reasons, I guess. I wanted to stop all the lies."

Suddenly I can see the full implication, the consequences of my actions if I tell Manny the truth. I will have to share my son with Manny for the rest of my life. Because I want to shed my secret, I'd essentially be taking my son from his real father, Matt. Manny would be a disruptive element in our lives forever.

"What do you want to do, about us, I mean?" Manny asks.

"Us?" I am puzzled, and finally back in the here and now where I belong.

"We'll keep seeing each other, of course," he states. "This is a very cozy setup. I can get away as often as you're available."

"Available?" I can't believe what I am hearing. Does he think I am some kind of call girl? *Yes, Mr. Gellar, I can squeeze you in next month.*

"What about Nita and Matt?" I ask. Do I really have to point out the obvious to him? Even Manny couldn't be that dense.

"No one has to know," Manny responds. "That way, no one gets hurt. No regrets."

I am already regretting my error in judgment, sorry I have come so close to cheating on my husband with this slimy serpent and deliriously grateful that I haven't spilled my precious secret to him.

"I can't believe you just said that."

"Julie, you don't understand," he says, when he sees how angry I am, but I can tell he really doesn't get why.

"Oh, I understand perfectly. You want me on the side. Well, I deserve better than that, a lot better. I'm just sorry it's taken my whole life to realize it."

Something wild and wicked has blown in on the winds of this hurricane, shaking my world to its very foundation, uprooting palms and shaking loose relationships like so many coconuts, loosening the ties that bind. The ties that bind me to Manny are breaking apart, finally freeing me from him. The hurricane and my near-death experience has somehow cleared out the cobwebs in my mind. I finally rid myself of my rose-colored memories that are more bitter than sweet, pull my head out of the sand, and shake it until my mind is no longer muzzy.

Earlier today Manny and I talked a little about what-ifs. What would our life together have been like? But it was just talk. We spoke mostly about the past, which is where we exist, frozen in time. Our world is a static one. We never move forward. In our language, *past present* is a comfortable place, but there is no *future* tense. It does no good to talk about a future that can never be. We aren't going anywhere, literally or figuratively. Even in my wildest dreams about Manny, I think I know inside my heart we will never be together. And I am finally weary of living in a dream world.

Of all the times I fantasize about seeing Manny naked again, I've never dreamed I'll wake up to a scene from "The Emperor's New Clothes." Suddenly he is exposed, and I am scrutinizing him with a critical eye for the very first time. Manny's love for me has never been genuine. *I have no trouble spotting fake diamonds at Stones, so why has it taken me so long to recognize that Manny is just an imitation and I had the real thing all along?* I am fifty years old, and I haven't learned anything. Well, better late than never.

Over the years, I have only played a minor walk-on part in Manny's drama, where he mostly took center stage. My role was to come when he called and perform on command like some submissive spaniel. Going along is what I do best. Looking back, I know that being with him would have been too much of an effort. He is exciting in spurts, but living with his colossal ego would have been exhausting. Manny gets along with everyone, but he loves himself more than anyone, prefers his own company. If we had been married, I might not have survived the union. With Manny, I would have been eternally fragile, never truly certain of his feelings for me.

Matt, on the other hand, makes me feel strong. He isn't nearly as hard to figure out. What you see is what you get. And that is more than enough for me. At times, Matt seems too good to be true. But the truth is, his claims live up to their billing. He is a good man. Better than I deserve.

Even though my choice about who to marry was impulsive, it was instinctive. I realize I don't want this man in front of me. That I have been blinded by the memory of who I thought he was. I also realize I made the right decision in marrying Matt. That my relationship with Manny was toxic from the beginning. That our love was lopsided. That Manny never loved me as much as I loved him. I conveniently blamed Nita for ruining my life, but she didn't hold a gun to his head when he married her. *Like my father almost literally did to Matt.*

However our marriage came about, I realize I do love my husband, truly. I fought it for a long time, but in the end I can't resist Matt's loving ways. Matt has done everything for me, will do anything for me. I'm remembering that now. Over the years, love somehow snuck up on me, bound me to Matt, safely and securely.

"Thank God I didn't marry you, you unworthy rat bastard," I utter to Manny, morphing into the mouse that roared. "I guess I came here looking for some signs of emotional maturity. You're still unwilling to commit to anyone. You're cheating on your own wife, even if it is with me. I don't know how many other women there have been. And I'm not convinced there won't be others in the future. I guess it all boils down to whether or not I can really trust you. I realize I don't even know you, who you've become."

Manny is getting mad. He is unused to my honesty where he is concerned. When it comes to relationships, he prefers his sugarcoated, and that's what he usually gets with me.

"I've been having problems in my marriage, and I was susceptible to you when you got back in touch," I explain slowly. "I always have been. The truth is, I don't think I ever got over you, and I don't think I'll ever shake you completely." *Having Josh will be a constant reminder.* "I love what we had then, and we recaptured some of that today. And no, I'm not sorry we got together. Today was beautiful. It was exactly what I needed. Honestly, it was very cathartic."

"What you needed?" Manny was incredulous. "Cathartic? Do you know how that sounds?"

"Why don't you enlighten me?" I prompt, stifling the urge to giggle.

"What do you want me to say, 'I'm glad I could be of service?' It didn't go that far, but what I want to know is, were you just looking to get laid?" he accuses, laughing harshly. "To scratch an itch?"

"That's rich, coming from you." Talk about role reversals. "What it boils down to is this. I'm not going to leave Matt. He needs me and I need him and I love him. I'm going to try harder. He's my husband, and I want us to work things out if we can. And I don't want you to contact me. No X-rated e-mails, no Internet come-ons. And if you do send me anything, make sure to screen it so it's acceptable enough to show my husband. I'm sorry if that hurts you, but that's the way I want it."

"I don't even know you any more, Julie."

"I don't think you ever did. I'm not that same starry-eyed teenager you seduced in college or the girl who hung on your every word in high school. That girl is gone. And you only have yourself to blame."

"What's wrong with you?" Manny demanded.

"There's nothing wrong with me. I just woke up and smelled the coffee."

"You don't even drink coffee, and you can't smell."

"Well, maybe that's been my problem all along. I didn't smell a rat when I saw one."

"And what if I threaten to tell Matt?" he says. Manny is the type who will follow through on his poisonous threats.

"I'm going to tell him myself, about everything. He deserves that."

"You won't tell him," Manny challenges. "You can't."

"I can and I will," I respond. "Just watch me. I could call Nita and blow your marriage right out of the water. You'd have to kiss your cozy career goodbye. But I won't do that to her. So relax. You'll get away with it. It probably won't be the first time, and I'm sure it won't be the last."

As if to punctuate my statement, the bedroom door blows off its hinges, knocking us onto the floor.

"Get into the closet," I scream.

"No, the bathroom is better," he argues, dragging me with him around the corner of the room, probably saving my life. He closes the bathroom door behind us and we crawl onto the floor of the shower, pulling the mattress over us.

This is not the time for an argument or a deep discussion. We are beyond exhausted, and too scared and stiff to move or tussle, like survivors of some great battle. So we verbally joust a minute more until we fall asleep facing away from each other under our respective duvet covers. Somehow, during the night, our positions shift.

Chapter Twenty-Six:
Let's Start Now on Forever

That's how Matt finds us, huddled on the floor of the walk-in shower, tangled together like the pair of lifeless chipmunks I found last month curled around each other at the bottom of our pool, looking peaceful, like they were just asleep. The storm is over. It is still sprinkling. There's a slight breeze, and I can see the sky through the opening in the roof.

Matt nudges me awake with his toe. I am soaked and chilled, cramped and disoriented, when I finally rouse to focus on him. He is showing signs of exhaustion. His eyes are bloodshot. He looks like he's been doing battle. But even at his worst, Matt is the best thing I've ever seen.

"Matt, what are you doing here?" I smile, momentarily startled. Forgetting where I am, I scramble up to hug him, I am so glad to see him. But I can hardly stand. I have lost all feeling in my legs.

He is staring at Manny and me in disbelief, looking genuinely perplexed and stunned to find Manny in our condo.

"What are *you* doing here, Gellar?" he demands. "Get your Goddamn hands off my wife."

And then, for that split second, that one last moment before realization dawns on him, I am still innocent in his eyes. Until I see a lifetime of trust shatter, then break, and land with a sickening thud. It isn't until that very moment that I realize the full consequences of my actions. Our easygoing relationship, though far from perfect, is gone, destroyed, by me. I see the look of hurt register in my husband's eyes, and turn to betrayal and contempt, before it boils over into anger. And the blame lies squarely where it belongs. With me.

I can lie and lay blame and make promises from now until the cows come home, and it won't matter. I can tell him I'd blundered into it, but this tryst has "premeditated" stamped all over it. I am caught. What is done cannot be undone. I can never take back the hurt I've caused him.

And then come the recriminations.

"Did you have sex?" Matt asks, his voice tightly controlled. "I hope it was good, Julie. I know that's what you wanted."

"No, we never—" But I catch myself when I realize how inadequate that sounds. I may not have followed through or done the deed, but I had wanted to, and the desire I felt was real, and just as damning. I had kissed Manny willingly and let him hold me, touch me, and I had enjoyed it. I was guilty of getting carried away and betraying Matt in every important way.

"I'm sorry, Matt," I say softly.

"You're sorry?" Matt is curt. "Is that all you have to say? How was it?"

How can I explain to him that being with Manny again was everything I remembered and expected but it still wasn't enough?

"That good?" Matt ventures awkwardly when I can't answer.

"Matt, don't."

"In our bed?"

I shake my head remorsefully. *At least not that.*

With deadly calm, and murder in his eyes, he drags Manny up by his shirt with both hands and jerks his rival to his shaky feet.

"Do you know how much I want to tear you apart right now?" Matt seethes, his face turning an ugly, twisted shade of purple. "So help me, I want to kill you, dammit. And I will if you don't get away from my wife and get out of here. The game's over. I'm calling Nita. So go home to your own wife or go to hell. I don't care. I don't ever want to see you anywhere around Julie again. Is that clear?"

"No, Matt," I beg, as I stand before him. "I know you have every right to, but please don't call Nita. She doesn't know anything. It will just hurt her." It surprises me that I want to protect the White Witch. Or am I still trying to protect Manny?

"But it's okay if I get hurt?" Matt says bitterly. "I never would have expected this from you, Julie. Never in a million years.

"I don't blame you, entirely," Matt adds. "This creep knew you were vulnerable. He played you all though college. But you still can't see through him to what he really is, can you?"

Matt lets go of Manny in disgust. Manny looks at me, and I nod, indicating that he should leave. He looks relieved to get away from Matt's grasp. And he can't get away fast enough. All that bastard cares about is saving his own skin. He doesn't even pretend he wants to defend me, defend us, fight for us. If I ever needed further proof about his character or his motivation, it is staring me right in the face.

I think Manny knows that in a fight he'd come out the loser. He is taller and broader than Matt, but he has gone to seed. Matt is more compact, in much better shape, and angrier.

"And Gellar," Matt says, "I haven't decided yet whether I'm going to call Nita. I'll let you stew on that while you're driving home."

Now Manny looks scared. In that brief blinding moment I wonder what it is I ever saw in him.

Manny walks out of the bedroom and into the hall before I hear him shout. "Holy Shit! Jesus. The whole side of the condo is gone. There's nothing left. Oh, my God!"

A few minutes later he risks wandering back to the guest bedroom.

"The elevator isn't working. How am I supposed to get down?"

"You could try jumping," Matt suggests. "Oh, and Gellar, I hope your car wasn't parked in the garage."

Manny's face twists.

"Water washed away the garage and the first floor," Matt reports. "What kind of car were you driving?"

"A blue BMW," Manny answers, not realizing Matt is baiting him. He already knows.

"You mean that fancy sports car I just saw floating in the pool?"

Manny swears and runs out the bedroom door to look down at the pool. Then he starts making his way down.

"That was mean, Matt."

"I wasn't joking," he says, almost smiling. "He can

try climbing down, but I'm not taking a chance with you. We'll wait here until the police come. What about your car? I didn't see it when I came in."

"It's parked at The Home Depot," I answer.

"You hate The Home Depot," Matt says.

"I had this idea that I could fix our marriage myself," I explain lamely.

Matt has spent a lifetime trying to make sense of my convoluted logic, but he still looks stymied.

"And, well, I guess I thought that if I left my car there, it wasn't like I was really going to the condo to, you know—"

"I think *cheat* is the word you're looking for."

I could only stare hopelessly at him.

"Julie," he ventures, in a more serious voice, low and level and infused with hurt. "I think you owe me an explanation." He is standing right in front of me, arms folded, looking straight into my eyes.

I have never seen Matt this angry, and it is one hundred percent worse because his anger is directed right at me like a laser and I cannot deflect it. I cannot get the words out.

"I know things haven't been great between us. But I never believed you would do anything like this." He leaves the accusatory words hanging there.

I look at him and still can't find my voice. Then I look down.

"How long?" he demands. "How long has this been going on? Look at me, Julie." He grabs my chin roughly and forces my face back into his line of sight. I flinch.

"Don't bury your head in the sand, Scarlett. For once, face up to what you've done." His breath is coming out in short, heavy spurts.

Matt has never been this cruel to me or anyone else. But it is no less than I deserve.

"Why would you do this to me? Have I ever given you cause to behave this way? I've never so much as looked at another woman or had thoughts of anyone else. And don't think I haven't had plenty of opportunities. But it was you, always you, for me."

I can barely speak. I am suffocating. Something is welling up in the pit of my stomach and choking my air passage. At least I don't have to run far for the bathroom. Without moving, I vomit into the duvet cover.

"Now you know how I feel," Matt rages. "You make me sick, both of you. Go clean yourself up. You stink of him." He is not ready to let his anger go. Cringing, I walk over to the sink and, finding that the water system doesn't work, realize I can't even rinse off the scent of shame and the stench of my betrayal.

"How long have you been making a fool of me?" he rants. I have never seen Matt so out of control, never even caught a glimpse of his temper. I didn't know Matt had a darker dimension. Apparently, there is a lot I don't know about my husband, have never bothered to learn.

"I know it doesn't change anything or excuse my actions, but this is the first time we've seen each other, and we really didn't do anything. You have to believe me, Matt," I finally manage, speaking quietly while I wipe my mouth with a paper towel. "We met here yesterday. It was supposed to be for lunch. Only for lunch."

"That's weak, Julie. That's like saying you're only

a little bit pregnant."

"And then the storm came," I say, refusing to be derailed, desperately needing to explain. "We had been in touch on line before that. He couldn't get home because of the storm. I'm sorry. So sorry."

"Do you honestly expect me to believe that you never saw your old boyfriend on all those trips you took to Miami this past year?"

"That's not why I—" I look down at the pattern in the tile floor. "I'm sorry."

"You're sorry," Matt rants. "You're carrying on with your old boyfriend behind my back and that's all you can say? Admit it—you never got over him, did you? Did you ever love me, Julie?"

"I did love you," I say, then correct myself. "I do love you." I mean it, too. A lump is forming in my throat, and I know I am going to cry, but I try hard to hold back the tears. "When he started e-mailing me, things between you and me were, well, you know how they were. You were gone all the time. I was so alone. I thought you didn't want me anymore. You never, we never, well, I thought maybe you and that woman from Germany… God, Matt, I thought it was over between us anyway. I still had a lot of unresolved feelings for Manny. I had to find out whether there was anything there. I wanted it to stop. Matt, there's no comparison between you. You're so nice and he's so—"

"I'm tired of being a nice guy," Matt says scornfully. "You don't like nice guys. You seem to gravitate toward scumbags like Gellar. Did you know when he first introduced us, he gave you a half-hearted endorsement and made it clear the package came with a warning? Hands Off."

"The package?" I am confused.

"You," Matt clarifies. "I spent our first date wondering why he was just handing you over to me. I thought there had to be something wrong with you. Then I tried to resist you, and by our second date, I couldn't, and then it was too late. All bets were off, and I went after you. By the time I figured out his angle, I realized that your old boyfriend had no intention of ever handing you over to anyone. He was just creating a diversion to keep you hanging on, grateful and dazzled by his power to arrange things."

"He wasn't my boyfriend," I protest, sick about this further evidence of Manny's manipulation.

"Well, then he was the biggest fool on the planet. Look, if you were so unhappy, then why didn't you come to me, tell me? Talk to me, before you ran off to him in Miami?"

I answer only after an uncomfortable silence. "I don't know. Matt, I didn't go to Miami to see Manny. I went to help out at Stones…and to see Little Jon."

"Little Jon?"

"He was helping me to—I was depressed—and he was helping me with that, helping me to get better."

"Jesus." I can't read the look in Matt's eyes. Disbelief? Fury? Disgust? Guilt?

Matt takes a deep breath and shudders, trying to process this new information, Manny's presence in our condo, everything. "Julie?"

He is pleading with me for verification, and I nod.

"And you couldn't tell me? Little Jon never said a word to me."

"No, I couldn't talk about it. I made Little Jon swear not to tell you or Mackie. I was too embarrassed.

Matt, I have to know, is it over with us?"

I watch my husband with a mixture of emotions. What I want more than anything is his forgiveness, though I know that's the last thing I deserve. I want our life to be the way it was before. *Take me back, Matt, please.*

"I know, that's up to you, but I hope not," I say in answer to my question. "I do love you, Matt, and I love being your wife. What I did was unforgivable, I know that. I did what felt good at the time. I didn't think about how it would hurt you, what it would do to us. I just didn't think. Will you ever be able to forgive me?"

"I don't know if I can," Matt answers truthfully. "I don't know what happens next. I can't stop thinking about him touching you, kissing you, screwing you. Oh, God, Julie."

"He didn't. We didn't. I promise you, Matt. It didn't get that far." Matt is still scowling.

"When I couldn't reach you, I imagined the worst," Matt says. "But I was wrong. This is worse. I'm going to need some time…" Rubbing his face with his fists to hold back the tears, he continues, "Time to get over this, if I can. It hurts, Julie."

"Can we talk about it?" I ask. "It's something we needed to do a long time ago, I know."

"What I need is some time alone to think, away from you," he says, reaching out to touch me, seeming to need the physical contact, then reconsidering and pulling back his hand. "But right now we don't have that luxury. We're stuck here until someone rescues us. So I guess, yes, we don't have any choice."

Then his shoulders heave, and I think he is going to break down. I want to comfort him, but I can hardly do that, since I am the source of his agony.

And the miracle is he doesn't make me wait any longer. He meets me more than halfway. He doesn't even hesitate. He looks deflated, like he is winding down, his anger spent. The mad just goes out of him as quickly as it has come on, and his face crumples.

Suddenly he is pulling me into his strong arms and holding me against his sturdy body. Just holding me. He is holding on so tight I think he might smother me. I lose control and clutch at his shirt and can't stop sobbing as I burrow my head into his chest.

Then I wrap my arms around his back in a death grip and hold on for dear life. But I can't look at him yet.

"I made a horrible mistake, Matt, I'm so sorry," I keep repeating. "So sorry."

"God, Julie, I thought you were dead," Matt says as a flood of emotion pours out of him. "I was so worried. You could have been killed. The storm was stalled on the coast, and then it took a turn at the last minute. By the time it came ashore on Palm Coast, it had intensified into a Category Five. It was a direct hit, with a monster storm surge, and a tornado that ripped right through the place like it was a Caribbean shack. When I got here and saw the rubble, I thought I'd lost you."

"I'm okay, Matt. You can see that I am. You haven't lost me."

Matt still looks desperate.

"Not to the storm," he whispered, and then I understood.

"Do you hate me?" I ask, licking away at the salty tears streaming out of my eyes and staining his shirt.

"I hate what you did to me, to us, but I could never

hate you," he assures, trying to compose himself. "I called your cell about a million times," says Matt, who isn't normally given to hyperbole.

"I turned it off to conserve the battery in case of an emergency," I explain.

"You didn't consider this hurricane an emergency?" Matt asks, bewildered but not surprised.

I shrug, and he massages my shoulders.

"When you didn't answer your cell, I panicked," Matt says, squeezing me tighter. "Oh, God, Julie, I'm so glad you're okay. If anything had happened to you— I don't know what the kids and I would do without you."

"I thought you were going to be out of town," I say, raising my head away from Matt's chest so I can bring him into focus through my tear-stained eyes.

"When I saw where the hurricane was headed, I just wanted to make sure you were safe. There were no flights into the area, so I drove all day and all night to get to you."

"How did you get to the condo, anyway?" I ask. "The bridge is closed."

"When I arrived, the eye wall was passing over Palm Coast, and I paid a guy to take me across on his boat. Then I walked the rest of the way and took shelter in the clubhouse until it was calm enough to come out."

"You crossed the Intercoastal in the middle of a hurricane? You could have been killed! Why did the man agree to help you?"

"Did I tell you I paid him a *lot* of money?"

"How much is a lot?"

"I offered to buy his boat."

"Matt, you didn't."

He gave me a sheepish grin, with crinkly lines around the beautiful green eyes I love.

"You always wanted a boat. Well, now you have one. At least I hope you still do."

"You rescued me, Matt," I say, sniffling and burrowing further into him. "I was hoping you'd come for me." Matt is my hero, and this is one time I don't mind being saved.

"Frankly, I think we're both going to need to be rescued," Matt admits. "I don't know how I made it up here, but someone is definitely going to have to help us out. And don't be so fast to make me out the hero," Matt cautions, taking a big breath. "I don't blame you for coming down here to meet Manny. I know I haven't been available either emotionally or physically. I let things get out of hand. I'm sorry I wasn't there for you. I knew how you felt about Gellar. I knew it when I married you. But I loved you, and I wanted you too much to care."

"I've always loved the way you loved me, Matt," I say softly. "So constant. No matter what I did, how I screwed up, how I treated you. It never changed the way you felt about me. I know I don't deserve that. Don't deserve you, now."

"I could see you were losing interest in me," Matt acknowledges. "I know I'm not exciting. I even bore myself, sometimes."

"Loving someone is not boring," I correct him. "Please don't ever apologize for loving me. I think we both just got a little too used to each other, took each other for granted, got on each other's nerves, maybe. After so many years, I think that's natural."

I am stalling, and he can tell I have more on my

mind. If I am going to come all the way home to Matt, I will have to be completely honest with him. I dread doing it. In the face of my betrayal, it is just plain cruel, and I don't want to hurt my husband any more.

"Matt, I know you're going to be mad, but there's something else I have to tell you. It's about Josh."

Matt places his hand on my shoulder and says quietly, "Stop. I already know what you're going to say."

I look up at him with questioning eyes.

"I think I knew Josh had to be Manny's son from the beginning."

I am stunned. "You knew? I thought you thought he was, you know, Fabio, Jr. How did you know?"

"I know *you*," he answers. "You weren't the kind of girl who slept around. You hadn't been with me, so there was only one person it could have been. And then when Josh started growing up, well, all you had to do was look at him. I'd have to have been blind not to notice the resemblance."

"Why didn't you say something sooner? I've been holding this secret inside for so long."

"I had trouble admitting it even to myself. It was too painful. You offered to tell me once, but not talking about it made it seem less real. I love Josh. I wanted to keep thinking of him as mine."

"Of course he's yours. You raised him."

Matt's face fell as another thought occurred to him. "You didn't tell Manny about Josh, did you?" he asks nervously, pulling slightly away from me.

"I came so close, Matt," I admit. "He and Nita were never able to have children. And I thought we were going to die in the storm. I wanted to clear my conscience, but thank God I didn't."

Matt's relief is palpable.

I can tell he thinks there is a possibility Manny might still try to take Josh away from him even though our son is already grown and is his own man.

"Manny's missed out on a lot," I say.

"He missed out on you," Matt says. "I know Manny wanted you, wanted the baby, but I interfered because I wanted you more. I cheated Gellar out of his son and a life with you. I realize that wasn't right."

"Don't apologize," I say, still struggling with tears. "You stood in for him. You stood up for us. Manny made his own choices for his own reasons. If he had wanted me, really wanted me, he wouldn't have let things turn out the way they did. And now, I'm glad he didn't interfere."

"Maybe breaking it to Josh is the right thing to do," Matt equivocates.

"No," I disagree vehemently. "I think it's for the best that Josh doesn't know. What good would it do him now?"

"If Josh ever finds out, he'll hate us, both of us," Matt says. "He'll never understand how we could keep something like that from him."

"I would deserve all the blame," I insist. "I'm the one who lied to him."

Matt shifts uncomfortably. "If the worst happens, then we'll handle it together."

"Manny and Nita are on the guest list for the wedding. In light of everything that's happened, I don't want them there, but I think we have to let them come."

"What if I said I was *not* all right with that," Matt asked, weighing his words carefully. "What would you do?"

"I'd make sure they weren't there," I assure him.

"I guess it will be okay if they come to the wedding, although I can't stomach the guy. I don't know how I'm going to be able to be in the same room with him again, and I really don't want him in the same room with my son."

"I know."

"But he did give us Josh," Matt admits. "Josh is a great kid, isn't he? We are lucky to have him. I still can't believe he's mine. I'm so proud of the way he turned out. I'm proud of both of the kids."

"They have a great father in you," I say, welling up, afraid I will cry again. "You're too good for me."

"That's not the way I see it," Matt says, enfolding me in his arms. We are enjoying our new closeness. Then he starts to speak.

"Before you go nominating me for sainthood or anything, I have a confession to make, Julie. I'm not as noble as you think. This—you and Gellar—didn't come as a complete surprise to me. I read some of your e-mails."

My eyes widen in shock as I remember some of the personal content of the correspondence, intimate things I never in a million years would want Matt to read. I don't think it is possible to feel any worse than I already feel. Ordinarily I would be furious that he has invaded my privacy, but I am not exactly in a position to lay blame.

"When?" I ask.

"About a year ago," Matt admits. "It wasn't hard to figure out who The Big Man at gellargroup.com was. The creep is not exactly subtle."

"A year ago? Why didn't you say anything?" I am getting angry now. I know I am mostly at fault, but Matt has put me through hell the past year by practically deserting me. And then there is the Gretchen issue that still has to be resolved.

"I don't know," he answers. "I didn't want a confrontation. I was hoping the whole thing would go away. I guess you're not the only one who sticks your head in the sand. I was afraid I'd lose you and Josh if I brought it up. That if it came down to it, you would choose Manny over me. That's the reason I moved us to Atlanta, to get you away from him. You two were steaming up the screen, but it seemed sort of one-sided. I didn't think you'd ever actually cross the line, but I didn't want to take any chances."

Suddenly Matt's disinterest over the past year makes sense to me. The distance between us is explained. It's why he has been so closed off. Why he's looked at me sometimes as though he hates me. Why he can't or won't sleep with me—because he is worried about me betraying him with another man, the same man. How that must have grated on him, eaten away at him.

And maybe I was subconsciously punishing Matt for pulling my life out by its roots and pulling away from me. And maybe his careless attitude toward me after he discovered I was deceiving him just fueled my susceptibility to my old love.

Had my mother known, too?

Of course she had. And that's why, although she never would have wanted me to leave her, she encouraged me to make the move to Atlanta with my husband. She was well aware of the dangers posed by a renewed relationship with Manny Gellar. She had known I might not be able to resist that strong connection.

"Couldn't you tell there was something seriously wrong between us?" I ask. "Matt, I was really mad at you this past year. You neglected me. I was this close to leaving you."

Matt looks truly shocked.

"I was waiting for you to say something, to come clean with me, but you said nothing," Matt countered, looking like he wanted to shake me. "It really burned me. I could hardly bring myself to touch you, I—"

"I don't blame you," I say, "now that I understand."

"Did you ever think that our problems might have started when Josh and Natalie went off to school?" Matt asks.

"I guess that made me more susceptible," I admit, "but it was more than just that."

I wanted to set the record straight.

"Let me tell you something about Manny Gellar that I think I've always known but just admitted to myself. He's shallow, he can be crude, he's not genuine. And he's not *you*. I think he's more in love with himself than he ever was with me, *if* he ever was with me. I romanticized what we once shared. The reason I came here was to try to get him out of my system so I could start over with you. I've done that. I know it doesn't mean much to you now, but I'm glad I married you, Matt."

"It means a lot," Matt says.

I look into my husband's grateful eyes and take his hand, trying to coax him out into the hall so I can see the storm damage for myself.

"I'm warning you, the place is a disaster," Matt says. "You don't want to see it. It's going to break your heart, honey."

Like I broke yours.

He must have sensed my thoughts because he added, "It's a mess. I'll start cleaning it up. But it's nothing that can't be fixed." He loops his arm around me as we walk out of the guest bedroom.

"The only thing that's left in the living room is that ugly-ass palm tree lamp you love so much, thank God," Matt says. "It survived without a scratch. Somehow, that makes it all bearable."

He says it with such amusement in his voice that we both burst out laughing, and it breaks the tension between us. It has been a long time since we've shared a joke together.

But as soon as I see the ruins of my beautiful condo, my tears start flowing again.

"Hey, honey, I think there's enough water in this place already," he says to reassure me.

"Look, Matt, everything's gone," I sob, and my breath catches in my throat. "Ruined."

"Not everything," Matt says, folding me into his arms. "They're only things, Julie." He places a light kiss on the top of my head. "Things can be replaced."

"You were right about building on the ocean," I sniffle. "It was a bad idea. It was a sign."

"This was an act of God, not a punishment. You know that, don't you?" Matt says, but I am not so sure.

"We're going to rebuild," Matt announces. "This time we'll buy an oceanfront lot and build a house."

It all sounds so permanent, and I wonder if Matt

has really thought it through.

"Matt, will you ever be able to forgive me, really?" I ask.

"I want to," he answers honestly. "But you'll understand if it takes time? You're not the only one who needs to be forgiven, though. There's enough blame to go around for both of us. I was inattentive and inconsiderate."

"With you traveling all the time and the kids gone now—you need to understand things from my point of view."

"I do, Julie. I had plenty of time to think about that on the drive down here. I haven't been there for you, and I don't want that to happen again. I know we've had some rough times lately, but I hope you know that no one could love you as much as I do."

"Matt, I don't know what to say. I wasn't even sure you cared anymore. I thought you must not love me."

"I know I didn't always show it, but—stop loving you? I'd sooner stop breathing than stop loving you."

Matt runs his hand through his hair and tries to explain. "You don't realize the pressure I've been under, doing this deal with the Germans. The IPO, merging the two companies. I haven't had any energy or urge to do anything else this whole year. I was so engrossed in work that I didn't have much left over for you. And I was so mad at you about the e-mails and at the same time so afraid to confront you because I was sure I would lose you to him."

"Matt, all that time, I needed you. I was so lonely. I know that doesn't justify my behavior or excuse it. Now that you know everything, what are you planning to do with me?"

"Take you home," he says, nuzzling his face against my hair, "and love you…forever, if you still want me."

"I don't think I can wait that long," I say, biting my bottom lip while Matt rubs my arms rhythmically, sensually, to get some warmth back into my system. I am numb, and I just want to feel again. In fact, I am starting to feel something that is suspiciously akin to, well, frisky. I ruffle Matt's thick, wiry hair, feel it spring back to my touch, and then grab his shirt.

"So, do you think you'll keep me around for a while?" Matt teases.

"Yes," I answer breathlessly, as a tingly feeling spreads, my breath quickens, and I hear myself say, "Are things really all right between us?"

The corners of his mouth turn up and his green eyes sparkle. "You know, Julie," he says in his best Horatio Caine imitation, "I think that they are." But this time the slow cadence of his voice isn't pissing me off, it is turning me on.

"Since we're going to be here for a while, why don't we start fixing things right now," I suggest hopefully, walking my fingers gingerly up his arm and massaging his back. He doesn't look alarmed that I am touching him, not even close. In fact, he is responding to me.

He leans down and kisses me, first tenderly and then with the thirst of a man who has been wandering the desert and finally comes upon a source of water. He lifts me until I am pressed firmly up against him, molded to him. I feel his need, and I want to answer that need with all the love I have to give. I want to feel him so far inside me I will never let him go again. But not here. Not in this place that I have violated by being with Manny. Not this soon. That would be wrong. The need is there for both of us, but the trust will take longer to restore. So we will take things at a slower pace until we find our rhythm and our way back to each other.

Holding on to Matt with everything I have, I whisper, "Let's start now on forever."

Chapter Twenty-Seven:
More Secrets

Atlanta

Jewels@aol.com: Mercedes found a new way to pick up guys. She was in the travel section of the bookstore yesterday and accidentally-on-purpose dropped a book in front of this hunky guy. He picked it up and asked her to go for coffee. The rest, as they say, is history.

DoubleMac@aol.com: The Cognitive Cinderella. To hell with the slipper. That's what Little Jon would say.

Jewels@aol.com: Does your husband always have an answer for everything?

DoubleMac@aol.com: No, he typically doesn't provide answers. He reflects. He's a damn parrot. If I say, "Little Jon, I'm really having a problem with a student at school," he'll say, "A problem with a student at school?" Or yesterday I almost cried when one of my students improved and I moved her up a level in her reading group. And Little Jon said, "One of your students improved?" I can never get a straight answer or an original thought out of him. I think psychiatrists must have a problem with commitment.

****

"I'm calling to RSVP to Josh and Zandy's

wedding," Mackie announces shrilly.

"You didn't have to call," I remind her. "It's Thanksgiving weekend. I already know you're coming up for dinner. I've put you down for three."

"Well, you'll have to change it to two."

"Why? Won't Greg be able to make it?"

"I want you to disinvite Little Jon."

"Disinvite him? What do you mean?"

"I'm leaving him, Julie."

"What? Are you serious?" I am totally shaken. I can't imagine Mackie without Little Jon. The world is suddenly crumbling.

"I'm deadly serious. I haven't told him yet, but I've made up my mind."

"Why would you want to leave Little Jon?" I am truly horrified.

"He slipped," informs Mackie curtly. "I believe those were his exact words."

"As in tripped and fell?" I am confused and slow to comprehend.

"As in *slipped up*," Mackie corrects, this time with unmistaken venom in her voice. And once she got wound up, she couldn't stop.

"He's been unfaithful to me. There's more happening on his couch than therapy. And this isn't the first time, either. I didn't want to believe it. I didn't even see it coming. He denied it, of course. Then there were the little inconsistencies I couldn't ignore. He wasn't where he said he'd be, there were the unexplained restaurant and hotel receipts, the smell of his women on his shirt, all over him. Then when I confronted him, he was all contrite and swore up and down it would never happen again, and so, dummy that

I am, I let it slide. Then things were better for a while. He was sooo romantic, in an overboard kind of way. And then it would happen all over again. I don't think he can help himself. He's a serial cheater. Now we have a 'don't ask, don't tell' policy. I don't ask Little Jon whether he's cheating and he doesn't tell me."

"You don't really believe he's cheating on you with his patients, do you?"

"If he's not, he's hanging on to his professional ethics by a thread," Mackie replied. "I always thought he should have been a gynecologist, but apparently it's more of a turn-on to get into a woman's mind than her pants."

"When did you find out?"

"He's pretty much been doing it on and off for years," Mackie confesses. "The White Witch was right. I should have listened to her when she told me about that bimbo waitress at the pledge class reunion. And that was *before* we got married. Actually, now that I've gotten to know her, Nita's really not so bad. Since you moved away, we've become, um, friends."

"Oh, great. First she steals Manny from me, and now she's stealing my best friend."

"Don't be a drama queen," Mackie says. "We don't still hate her, do we?"

"I do, and if I do, you do." I am adamant.

"I thought the statute of limitations had run out on condemning witches. Besides, Nita and I are both in the same boat."

"What do you mean?"

"Ever since Matt moved away, Little Jon has no one to play with, so he's been hanging around with Manny. Manny and Little Jon are two peas in a pod.

They feed off each other. I'm surprised you didn't know. I've got the garden variety Wandering Jew right in my own backyard."

"Why didn't you tell me?"

"About Little Jon, or Manny?" Mackie asks sarcastically.

"Little Jon," I say, sounding offended, but I am wondering why she never told me she knew for certain that Manny played around. It could have saved me a lot of heartache. But Mackie is pouring out her heart, and she is hurting.

"If I had told you about Manny," she begins evenly, "I'd be admitting that Little Jon was guilty of the same behavior, and I wasn't ready to do that, to you or myself. I tried to warn you."

"I'm really sorry, Mackie. I had no idea. Are you sure?"

"As sure as I can be," she confirms.

"How are you handling it?"

"I'm trying to will myself into tranquility. I recite the rosary three times a day. I go to church as often as I can. I'm thinking of getting Little Jon to prescribe some drugs for me."

"You want your husband to prescribe medication so you can recover from what he's putting you through?"

"You have any better suggestions?"

"Confront him," I suggest. "Talk to him."

"I'd rather stick my head in the sand," Mackie says. "It's always worked for you."

"Do you want me to talk to him?" I offer, choosing to ignore her remark.

Mackie starts laughing, almost hysterically.

"You're part of the problem," she states cryptically.

"Me?" I say, bewildered.

"You didn't know Little Jon has the hots for you, always has?" she asks suspiciously. "Has he ever come on to you?"

"No. I mean, he flirts and jokes around, but I never take him seriously. He does it right in front of you. Little Jon has always been the touchy-feely type. That's part of his charm. It's just Little Jon being Little Jon."

"I'm sorry, Julie, but there's nothing charming about a cheater," Mackie says sullenly. "He finds your body type attractive. He's really into you, Julie. He fantasizes about you."

"How do you know that?"

"He's sighed your name a couple of times while we were having sex. It just slipped out. I don't think he was even aware of it."

I can't believe what I am hearing.

"You must hate me, then," I say quietly.

"I don't hate you," Mackie says. "Correction. I did hate you, but I understand what you did."

"What I did?" I ask, confused.

"I didn't want to have this conversation over the phone," Mackie says.

"What are you talking about?"

"I know you've been with him, Julie," she says evenly and then pauses. "But I've forgiven you."

"What?" I shout. "You don't really believe I would—"

"Remember that last night before you moved to Atlanta, when you still lived in Miami? Matt was out of town. He called in a panic and insisted that Little Jon drive over to your house to make sure you were all right."

I could barely breathe. I thought I had locked the vault on that night. Safely submerged all thoughts, blocked all memories of that horrible time. If I ever recalled it, I thought it had all been just a bad dream.

"He never came home, Julie. I know he was with you."

"Yes, he was at the house," I admit, "but it wasn't what you think. Natalie was there. He spent the night on the couch. I was—he was—" I was so distraught I hadn't even thought to consider what that night might have looked like to Mackie.

"You needed him, Julie. I know that. Little Jon is very comforting. All his women think so."

Then Little Jon hadn't told her the truth about that night.

"I needed him as a *friend*, Mackie, that's all. As a doctor."

"Then why, when I asked him, wouldn't he talk about that night?" Mackie wanted to know.

"Because I made him promise not to," I say simply.

"Why not?" Mackie insists.

"I was out of it, Mackie. I was at the end of my rope. I was in a dark place."

"What exactly do you mean by 'a dark place'? That you turned the lights out?" I recognize that sarcastic tone. Mackie is working herself into a frenzy, and I can almost hear Matt's voice on the telephone the way it sounded just over a year ago, before Little Jon came to my rescue.

"Have you eaten dinner yet?" he asked from his hotel room.

"No," I answered, curled up on the couch, clutching Abercrombie. The dog was trying to wriggle away, but I wouldn't let her go for anything. "There's nothing in the house. Everything's packed up. The movers are coming tomorrow, and you were supposed to be here, remember?" I said, managing to inject a modicum of acidity into my tone.

"You're an adult. You have a car. Go to the store and buy something," Matt chided gently.

"I don't feel like going out right now. I'm tired." Of course I'm tired. I'm tired of cooking for people who don't want to eat. Tired of being the only one in the house who seems capable of clearing the table, loading and unloading the dishwasher, or changing a roll of toilet paper. Tired of being a wife without privileges. The bottom line is, I'm just plain tired. "You know I hate it when you scold me."

"I'm not scolding you. You're just being overly sensitive. Where's Natalie now?"

"She's up in her room, exercising. She thinks I can't hear her jumping around up there like a wild woman."

"Why haven't you eaten?" Matt prodded again.

"It's no fun to eat alone. Josh is out with friends, and it's too much trouble to cook for myself."

"You could have ordered take-out."

"I'm not hungry, Matt," I argued.

"Julie, you have to eat. I don't want two starving women in the house."

"Abercrombie ate her whole bowl of dog food. She's a woman."

"She's a dog, Julie."

"More like a pig, actually."

"What did the doctor have to say today?" Matt asked, trying to get the conversation back on point. And the point was that Natalie was the only one left in this house he was really interested in.

"He said that one day Natalie would just wake up and decide to get better and start eating normally again. But that the whole recovery process might take up to three years."

"Well, good, then we only have one year left," Matt said, trying to make light of the situation. "What about the pediatrician?"

"She gained half an ounce, but it turns out she was hiding a weight in the hem of her jeans. He said if she gets below seventy pounds she's going to have to be hospitalized."

"It's not going to come to that," Matt said. "Dammit, I should have been there. I'm sorry you have to handle this by yourself—the doctors and the move."

"There shouldn't have been a move." I sighed. "Josh is a big help. He went to both appointments with us. He's been great. But he's missing out on his own life. He should be out playing football, having fun, or something. I'm letting him spend the night with some friends. It's his last night here, you know. And he wants to spend some time with Zandy. He needs to get away from everything. From me. I'm not exactly a barrel of laughs these days."

I debated whether to tell Matt the whole truth about the visit to the psychiatrist.

"The doctor says that Natalie thinks I favor Josh, that I like him better," I whispered. "That she might be doing this to get my attention."

Matt didn't say anything.

"It's not true, Matt. I love both of my children equally. You know that."

Matt was quiet.

"Well, say something. You don't think it's true, do you?"

"I never said that. Why don't you order out a pizza or Chinese? Or make some eggs. I'm worried about you, honey. You're wasting away."

"No, Natalie is wasting away," I said, raising my voice and trying to hang on to my sanity. "I can't think about food while my daughter is going hungry."

"I think you may be depressed," Matt said softly.

I took a deep breath and closed my eyes. When had the everyday business of living become such a chore? Was I depressed?

"Well, maybe I am," I replied, feeling sorry for myself. "Can you blame me? You've rearranged my life to suit your own needs. My daughter is starving herself to death, and I can't take it any more. I hate my life. I'm a miserable failure as a mother. I'm no good to anyone."

"Don't say that, honey. You know you don't mean that."

"How do you know *what* I mean?" I started crying. "You're never around."

"Julie, do you want me to fly home?" Matt offered.

"This isn't home any more, remember?" I said, petulantly. "You're taking my home away from me. I don't want to leave Miami, Matt. Why do we have to move to Atlanta?"

"Julie, please. I can come home early."

"You have an important meeting tonight. I know you can't." *Won't.* With all my heart, I wanted him to.

He was probably with Gretchen. I bit my bottom lip until it bled, but the steady stream of tears wouldn't stop.

"Why don't you call Mackie or Little Jon and have them come over and stay with you tonight?"

"Little Jon is sick of hearing about my problems. I'm sick of me, too."

"The point is, you're the strong one in the family. You're the one who holds us all together. Natalie needs you. Josh needs you, and I need you. I'll be home tomorrow morning, before the movers get there. Like I promised. Can you hang on that long? Stay in a holding pattern, Julie. Stay in a holding pattern." My husband had logged so many Sky Miles he was even starting to sound like a pilot.

"Stop treating me like a baby, Matt." Now I was sobbing uncontrollably, so I hung up the phone, before he could say, "Well, then stop acting like one." I released Abercrombie from my death hold and looked around my beautiful, soon to be ex-home. The home I'd never see again after tomorrow. No one understood how much it meant to me. The lights were off, but I walked through every room, by feel, and drank in the memories, the good times we'd had in the house where we'd raised our children. Mostly I tripped on boxes and almost tripped over Abercrombie. Then I scooped up the dog, tiptoed up the stairs, and paused outside my daughter's room. She was still exercising. The music was blaring. I tapped on the door and let Abercrombie down on the rug to hobble into our bedroom.

"Natalie?"

The noise stopped. I gave her a few minutes before I walked in. She was curled up in the coverlet like a crepe.

"I'm going to bed," I whispered. "But I just wanted to tell you I love you. A lot. The most." I leaned down and hugged her fragile frame tightly, while she feigned sleep. I sighed and walked out her door.

I turned out the lights in the hall, walked into my bedroom, and crawled into bed completely dressed, pulling the covers over my head.

I must have slept a little, because I woke up sometime later, rumpled and groggy.

I had been dreaming I was on a deck chair staring out at the blue Atlantic from a pink sand beach in Bermuda. Away from the daily drama of dealing with an anorexic daughter who had left me emotionally drained. Away from arguments about psychiatrists, nutritionists, fights about food, doctor's visits to draw blood and weigh in, and the repetitive mantra of the anorexic, "I hate myself. My stomach is too fat. I look like a whale." *More like a whalebone.* This from an eighty-pound girl who looked like a Biafran or a concentration camp victim—in America—in the new millennium!

I would never forget the day I recoiled in horror when I walked into the dressing room at Macy's, where Natalie was trying on a bathing suit. Was this really my child? She was emaciated, nothing more than a skeleton. Why hadn't I noticed it before? Why hadn't Matt? Because it had been winter and Natalie was hiding underneath layers of clothing. But this...was unthinkable. Apparently it had been going on for months, right under our noses, and we never even had a clue. Apparently I still had my head buried in the sand. It turned out Natalie was throwing food away behind our backs and eating no more than a few lettuce leaves, like a rabbit.

I thought the root of the problem might have been Matt's obsession with exercise. He was always encouraging Natalie and me to keep in shape. Before Natalie got sick, I remembered Matt making a comment about how Natalie needed to lose a little weight. And according to all the literature I read about anorexia, one comment was all it took to trigger the downward spiral.

Every day was a struggle. Just as things seemed to be going right, they'd slip away, out of control. And then the horror would start all over again.

Matt and I tried everything, but Natalie was a clever girl. My sweet, perfect little Natalie was becoming deceptive, a person I barely recognized any more.

The books I read all said she was hearing voices, the good voices, and the bad voices causing her to stop eating whenever she was making progress. But I didn't believe in voices. I believed you had control over your own life and that you could cure yourself if you really wanted to. My daughter knew all the tricks—feeding the food to Abercrombie under the table, putting weights in the hem of her jeans for the weigh-in at the doctor's office. But Natalie, who had been so close to borderline, had never had to be hospitalized.

Mackie's husband, Little Jon, had been a lifesaver. I don't know what I would have done without him, truly. He had been there for me, listening patiently, providing a shoulder to lean on, someone to cry my heart out with. I'd really abused his friendship, calling him at all hours of the day and night with a million questions about Natalie.

The psychiatrist Little Jon recommended to treat Natalie had done wonders for her. He helped us cope with the monotony and anguish of a disease where parents had to watch their child disappear right before their eyes and were powerless to do a thing about it. He didn't lay blame, but he concurred that Matt's obsession with exercise was not helping matters, and he also intimated that my obsession with perfection was something Natalie had picked up on and perhaps was emulating.

I had always thought my life was perfect—perfect children, perfect home, perfect clothes, perfect car, perfect jewelry, perfect shop. But in fact, right now, everything was a perfect mess.

While Natalie was showing signs of improvement, my life was spinning out of control. Some nights things looked so bleak that instead of taking out my frustrations on Natalie, Josh, or Matt, I turned in toward myself and felt so hopeless I wanted to scream or run to my room to hide—to stick my head in the sand. The evening before we were scheduled to move to Atlanta was one of those nights.

Waking, disoriented, I don't remember feeling anything at all. I must have carried my dark thoughts into bed with me; they must have invaded my dreams.

My head was pounding. Pounding. Pounding.

I wanted all the pain to come to an end. I got out of bed, turned on the bedside lamp. I stood in front of Matt's dresser drawer and picked up his loaded blue-steel Luger .357-caliber magnum, the gun my father had given him as a wedding present. Someone was at the door. Was it Matt? I stared at the weapon for the longest time. I imagined slowly pulling the trigger, thinking that all my problems would be over. What would that feel like? Did I really hold the gun up to my head or just imagine doing it?

"Julie, open up. Are you in there? Unlock this door or I'll kick it down."

Little Jon's voice sounded like it was coming from the bottom of a well. I was frozen in place. I couldn't make my legs work. I was sweating, and I tightened my grip on the gun.

Little Jon rattled the bedroom door and then splintered it as he kicked it in.

The ceiling light blinked on, and I looked up to find my best friend's husband standing there in disbelief. He scrambled over the bed, grabbed the gun out of my hand, and wrestled me to the carpet.

"You little idiot," he said. He wasn't yelling. He was talking calmly, evenly, shaking me gently. "What the hell do you think you're doing?" I took a deep breath and started sobbing.

Little Jon pulled me up against him, and I latched on. He held me for a long time, putting a comforting arm around me and smoothing my back with his other hand until I came out of that dark place.

"Go on and cry it out, Julie girl, it's okay to cry. How long have you been feeling this way?"

"A long time. I don't want to go on anymore. I can't cope with it. I don't have anything left to give. I can't even help my own daughter. I'm so alone, Little Jon. I don't want to be here anymore."

"I understand, Julie, but there are people who rely on you. I know things feel hopeless now, but Matt and Josh need you, and mostly Natalie needs you. I don't know what any of us would do without you. You need to try to put things in perspective."

"And how am I supposed to do that? Things are piling up, and I can't deal with them anymore." I wiped the tears off my face with Little Jon's shirt.

"You can start by letting go," he said, taking my hand. "Relinquishing control. Not everything has to be perfect, and no matter how hard we want it to be, we can't be in control of everything, sometimes not anything. We can't take responsibility for everything. Perfection is just a veneer, Julie. Living with Natalie's illness should have taught you that. You have to learn to welcome imperfections as a part of life."

"I'm drowning, Little Jon."

"Then hang on to me," he said in his soothing clinician's voice. "Let me help you find your way back."

I looked up at Little Jon through my tears and asked, "Why are you here? Matt should be here."

"Well, he's not here now, is he?" Little Jon murmured softly. "So I'll have to do. Matt called me after he talked to you. He could tell something wasn't right. He told me to get over here and bust down the door if I had to."

"Do you always do what you're told?"

He laughed. "There, you see? You made a joke. Things aren't so bad, are they? You scared the hell out of Matt," Little Jon admonished. "He'd go crazy if anything ever happened to you. We will just deal with this, now, Julie, together."

"Is that the royal 'we'?"

Little Jon smiled. "You see? You made another joke. That's nice. I want you to come to my office in the morning. I want to put you on something to help with your depression."

"I don't need drugs, Little Jon. I'm not depressed."

"You sure as hell are depressed if you were thinking about taking your own life. This isn't normal behavior, Julie. This is not like you."

"I just want you to know that I wasn't really going to pull the trigger," I insisted, biting my bottom lip, but I wondered if I knew I was deluding myself. "I heard an intruder." I started trembling, and Little Jon took me back into his arms.

"Jesus, Julie. I'm sorry, but you have to face up to this. You have no other choice. Natalie is depending on you."

"Do you swear at all your patients?"

"You're not my patient," Little Jon said as his eyes met mine.

"But you think I need to be," I challenged.

"Do you think you need to be?" he countered.

"Can't you ever give a straight answer to a question?"

"Yes, I think you need to see someone, okay?" Little Jon said patiently, ignoring my insults.

"What I need is Matt, and he's never here for me," I said stubbornly, sniffling.

"Of course he is. And so are your friends and your family. We're all so proud of the way you're handling this. Just promise me you'll never think of doing anything like this again."

"If you promise me you'll never tell Matt or Mackie. I'm so embarrassed."

"I promise." Little Jon was a doctor. I knew he had to keep his promise. "But there's nothing to be embarrassed about."

I shook my head, and he brought me gently over to the bed and sat down beside me.

"How can you help me? I'm leaving tomorrow."

"You need a hand. You've hit rock bottom. I can be a jerk sometimes, but I'm good at what I do. I think I can help you. I *want* to help you. But, for a lot of reasons, it shouldn't be me. I can recommend someone."

"No, Little Jon, it has to be you. You're the only one I'd trust."

"Why haven't you told Mackie, your best friend, about what's happening with Natalie?"

"I'm too embarrassed. I don't want Greg to find out."

"You don't think Greg knows? For Christ's sake, Julie, he's Natalie's best friend. And that's what you need. Support from your best friend. Keeping this secret is only making things worse."

"No, Little Jon. You have to swear you'll never tell Mackie."

Little Jon hesitated, considered his options, and then spoke. "Mackie told me you'll be flying back to Miami to work at Stones once a week, so if you want, we can find time to fit in a session while you're here."

I nodded, my head throbbing. Little Jon was rubbing my arm, and I felt a stinging sensation like an insect bite. Suddenly I felt woozy and I just wanted to go to sleep.

"Little Jon?" I looked at him in confusion.

"Now I'm going to get Matt on the phone," he said carefully, treating me as if I were an unstable jumper he had to talk off a ledge, afraid to say the wrong thing, to upset the precarious balance. He began dialing.

"She's okay, buddy," Little Jon said as soon as he heard Matt's voice. "I'm here at the house, and everything is okay. Julie is going to sleep now, and I'm going to be right downstairs in case she needs me. I'll let you talk to her." He placed the phone up to my ear because I no longer had the strength to hold it.

"Julie," Matt began.

"Matt?" I said tentatively, tearfully.

"I'm at the airport, and I'm booked on the next flight out. I'll be home soon. So hang on, honey."

"Come home, Matt. I need you so much. Just come home." I could hardly form the words. Little Jon took the phone from me and tucked me firmly under the covers. He lowered his voice to a whisper, but I could still hear his angry words to Matt before he hung up the phone. "You'd better haul your ass the hell back here now, or you won't have anything to come back to." Little Jon slicked his hands through his hair and shook his head.

Then he turned to me, and in the tender way you talk to a sleepy child, like he was tucking in Greg or Natalie, he said, "There, Julie girl. You're snug as a bug in a rug. I'm going to spend the night. I'll make myself comfortable on the couch downstairs. I'll check on Natalie first. I know Josh is out for the evening. Call out if you need me. Just sleep, Julie. Things will look better in the morning. I promise. Do you trust me?"

I nodded, spilling a few more tears before drifting into a sound sleep, which was later interrupted by the crack of a door closing and the sound of flowing water.

When Matt came up the stairs, he walked quietly into our room and began massaging my back.

"You okay, honey?" he whispered.

I was breathing heavily. My head was face down on the pillow.

"I heard the water running," I said.

"There's a sink full of dirty dishes downstairs," he answered.

I refused to look at him.

"If it bothers you so much, then do them yourself," I snapped, keeping my face buried in the pillow.

"It didn't and I did," he said. "I wanted to do—something for you."

"I don't need help with the dishes," I said. "I need help. I need you." Then I turned into him, and he held me tightly like he'd never let me go. And I cried out all my leftover tears in anguish. Healing tears.

The morning after the incident, the gun that almost tripped the trigger and precipitated the slide that would have sent me hurtling even further into myself, or worse, had disappeared. I never found out what had happened to it or what Little Jon told Matt about that night. Digging deep into my impressive arsenal of conflict avoidance, I didn't ask any questions and neither did my husband.

"Julie, are you still there?" Mackie's voice brings me back to the present.

"Little Jon may have stopped me from killing myself, okay?" I confess. "I had a gun, and he got there right before, right before—and now it all seems so unreal. I can't imagine I would have done something like that. But back then—"

I can tell by her silence that Mackie is backing off.

"I didn't realize things had gotten so bad," she says after an uncomfortable pause. "Why didn't you tell me? I'm your best friend."

"There's a lot I didn't tell you. I didn't even tell Matt. If Matt hadn't called Little Jon, and if he hadn't come when he did, things might have turned out very differently. He saved my life, Mackie. I begged him not to tell you or Matt. He put me on some medication. I started seeing him, professionally. I was his patient, Mackie, after I moved away. He never crossed the line with me. I swear."

"You know, for a while your moving away was the best thing to happen to my marriage," Mackie admits.

It feels like I've been slapped in the face.

"I know it's hard for you to hear, but it's even harder for me to say," Mackie continues. "Thinking that my husband and my best friend were—"

"There was never anything going on between us," I assure her. I thought back to that night. Was there a moment when Little Jon's comforting hug could have turned into something more? When his strong arms, soft words, soothing tone, light touch, and tenderness could have turned hungry? When I looked into Little Jon's eyes and saw longing? Yes, if I'm honest with myself, yes. I could easily have given myself up to it. But I never would have let that happen, never in a thousand lifetimes. Mackie's friendship means everything to me.

Mackie doesn't say anything, but she starts to cry. That touches off a chain reaction, and my tears start flowing.

"If I had known what you thought," I begin. "I can't believe how screwed up I was back then. How depressed."

"You? Miss Perfect in Every Way?"

"I'm far from perfect, and I wouldn't want to be.

Perfect is boring. Little Jon taught me that. If I came from The Home Depot, it would be with instructions that read, 'Needs Some Assembly.' In a foreign language. So no one could ever figure me out."

We had talked it out, and Little Jon had helped me understand what was happening. During the stress of Natalie's illness, Matt and I went about dealing with our daughter in exactly the wrong way. Instead of wrapping her in love and devoting every waking hour to feeding her constant demands for attention, not to mention feeding her, we both lost ourselves in our worlds of work, me at Stones and Matt in his mergers and acquisitions. We were both seeking sanctuary in an area of our lives over which we thought we had some level of control.

We were so consumed with Natalie's sickness we never addressed our own problems or noticed the growing cracks in our marriage. Although our marriage survived the stress fractures intact, it was sorely tested, and sometimes only limped along.

"I'm glad I had Little Jon."

"And I'm glad I have you," Mackie sniffles. "You know, I think I could live without Little Jon, but I could never make it in this world without my best friend."

"The feeling's mutual," I reply, adding hopefully, "so are we all right?"

"We're more than all right. You know, I've never told you before, but I've always wanted to be you," Mackie admits.

"And I've always wanted to be more like you," I reply.

"I'm sorry for doubting you," Mackie says.

"Look at us," I say, placing the phone on the couch

for a minute and wiping my eyes with the back of my hand. "We're quite a pair. Both of us were going through hell and too damn proud to ask for help. I miss you so much, Mackie. This past year has been one of the worst years of my life."

"Well, thank goodness for *The Colonoscopy Club* and cell phones," Mackie jokes. "Julie, what am I going to do?"

"Little Jon is in love with you. I'm sure of it. He'd be lost without his Little Bit."

"Oh, I know he loves me, but I think he's getting tired of living with an angry pixie. You're tall."

"I'm not that tall," I respond.

"You're taller than me." She sounds miffed.

"Everyone's taller than you," I laugh, glad to have Mackie back.

"Bite me," she retorts.

"I would, but I'm afraid you'd bite back."

"You're sexy, sweet, and needy," she rants. "That's an irresistible combination to a man. I think Little Jon had visions of riding to your rescue and how grateful you'd be."

"You think I'm needy?"

"Don't make this about you, Julie," Mackie says. "Well, normally you're not, but back then, when you were going through whatever you were going through, yes, you definitely were."

I know that's true.

"Well, I've ignored Little Jon's bad behavior for too long," Mackie says. "At first I stayed with him because of Greg. But Greg is in college now. I can't use my son as an excuse anymore. I've stayed with him all these years. What does that say about me?"

"That you love your husband. That you still want him in your life. That you need each other. And, if you think your marriage is worth fighting for, that you forgive him. I've learned a lot about forgiveness from Matt in the past few weeks."

"Well, I can either accept him for what he is, with all his faults, or leave him. If I don't leave him, I'm just plain stupid. I don't like feeling stupid. But I can't imagine my life without him. A bad day with Little Jon is better than a good day without him. He's a complicated man, but I love my husband, Julie. Right now I hate him, but even while I'm hating him, I'm still in love with him. How lame is that?"

"Loving someone is not lame," I say calmly. "It's the most important thing there is in this world."

Chapter Twenty-Eight:
Don't Ask, Don't Tell

After our conversation, I pull out Natalie's photo album, sit back down on the sofa in the den, and start flipping through the pictures. Pictures of Natalie and Greg and our family and the Shacks on countless vacations. I have been keeping a close eye on my daughter for so long, it is hard to let go.

I am missing Natalie, so I call her on her cell phone. She is walking to her sorority house for lunch. At least I hope she is going to eat lunch.

"How's Greg doing?" I begin. I am worried that Greg might have picked up on the tension between his parents.

Greg and Natalie have been best friends their entire lives, which is why Greg decided to follow Natalie to college in Florida. Mackie and I had hopes that one day we'd be in-laws. But Barnyard is getting in the way.

"Mom, you've got to stop that. You're so transparent."

"Have you been out with Greg since you've been to college?" I ask, ignoring the warning signs.

"I always go out with Greg. We went shopping together yesterday. But we're just friends. I like Bernard."

History is repeating itself. I remember when Manny and I were inseparable and my mother and Mrs.

Gellar were hatching their big plans for the two of us. Plans that never materialized. Plans that gave me false hope. And now I am guilty of doing the same thing with my daughter.

"You went to the prom together," I remind her lightly.

"We only did it to make you and Greg's mother happy, and because we truly care for each other and wanted to spend that special time together. But there's nothing between us. So stop forcing it. I'm going to hang up if you say one more word about it."

"But he's so handsome. And smart. You could do a lot worse. He'd make a good—"

"Greg is *gay*, Mom. Okay?"

For the second time that day, I am speechless.

"Aren't you going to say anything?" she challenges.

"Are you sure?"

"Of course I'm sure. Greg is fine with it. He has tons of friends. He's very happy here."

"I'm sure Mackie doesn't know. She would have said something to me."

"Do you tell each other everything?" Natalie asks.

I had thought so, until recently.

"Greg is going to tell his parents at Thanksgiving," Natalie says.

"At our house? You know the Shacks are flying up to Atlanta for Thanksgiving, right before the wedding," I say. I don't think it is my place to tell Natalie that they probably won't be coming to dinner now, and that the family might not even be intact by then.

"Greg thought it would be better if there were other people around. He's not sure how his father will react to the news."

"I think he's picked the wrong holiday to come out of the closet," I say.

"What do you mean?"

"Fourth of July would be more appropriate."

"Why?"

"Fireworks."

"Well, Mrs. Shack will be okay with it. She's cool. And Greg thinks she may already have sensed it. And that's why she's so desperate to push the two of us together."

"Mackie wouldn't do that, not if she really knew." With all the secrets we'd been keeping from each other, do I really know what my best friend would do? Or wouldn't do? Or what I would do if I were in the same situation? Didn't I subconsciously encourage Natalie to turn to Greg when she was sick, thinking his love and friendship could somehow make my little girl normal again? Whatever normal is.

"How do you feel about it, Mom?"

"I think Greg is a wonderful boy. That will never change. I just hoped, we hoped—"

"I know what you hoped. You're just going to have to get over it. I did. And it was a lot harder for me." Then she sighs, and I can practically see her heaving her shoulders.

"That's why Bernard is so important to me," she continues. "He can never replace Greg, but, if it makes you feel any better, it's something I would have wanted too. If Greg were interested in me that way, he'd definitely be the man I'd want to be with, Mom. But hey, I'm growing to like Gay Greg way better than Straight Greg."

"I wish you would have come to me, told me sooner," I say gently, wishing I could help heal my little girl's broken heart.

"What could you do about it? I wasn't even sure you'd understand. His father is going to freak when he finds out," Natalie predicts. "He's such a *man*." And by the way she says it I can tell she means it in the worst possible way.

I cringe. Knowing Little Jon, I know she is right. He's going to have a lot to deal with at once. And I am determined to be there for him if he needs me. Because you don't desert your friends.

"Dr. Shack is trained to deal with those types of issues," I say.

"Not if it's his own son," Natalie points out. "I know Dr. Shack. He'll say Greg just has deep-seated gender issues."

"You may be right," I acknowledge, and wisely change the subject.

"Does the bridesmaid dress I sent you fit?" I inquire, when what I really want to know is whether she has lost any weight since the dress was altered.

Natalie hesitates. "Yes, it may even be a little tight."

"Really?" I respond, barely able to conceal my joy.

"No, not really, but I thought that would make you happy." Natalie laughs.

"It won't make me happy unless it's true," I chide gently. "Are you eating your porridge, Goldilocks?"

"Yes, Mama Bear. But I think you're in the wrong fairy tale. You're more like the witch in Hansel and Gretel, always trying to fatten me up." Natalie laughs again, and since she feels comfortable laughing about it, so do I.

"To answer your question, truthfully, the dress is a perfect fit," Natalie admits.

"Good," I breathe. "I still think the color is a little out there. Pink might have been nicer." Do I always have to stick my two cents in where it doesn't belong? Apparently, yes.

"Zandy's not a huge pink person," Natalie responds. "Any other questions?"

"Are you still getting along with your roommate?" I wonder.

"When she's not trying to impress me with her uniqueness. But she's hardly ever home. She gets picked up every night at parties, multiple times, so yeah, we get along great. I think deep down she's just insecure. I was wondering if I could bring her home for the weekend." Natalie paused, then announced, "She's anorexic."

"Good," I reply cheerfully. "Then I won't have to do any cooking, will I?"

I can look back on those days now, because thankfully the worst of the ordeal is behind us. When Natalie went off to college, I threw away all of her old clothes I associated with her illness. I even tried to wipe away all the old memories by having the entire house repainted. I covered the cool, elegant taupe walls with pastel pinks and yellows and white, reminiscent of the bright colors of Bermuda. It didn't help Natalie, but it lifted my spirits.

Although Natalie no longer has to see her therapist, she still has "food issues." And I still feel as if I have to watch her like a hawk. I'll always wonder whether it was somehow my fault. Was Natalie chirping for my attention like a hungry baby bird in the nest? Was she sick because of something I had done? Or hadn't done? But now, whenever I have doubts, Mackie tells me to stop blaming myself.

"It's out of your control now. She's already baked."

Together Natalie and I, out of sheer stubbornness, got through the roughest period, and Natalie triumphed over her sickness. She relied on my strength, and I relied on Matt and Josh and Little Jon. I am so proud of my daughter. We have accomplished what we set out to do, and in my mind, that chapter in our lives is closed. Even though I know I'm probably compartmentalizing and sticking my head in the sand.

In time, I have gained a new perspective on Natalie's problem and lost some of my intensity. In fact quips like the roommate remark, that would have previously set me off, today simply roll off my back.

On to the next controversial subject.

"Well, then, how are your grades?" I ask.

"I'd rather talk about Greg."

"Why, what's wrong?" I probe.

"I got a C on my last macroeconomics test," Natalie reveals sheepishly.

"A C?"

"A high C," she qualifies.

"Hi-C is a drink, not a grade," I say, before I can stop the words from coming out of my mouth. I have to stop expecting perfection from my children and myself. "C's are nice," I amend, almost choking on my words before we say our goodbyes.

Natalie is facing the challenge of college, losing the man she thought she would spend the rest of her life with, and learning to love again. She is still struggling with getting over the hurt of not having Greg love her back completely. But I know she'll survive it. She's already survived worse than that.

Still, I have to catch myself every time I have the inclination to interfere in Natalie's new-found independent life. Likewise, should I just mind my own business and stay out of my best friend's marriage before I do any more damage? Or should I have a talk with Little Jon, return the favor and repay him for all the help he's given me and Natalie? If it weren't for Little Jon, I might not be here today, about to celebrate my son's wedding.

Chapter Twenty-Nine:
The Suarez-Paver Wedding Reception

Three Months Later

Mattb@globalshipping.net: Hey, baby, can you get away after the wedding?

Jewels@aol.com: Sure. I'm up for anything, if you are.

Mattb@globalshipping.net: You looked incredible in that dress this evening. I can't wait to get you out of it.

Jewels@aol.com: What about your wife? Won't she mind?

Mattb@globalshipping.net: My wife is a very understanding woman.

Jewels@aol.com: Up to a point. Don't keep me waiting, Schatzi.

****

"So that's the infamous Barnyard," I say to Natalie, observing my daughter's boyfriend as he ambles across the room toward her.

"Mom, it's *Bernard*. Don't you dare call him Barnyard to his face."

"Don't worry. He's kind of cute. Does he bray?"

"Mom," Natalie implores. "You're impossible. Stop it right now. He's coming over, and I want you to behave."

"No more animal jokes. I promise."

Out of the corner of my eye I notice Manny walking over to Josh and Zandy. I grab Matt's hand in alarm and direct his attention to the head table.

"Relax," Matt says. "Remember, he doesn't know. It's our secret now."

I take a deep breath. It looks like Manny is having a "man-to-man" talk with my son, no doubt trying to give him the *benefit* of his *limited* expertise on women. But Josh is too busy looking at his new bride to notice. She is beautiful, as a young bride should be, and he is over the moon. I presented the emerald medallion to Zandy this morning as a special wedding gift because I want it to remain in the family and because I am finally ready to give it up. My emerald medallion—now Zandy's emerald medallion—sparkles brilliantly against her white satin wedding gown and her rich, olive skin. But the light of love shining in my son's eyes, reflected back in his wife's, is even brighter.

I see Manny hand Josh an envelope and urge him to open it. Then I see my son shake his head and try to press the envelope back into Manny's hand, but he refuses to accept it. My son looks shocked. Manny says a few words to him and then walks away.

Josh strides over to us. He seems agitated.

"What did he say to you?" I ask evenly.

"He gave me this," Josh says, and handed me a check.

My mouth falls open.

"Five thousand dollars. Mom, that's creepy," Josh says. "I told him we couldn't accept it. It's way too much. He wouldn't take it back."

I look at Matt and frown. Could Manny have

guessed somehow?

"His mother and your grandmother are best friends," Matt explains. "Manny has been a friend of your mother's her entire life. He can afford it. You know he doesn't have any kids of his own. He probably thinks of you like a son." I know that is hard for Matt to admit.

"What did he say to you?" I repeat, squeezing Matt's hand. "I want to know exactly what he said to you."

"He said, 'Be happy. Just be happy.' "

I breathe a sigh of relief.

"Thank goodness you didn't tell him," Matt jokes when Josh walks back to Zandy. "He'd probably slip up and leave Josh all his worldly possessions when he dies, although that day couldn't come soon enough for me."

Matt gets more serious. "You know, we should probably tell him the truth one day, Julie, or it will eat us both alive. It's probably the right thing to do. We can't hide our heads in the sand forever."

"But you said Josh will hate us when he finds out we've kept something so important from him," I remind him.

"He's married now. Soon he'll be starting a family of his own. He's old enough to understand and forgive us. I trust my relationship with my son. It's Manny I don't trust. He's a loose cannon. He might figure it out. But we don't have to tell Manny about it unless Josh decides he wants to pursue the relationship," Matt reasons.

"I don't want Manny in our lives," I insist stubbornly.

"Julie, he's already in our lives," he says quietly,

taking my hands between his and rubbing them, so I'll know he isn't condemning me. "He's always been there between us, right from the start."

I can't deny that.

"But I'll respect your wishes," Matt says and smiles.

A few minutes later, as if he is reading my mind, Manny walks over to me.

"Don't you think you went a little overboard on your check?" I pose dryly.

Manny looks sheepish.

"You wanted to give more, didn't you?" I smile. "That's your style. Anything worth doing is worth overdoing."

"I figured I owed Matt, both of you," Manny explains. "I know your husband is pissed off at me. I appreciate you inviting us to the wedding and not saying anything about what went on between us to Nita."

"That's because nothing went on between us," I say easily. "And nothing ever will."

Locking onto my eyes, and leaking charm out of every pore, he flashes me his best killer smile. "How about a dance, for old time's sake, Jewels?"

"I think I'll sit this one out with my husband. Why don't you ask your wife to dance, instead?" Nita looks lovely and lonely sitting in the corner in her crisp white linen suit. Not at all like an evil witch.

"You're turning me down?"

"It looks that way."

He looks at me in disbelief. For the first time in his life he is speechless. *Nice try, Gellar, but you can't get to me anymore.*

"But you hate Nita," he states.

"It's true I can only take her in small doses, but she's the only wife you've got, so I suggest you start acting like she means something to you, if you want to keep her. And actually, no, I don't hate her. I sympathize with her." Then I walk away, taking the last word with me.

"I saw that rat trying to skewer you with his big brown bedroom eyes," Mackie observes a few minutes later.

"Yes," I answer. "Isn't it great? I don't feel a single palpitation."

"Not even a pitter-patter or a ping?"

"Not even a flutter. I'm finally immune to him, Mackie. I'm over him. No regrets. I've flushed him out of my system." Whatever I once felt for him is gone with the hurricane-force winds. "The White Witch can have him with my blessing," I add.

"The White Witch does have him," Mackie says, trying to gauge my sincerity.

"That's her problem, then. You know, I feel so generous I'm thinking of proposing Nita for membership in *The Colonoscopy Club*."

"Are you serious?" Mackie asks.

"I so am. Has she had her colonoscopy yet?"

"Uh, well, she, um—" Mackie stammers.

"What aren't you telling me?" I press.

"We had ours together, on the same day, at the same doctor's office."

I open my mouth to say something, and then I just close it.

"I'm sorry," Mackie says. "I guess you've changed your mind about membership, then."

"Oh, why the hell not? I'm getting tired of hating her," I admit. "After all she's had to put up with from Manny, she deserves a membership *and* a medal."

"I think she'll make a great addition," Mackie agrees. "Let's go over and tell her together."

"I'll offer the olive branch myself. Right now, I think there's someone else you should be talking to." I nod in the direction of the bar.

Little Jon is staring at Mackie from across the room, heading her way with a lovesick look in his eyes I haven't seen there for a long time. My heart-to-heart talk with him must have hit home.

"Hey, it looks like you two are solid again," I say. Mackie and Little Jon acted like lovebirds at Thanksgiving dinner, and Little Jon had been surprisingly understanding about the bombshell Greg dropped over the meal. That's because it wasn't really a bombshell. I had let Little Jon in on Greg's little secret in advance because I didn't want him to break his son's heart with what I thought would be his initial knee-jerk reaction. Of course, I'd sold the man short. His total acceptance of his son's new lifestyle was sincere.

"He's like a new man, Julie. It's great. I think he's really sorry he screwed up. He's trying his best to get back into my good graces, and I'm not making it easy for him. In fact, I'm almost done torturing him," Mackie discloses with glee. "And by the way, I meant to thank you for talking to Little Jon before Thanksgiving."

"He told you?"

"Yes, he's trying honesty for a change, and it's working."

"I was afraid you'd think I was interfering," I say.

"You were, and that's what best friends are for. I'd like to think he'd have handled the situation like a man, but actually, I was really afraid that he'd handle the situation like a *man*." We laugh together and it feels good.

"How is Greg?"

"*Greg* is fine, in fact, better than fine. It's the rest of his family that's screwed up." Mackie laughs. "And by the way, he approves of *his* best friend's choice in men."

"He gave Barnyard his official stamp of approval?"

"Yes, Barnyard is U.S.D.A. Prime Beef, according to Greg."

"Oh, my God."

"Well, aren't we the perfect pair?" Mackie muses. "Trying to match up Natalie and Greg. We're no better than your mother and Elena trying to push you and Manny together. We were kidding ourselves."

"Were we?" I risk asking.

"What did we know, right?" Mackie pauses and heaves a sigh. "I suspected," she admits. "But I guess I had my head stuck in the sand. They seemed to be in love."

"They did love each other, Mackie. Their feelings were real," I acknowledge. "We can keep each other company in that sandbox."

Let's make our next meeting of *The Colonoscopy Club* a spa day in Miami," Mackie suggests. "Then I want you to help pick out a nice, expensive piece of jewelry Little Jon can buy for me at Stones."

"I'll give him the family discount."

"Not on your life. I want that man to pay full retail price."

"I hear you, girlfriend, and that can definitely be arranged." I laugh. "But I'll refund the discount to you, in cash."

"I might even want to have a little affair of my own," Mackie's eyes sparkle. "I'm feeling kind of wicked."

"I hope you're kidding," I admonish. "Because if you're not, I have just three words of advice for you. *Don't ever cheat.* It will take years off your life, and at our age, we can hardly afford that. I thought I was living out my fantasy, but it turned out to be a nightmare. Matt's only just forgiven me, and things are better than ever between us, but it could just as easily have gone the other way."

"What if I catch Little Jon with another waitress?" Mackie wonders.

"I don't care if Little Jon screws every bimbo in the bar. Dump him, divorce him, or disembowel him. Just don't cheat on him. Don't punish yourself for his mistakes."

"That's not fair," Mackie complains. "Men think it's their God-given right to drop their pants whenever and wherever they get the urge, while women are supposed to remain faithful. Talk about unfaithful. Who's the amazing-looking blonde with her hands all over your husband?"

I turn to see über-Barbie cozying up to Matt. "He had me invite his very shapely sidekick, Gretchen, from the German office." Taking time to calculate her assets, I am hard-pressed to find any liabilities. Cripes, could the woman be any more magnificent?

I hightail it over to the bar before Homewrecker Barbie's hands can crawl any higher up or inside my husband's shirt. Could the in-your-face floozy be any more obvious about her intentions where my husband is concerned? Could her body-hugging silk sheath be any shorter or tighter? *I dare you to breathe in that outfit, Gretchen.*

The thought of another woman with Matt, especially this woman, is driving me insane. I am a thrower, so my first instinct is to look around for something to hurl. Instead, I exercise restraint when I approach, only glaring at my competition—viciously.

"Matt, schatz," Gretchen purrs, ignoring the warning signals, rubbing the fleshy part of Matt's arm as she offers him a simpering smile. Even hidden under his tailored tuxedo, Matt's muscles, bulging and buff, swell and take on a life of their own.

Schatz? Jeesh, I hope I'm not too late. What if they have already gone beyond the terms-of-endearment stage?

"Is this your wife?" she sneers, with a self-satisfied smile that dismisses me as only a minor threat.

I suddenly see what Gretchen sees in my husband, what I almost let get away. In the past year, Matt has made frequent trips to Germany, logging more miles than an airline captain. Don't pilots who fly international routes keep secret second families or lovers on the other side of the ocean? Maybe I should have paid more attention. I have so carelessly taken Matt for granted.

Matt makes the introductions.

"Julie, I don't think you've met Gretchen Kleinmann yet. Gretchen is my new sales vice president."

So this is Gretchen. She is worse than my worst

nightmares. If this woman is a sales vice president, I am a rocket scientist. I can see her particular qualifications spilling precipitously out of her plunging neckline. And so can every other man in the room. A sparkling diamond necklace bisects her two best assets. *My diamond necklace*. I am spitting mad. Matt, how can you do this to me? My newfound marital bliss begins to disintegrate before my eyes. I make some insincere welcoming noises and step over to massage Matt's other arm, determining to fight fire with fire.

"Matt, darling, sorry to take you away from important business, but the kids are ready to cut the cake, and they need us for pictures. You go on ahead. I'll catch up."

I think it is about time I brush up on my German.

"*Auf Wiedersehen*, girlfriend!" I warn Gretchen after Matt is out of hearing range. "Stay out of my business or I'll scratch your smug eyes out." *Translate that, you oversexed pit viper*. Then I walk off to take back possession of my husband.

"Should I be losing any sleep over Bavarian Barbie Dream Whore?" I whisper to Matt snidely as I glance over my shoulder at Gretchen, whose eyes are shooting daggers at me.

"Not unless it's because I'm keeping you up all night," Matt replies. "Does that mean you're jealous?"

"Of course I'm jealous."

"It's about damn time."

"You think I'm kidding? Stay away from her, *schatz*," I snarl. "She's messing with you, in case you haven't picked up on the signals."

"Oh, I've picked up on them." Matt laughs. "They're hard to miss."

"Are we still talking about signals here?" I joke. "She looks highly explosive."

"Can't argue with that. But so far, I've managed to resist the temptation."

"You're teasing me, aren't you," I say, tugging on my bottom lip. Matt smiles.

"Does she have a brain underneath all that—equipment?" I gesture in Gretchen's direction.

"Quite a big one, actually," Matt says. "Looks can be deceiving, and women can be so bitchy to each other."

"Well, I guess you work with her, so you have to continue seeing her, right?" I pout.

"You can trust me, Julie, honey. You know you can." No grief about how he can't trust me. No throwing anything back in my face. He has truly forgiven me.

"I know," I say quietly, lifting his hand to my lips for a kiss.

"But, really, you don't have anything to worry about," he assures me.

As we walk over to where the cake is displayed, I notice that Josh could care less about the cake. He can't keep his eyes or his hands off Zandy.

"Did you ever look at me that way?" I ask Matt.

"I'm looking at you that way right now," Matt smiles, as he links his hand with mine and kisses my lips softly. "Do you think it's appropriate for the parents of the groom to skip out early?"

"Probably not." I laugh. "But it's tempting. Do you remember our wedding day?"

"Yeah. I practically had to drag you down the aisle, kicking and screaming, and into my bed."

336

"I was so scared that night, Matt, so confused. I resisted you every step of the way. And all you did was love me in return."

"I know, honey. You're so passionate about so many things—jewelry, Stones, your old boyfriend, or at least the memory of him. I just wanted you to feel that way about me for a change."

"Love isn't always about unbridled passion," I say, remembering Little Jon's words. "You were always there for me. I love you so much, Matt. I never realized just how much until I almost lost you." I snuggle up against him.

"And I love you, Julie."

"You taught our son how to love, too," I marvel. "That's the greatest gift you could have given him."

"Now I have a gift for you," Matt says.

"Can't it wait until after the reception?" I smirk. Since we'd worked out our problems, Matt and I have been going at it like a couple of rutting rabbits. Sometimes we get lucky and hit the daily double, in a not-too-shabby attempt to shatter my brother and sister-in-law's shagging record.

"Get your mind out of the gutter, Julie. It's not *that* kind of gift." Matt laughs, wrapping his arms around me. "I'm saving that for later. Here," he says, handing me a beautifully-wrapped box from Stones. "This is for you to open now."

"For me?" I ask, confused.

"Who else would it be for?"

"What's the occasion?"

"Our son is getting married. Does there have to be an occasion for a man to give a gift to the woman he loves?"

I hurriedly rip off the wrapping paper, before Matt can change his mind, and open the box. I can't believe my eyes. Oh, God. It is the most magnificent diamond necklace I've ever seen. A perfect, multi-carat, single teardrop stone fashioned in an antique platinum setting. It overpowers Gretchen's necklace or even the emerald medallion in its brilliance and classic simplicity. It must have cost Matt a fortune. My eyes start to tear. "Matt, it takes my breath away."

"You take my breath away," Matt says softly. "Do you like it?"

"Like it? I love it. But I thought that—"

"You thought what?" he asks evenly.

I thought the necklace was for Gretchen is what I thought. "I mean, my mother told me months ago that you had bought a diamond necklace—"

"Your mother never met a secret she could keep, did she?" Matt laughs.

"And when you never gave it to me—and then tonight, when I saw Gretchen wearing—so I thought—Oh, Matt, you know what I thought."

"Sweetheart, I haven't given you any significant jewelry since your wedding ring. I know you can get your own anytime you want to, at the shop. And you were never without that emerald necklace that Manny's mother gave you."

"Matt, I'm so sorry. I know you don't think jewelry is important."

"But you do, honey. Your brother told me you planned to give Zandy your emerald medallion. It must have been hard for you to part with it. I know how much it meant to you, and, well, I wanted to give you something nice to replace it, so you'd know how much you mean to me."

"Oh, honey, I don't need a necklace for that." I grab on to Matt and don't let go.

"Should I take it back?" he teases.

"Don't you dare. Put it on me, honey. I want to wear it right now." Matt lifts the necklace from the box and places it around my neck. I hold the diamond while he attaches the clasp. Then he rubs the back of my neck before he places a tender kiss there.

"Sweetheart, I will never take it off, ever. I don't think I could love you any more than I love you right this minute. I love you so much it hurts."

He smiles, and I can tell he is pleased by my reaction. But he has more news.

"The renovations on the Palm Coast condo are almost finished," Matt says. "I want to make Florida our permanent home. That way we'll be closer to your family and to Natalie, and it will be easier for you to get to Stones if you want to help out on occasion."

"But you always said you'd be bored living in Palm Coast." I, on the other hand, could be content to join the Hammock Palms Civic Association, attend the annual covered dish dinners and beach barbecues, and get into all the local issues affecting the barrier island—zoning, water supply, ordinances to protect the native tree canopies. At this stage in my life, the peace, solitude, and brightness of living in a luxury condo on the beach in a small town appeals to me. In fact, it all sounds heavenly. I think that living in Palm Coast at this time in my life is exactly what I need. And as an added bonus, everyone in Palm Coast is at least two decades older than me.

"What about the sharks?" I warn. "Isn't Palm Coast

the shark-bite capital of the world?"

"That's Ponce Inlet," he corrects.

"What's to stop them from swimming a few miles down the coast?"

"We live on the water, not in it," Matt reminds me.

"But what about your job? You can't work in Palm Coast. You still have a year left on your contract. And what about Gretchen?"

"I worked it out. I've already let my board of directors know that I'm retiring early. That's why Gretchen flew in. She's going to take over for me."

Have I been too harsh and too quick to judge Gretchen? I don't think that pretty poacher's motives are entirely innocent.

"We don't need any more money," Matt is saying. "I need the time to start taking better care of you."

"You hate the beach," I stammer, stunned that Matt would give up everything for me when I should be the one to give up something important for him. But his actions shouldn't come as a shock. He has been making sacrifices for me throughout our marriage. I am not going to let him make another one. And I start to tell him so.

"But I *love* you," he replies before I can speak. "And anyway, after the hurricane, there's not much of a beach left. It's all been washed away. But we'll get it back."

I sigh and snuggle closer to Matt, into the space that is meant just for me, knowing he is talking about more than an eroded stretch of sand. Knowing I have the rest of my life to make it up to him and that we will work it all out together.

A word about the author...

Marilyn Baron, a public relations consultant in Atlanta, is a PRO member of Romance Writers of America (RWA) and Georgia Romance Writers (GRW), and winner of the GRW 2009 Chapter Service Award, a former GRW board member and past editor of the chapter's online newsletter. She also belongs to Marketing for Romance Writers and The Atlanta Writers Club. For The Wild Rose Press, Inc., she writes humorous women's fiction (*Significant Others, Stones*), historicals/romantic thrillers (*Under the Moon Gate* and *Destiny: A Bermuda Love Story*), and Romantic Suspense with paranormal elements (*Sixth Sense, Homecoming Homicides*). She has also written in a variety of other genres. She graduated from The University of Florida in Gainesville, Florida, with a Bachelor of Science in Journalism (Public Relations sequence) and a minor in Creative Writing. Born in Miami, Florida, Marilyn lives in Roswell, Georgia, with her husband, and they have two daughters.

Marilyn says: "What's unique about my writing? I try to inject humor into everything I write. I like to laugh and my readers do too. I tend to feature older heroines, because, let's face it, we're not getting any younger. I love to travel. I studied in Florence, Italy, for six months in my junior year of college and still love Italy and Italian food. Part of my novel *Stones* is set in Florence. I also love jewelry, which is why the jewelry store Stones plays such a prominent role in the book. And I'm planning a wedding for one of my daughters, so I can relate to Julie. I'm looking forward to my next release with The Wild Rose Press, *Murder on the Repositioning Cruise*, Book Three of the Psychic Crystal Mystery series."

Visit Marilyn's Web site at www.marilynbaron.com and her blog at http://www.petitfoursandhottamales.com/